FRAUDULENT TRUST

A PLANNERS AND DREAMERS NOVEL

BOOK TWO

LYNNE HANCOCK PEARSON

I owe a huge debt of gratitude to a multitude of people.
To Amy Wheeler, Sabrina York, Celeste Deveney, Natalie French, Brent Archer, Cat Hickey, Laura Luna, Beth Delescavage, Eliana West, Danica Sorber, Tina Radcliffe, and Sherri Shaftic, thank you for listening to my bellyaching, offering suggestions, answering my (often repeated) questions, and holding my hand.

To Leanne Fisher, our conversations and your suggestions regarding residential schools were incredibly helpful.

To Dawn McKay, Kim Hancock, and Carolyn Link, you stopped me from getting a big head.

To Joy and Will, thank you for the tattoos. You made me cry. To Matt, I'm so glad I let you use my library card that day.

CHAPTER 1

*D*elia used the camera on her phone as a mirror, reapplying her lip gloss and fluffing her hair. Judging where the best light was, she took a selfie in front of the shelves of law books. She tossed the phone into her bag and strutted down the long carpeted hallway to the office at the end. She poked her head in the open door. Her dad, Chuck Duncan Sr., sat in front of a desk loaded down with manilla file folders, across from a stern-faced woman in a no-nonsense suit. The woman behind the desk looked at her wristwatch before giving Delia a pointed look. Delia ignored her.

"Hi, Daddy." She kissed his cheek and settled into the chair beside him.

"Hi, sweet pea. Did you have trouble finding parking?"

"Nope." Delia smiled at the woman now tapping a manilla folder with a pen. "I don't think we've met."

Chuck Sr. gestured between the two women. "Delia, this is Naomi Sanchez. She's the administrator for the family trust."

Delia extended her hand, admiring her manicure and thinking how best to photograph it for her next Insta post.

Ms. Sanchez gripped her hand and released it quickly, as if she didn't have time to observe social niceties.

"Ms. Duncan. I told your father, while we were waiting for you, that while I'm new to you and your family, I'm quite familiar with the Duncan family trust. I've worked closely with Mr. Patel for the past few years, and now that he will be retiring, I will be the lead administrator."

"I see." Delia shifted to look at her father. "Why am I the only one here? Where are the other family members?"

Chuck Sr. opened his mouth, but Ms. Sanchez held up a hand. "I'll get to that. Let me give you a little background first."

The woman explained the history of the family trust. In 1872, Gweneth Duncan started buying up pieces of land along the Seattle waterfront after the death of her husband.

Thinking of the waterfront, Delia looked at her boots. She'd bought them at a divine boutique close to Pike Place. She twisted her ankle, admiring the sleek leather. Dammit! The heel was ripped. After this, she'd have lunch with Daddy and then buy a new pair. She bent to retrieve her phone to look up the store's hours. Shopping on a Monday was always iffy. She straightened at the lawyer's last words.

"Unless things change, the clause will be invoked on your thirty-fifth birthday."

"Excuse me. What clause?"

Her father looked pained. The lawyer looked annoyed.

"Ms. Duncan, unless you can prove that you're capable of supporting yourself on income you generate, your trust will be cut off."

Delia gaped. "Seriously? Why?"

"Your ancestor, the founder of Duncan Properties, believed in a strong work ethic. She had six children. Some worked in the family business, while others worked for themselves. All were successful except for a couple grandchildren who seemed to believe work was what other people did and were content to ride the coattails of their indulgent parents. Gweneth added the clause when she founded the trust to prevent any of her progeny from living exclusively off the work of others."

"But…why am I only hearing of this now?"

"The clause has never been invoked before."

"Never?"

The lawyer shook her head. Her father shrugged.

"Not once?"

"By their thirty-fifth birthday, every descendant of Gweneth Duncan has been able to support themselves without the aid of their trust. Everyone, that is, except you." Ms. Sanchez sat back, twisting her lips in a slight smirk.

"So, honey, between now and your birthday, you have to start earning an income on your own."

"Dad! I do earn an income." She flipped her hair and straightened her shoulders. She smirked back at the lawyer. "I'm an influencer. Perhaps you've seen my videos on TikTok. I brought down Southwest Savior Church when they were scamming donations from people." With 200,000 combined followers on TikTok and on Instagram, her post had started an investigation into the church's predatory practices. More than one unsuspecting soul had given away their life savings. The parents of her future sister-in-law, Beth Beckett, had their bank account wiped out by the church.

The lawyer crossed her arms. "I did see the post. How were you involved after making the video?"

"I kept the conversation going. My followers like to interact with me, and I responded to their comments with more questions. The post got picked up on Twitter and voilà." Delia spread her arms with a flourish. "In three days, the church backed down and rescinded their donation policy."

Her dad patted her hand. "Good job, honey."

"That was very commendable. Have you monetized your influencing?"

"People pay me to promote their products and events on social media." So many didn't understand the importance of a social influencer. She opened her mouth, prepared to educate the uninformed woman.

Pulling a legal pad toward her and picking up a pen, the lawyer spoke before Delia had a chance. "I must have missed that. Did you include that on your income taxes?"

"Well, I get paid in product, and I attend events for free."

"I see. So you didn't make any money off your *influencing*."

Warmth rose up Delia's neck and settled in her cheeks. "Well, no. But these products are expensive, and VIP treatment at a concert is worth a lot of money. I didn't pay for these things, and it didn't cost me anything to buy the products or attend the events, so I earned an income off them."

Doodling what looked like a giant question mark, the lawyer kept her eyes on the legal pad.

Her dad faced Delia. "Sweet pea, it doesn't work that way. There has to be a paper trail indicating money exchanged for goods and services. You getting a box of face cream in exchange for an Instagram post doesn't meet that criteria."

"I give away a lot of the products I get. I don't need to earn an income. I have my trust fund."

"Not for much longer."

The lawyer's words hung in the air, her lips curling in a smug little smile. Good manners and the presence of her dad were the only things preventing Delia from leaping across the desk and slapping the smile off her face.

Her father rose from his seat and reached out to the lawyer. "Ms. Sanchez, thank you for your time. We'll keep you updated."

Delia trailed behind her father. Her mind racing, absorbing what she'd just learned. They waited in silence for the elevator. Inside the cab, she turned to her dad. "You're cutting off my trust?"

"Not exactly. Unless you're gainfully employed and able to support your lifestyle all by yourself, the trust will be cut off on your next birthday."

"That's…that's three months from now!"

"I know."

"That's insane. I should have been told sooner than this!"

"Honey, you were told. Ms. Sanchez informed you in writing and also via email."

"I didn't get them." Maybe she did. She couldn't remember. If she didn't understand the subject line of an email, she ignored it. As to snail mail…

"Well, I did. I was cc'd on the emails, and when you weren't responding, Ms. Sanchez contacted me."

"Fine. But I don't have time to start up and run a successful business in three months! I mean, I can certainly start up a business in that time—how hard is that? Be a successful business? That takes time." She snapped her fingers and smiled triumphantly. "I know, I'll buy into a business!"

He rubbed the back of his neck and sighed. "Well, no, you can't do that. You need funds to do that."

"Not a problem. I'll take the money out of my—"

"No, sweetheart, you can't. There are restrictions on your trust that don't allow it."

The elevator doors opened, and they exited into the parking garage. Her father stepped to the side, and she followed him. "But I don't understand. I opened an interior design studio."

"Your mother and I funded that."

"You did? And the vegan boutique?"

"That too."

Delia contemplated her father's sympathetic face. She had started two businesses with her parents' backing, both of which had failed. How had she not known it was their money? "My condo? Do I pay for that?"

He beamed. "Oh honey, we gifted that to you on your twenty-third birthday. You won't have to ever worry about that." He pulled a key out of his pocket. "I need to get back to the office so I don't have time for lunch today. Let me walk you to your car."

He chattered about an upcoming Husky game while they walked. She slid in and waved him off. She stroked the leather seats of the sleek Lexus. She hadn't even paid for that. It was a Christmas gift from her parents. Her thoughts filling the interior until she felt confined, she got out of the car and walked up the parking ramp to the exit. Retail therapy would ease her jangled nerves.

She meandered along the sidewalks of downtown Seattle in a fog, stopping every now and then to stare sightlessly at window displays. She couldn't muster up the energy to open doors, go inside, and buy something, anything to take her mind off the past hour. Following the path of least resistance, she followed tourists toward the waterfront, squinting against the late afternoon sunshine. Construction blocked a sidewalk, and she turned down an unfamiliar street where there were fewer open shops. The buildings were old, some bearing signs of impending teardown and reconstruction. More gentrification in the city.

After a couple of blocks, she heard voices behind her, rough laughter, men making comments about her. She didn't pay any attention. She'd heard it before. The voices came closer. Delia glanced over her shoulder. Three young men, kids practically, leered at her. One of them blew a kiss her way and grabbed his crotch while the others laughed. They might be harmless, but then again, there was no one else around. Taking a firm grip on her bag, she lengthened her stride to reach the narrow opening ahead of her. A neon OPEN sign beckoned her.

She crossed the street, walking as fast as her high heels would take her toward the store. A man opened the door, picked up a sandwich board, and took it back inside. The neon sign winked out. Delia picked up her pace, pushed open the door, and ran into a flannel wall.

✳

The leggy blonde stepped back, glanced at Cal, then disappeared into the stacks of old books. It figured. No customers all day until he was ready to close up shop.

Cal studied the convex mirror mounted high in the corner. The woman had a hand on her chest and was breathing hard. She slipped into a door clearly labeled Employees Only. He took two long strides after her, stopping when he heard male voices outside.

Finally.

Three young men stood on the sidewalk, the one with his back to Cal wearing a familiar jacket.

Smiling, he opened the door. "Hey."

The jacket might have been familiar, but the kid wearing it wasn't. Shit. Cal raised a hand, palm out. "My bad. I thought you were someone else."

The tallest one, a pimply-faced blond, craned to look over Cal's shoulder. "No problem," he said.

Cal moved to block the doorway. "Can I help you? Need some reading material?"

"Wait, you sell books here? I thought this was like a pot shop, you know, Jimmy's Joint." The smallest one doubled over with laughter. The other two snickered. The shop had been around since Cal's great-grandfather opened it in 1948, and he was loathe to change the name.

"Sorry, guys. Hate to disappoint you. Can I interest you in a Jeffrey Archer novel? Maybe a Nicholas Sparks book?"

They looked at him like he was speaking Greek. "No? Then you all have a good day." Going back inside, he closed and locked the door.

Drifting over to a shelf next to the big front window, he pretended to rearrange the books. Through the window, he saw the boys point back at the shop and then up the street. One shoved another, and then they all took off, stopping and looking in each storefront they passed. Satisfied, Cal walked behind the counter, calling over his shoulder, "They're gone." He heard the door close, and he turned to face the woman.

She was clearly in the wrong part of town.

In heels, she was almost eye level with him. Without them, he guessed she'd be about five ten. She looked to be in her late twenties, slim-hipped and big-breasted. Cal knew nothing about women's clothes, but hers looked expensive: a lipstick-red close-fitting dress topped by a black leather jacket, and high-heeled knee-high boots. She pushed her long blond hair back over her shoulder and darted a glance out the window. "Thanks. They were following me and I…"

It was his shop, and he had nowhere to go. Cal nodded. "You can hang out here for a bit, if you want."

Hands tightly clutched around the shoulder strap of her big tote, she twisted her head as if taking in her surroundings for the first time. She slid onto one of the old chrome and red leatherette stools at the counter and dropped her bag on another. "May I have a coffee?"

Cal blinked and pointed at the big commercial machine behind him. "Sure. Help yourself." He settled onto his own stool at the far end of the counter, pulling his laptop toward him.

"Really?" Perfectly groomed eyebrows rose over big brown eyes.

"Yeah. This place stopped being a diner about fifty years ago, but you're welcome to some coffee."

Nodding, she rose and rounded the counter, heading to

the coffee machine. Her bright dress and her bright hair gleamed against the dull mirrored tiles that ran along the wall behind him. She grabbed a mug from one of the glass shelves and inspected it, then stepped over to the sink and rinsed it out. "Do you have a dish towel?"

He flapped his hand at her. "Paper towels are under the sink."

She bent to retrieve the paper towel, giving him a view of her perky butt and smooth thighs. Cal shook his head. He spent way too much time with romance novels. He stared at the computer screen, trying to remember where he'd left off in the story he'd been working on before she'd entered the shop.

"Oh my God!"

He twisted around to see the woman pour her coffee down the sink and fill the mug with water. She drank deeply. "That wasn't coffee. That's swill. That's motor oil. That's—"

"I get the picture. I happen to like my coffee strong."

"And old. When did you make that?"

Screwing up his face, he thought about it. This morning? Yesterday? "No idea. I flick the burner off at the end of the day and back on again in the morning."

"Eww," she said. "I'll just…have water."

"Knock yourself out." He tapped a few keys and then deleted the words, unable to work with the woman prowling around his store. From the corner of his eye, he watched her peek out the front window, then move to stand right in front of it and crane her neck left and right. She sighed. "I can still see them. Do you mind if I wait here for a while?"

Yes, he did mind, but he would be a jerk for saying so. "Not if you buy a book."

"Oh. Sure. I can do that." With a graceful sway of her hips, she walked over to inspect the bookshelves. She moved farther into the stacks, was silent for a moment, then came striding back, holding a book over her head as if it were a trophy.

Cal met her at the cash register and held out his hand for the book. They touched briefly, her small, pale hand a sharp contrast against his bronze skin. He ignored the jolt and concentrated on the tattered hardback. "Mary Oliver, eh?"

A smile animated the woman's face. "Yes. I'd forgotten how much I love her poetry. I used to have this book myself."

"Yeah? Can you recite any?"

She dug around in her tote and pulled out her wallet. "I used to be able to. Not anymore."

Cal keyed in the sale, and she thanked him. "I saw a table at the back. Okay if I sit there?"

"Sure."

Picking up her bag, she walked back into the stacks. Resuming his seat, Cal watched through the mirror as she pulled a large notebook out of her bag and settled it on the table in front of her. She read for a few minutes, then wrote in her notebook. Pulled out her phone and took a selfie. Took photos of the books behind her. He thought about where she was located. Why send photos of old self-help books to someone? It was none of his business, but he rarely had customers, let alone beautiful women who took up residence in the shop. Not that it was going to be his shop much longer, but he buried that thought and went back to studying his customer.

More things came out of her cavernous tote until the table was covered with whatever accessories women carried these days. Discarding her leather jacket, she rose from the table and perused the shelves. Her arms were bare and toned, almost pearly white in the gloom of the old store. She started pulling books off the shelves and stacking them on the empty chairs.

"What are you doing?"

She glanced up, looking for him. Turning around, she

spotted the mirror and addressed it. "I'm organizing your books."

"They're organized. They're in categories."

She gestured behind her like a game show host. "I'm going to keep them in their categories but arrange them by color. That way, they'll be more visually appealing."

Cal was on his feet and around the counter faster than he'd moved in days. He stomped toward her and waved at the shelves. "You can't do that. Readers expect to find books in alphabetical order within the subject. It makes sense that way."

"That may be, but it's not very attractive." She tossed her hair over her shoulder and turned her back to him.

"Attractive doesn't sell books." Grabbing books, he thrust them back onto the shelves, not paying attention to where they went.

"Really? How's that working for you? With the amount of dust on these, I don't think you've sold anything in days."

It had actually been weeks, but she didn't need to know that. In silence, he finished with the books and exited the stacks. Walking over to the window, he peered out, looking both ways and then down at his watch. He'd intended to close early and head home two hours ago. Letting Jimmy's Joint serve as a sanctuary to the haughty woman now meant he'd have to clean up after her. Fortunately, the punks were gone, and he wouldn't have to put up with her much longer.

"I'm closing soon, and it looks like the coast is clear."

She didn't say anything, but moments later, she stood next to him. "I've called a car. They'll be here in a few minutes."

He glanced outside at the growing dark. The punks weren't in sight, but this part of Seattle was not a good place for a woman to be standing alone on the sidewalk. "You can wait in here."

"That's so gracious of you." She didn't attempt to keep the sarcasm out of her voice.

He grunted and walked back to his laptop.

Standing stiff as a statue, she stared out the window until movement indicated a car's presence. Opening the door, she was out of there.

Moving to the window, Cal watched her climb into the back of a car and speak to the driver. She sat back, staring straight ahead, and the car drove off into the gathering dusk.

Inside the store, the scent of lavender lingered in the air, and Cal returned to his laptop and silence.

CHAPTER 2

The car service dropped her at the front door of her building, and she thanked the driver before angling out of the backseat. Pawing through her tote, she pulled out her keycard and walked toward the entrance. First the lawyer, then the stalkers, then the bookstore owner. People were so rude! Her shoulders slumped with defeat, and she longed for her bed, even if it was barely seven o' clock.

A young woman with short, spiked hair opened the door in front of her, nodding and gesturing for Delia to enter.

"Thank you."

The woman smiled politely and walked back to the small office that opened off the lobby. She entered and then appeared at the concierge counter.

"Hi," Delia said. "Are you new here?" Now that she was looking, she could see the woman wore a navy blazer over a white blouse and navy slacks. A name tag on her left lapel said Consuela Ortega.

"No, miss. I usually work the midnight to eight shift. I've recently switched to evenings."

Delia processed this. "Have we met before?"

Her face expressionless, Consuela nodded. "Yes, we have. A few times."

Delia had no memory of meeting her, but if they'd met in the wee hours of the morning, no doubt she'd been returning from a party. She hoped she'd been civil.

"I saw you arrived in an Uber. Is your car okay?"

Her car! She'd left it in the garage under the lawyer's office and forgotten about it. "I think so. It's parked in an underground lot. I'll pick it up tomorrow."

"Would you like us to retrieve it for you?" Consuela turned to a desktop computer, her fingers poised over the keys.

The beauty of living in The Arches was having someone take care of you. Dry cleaning, ready to be picked up, hung in the office behind Consuela. Delivered packages were stacked neatly beside her as well. If Delia had a pet, which she did not, the concierge would arrange for its care. The concierge service was part of her condo fees. They came out of her bank account automatically, and she had no idea what they cost. Shoving that thought to the back of her mind, she smiled and shook her head. "No, thank you, I'll take care of it." Her gaze landed on another computer, this one a battered laptop covered in stickers. Next to it sat an open binder filled with handwritten notes. She gestured at it. "Are you a student?"

Consuela's ears pinked up. Was she studying on company time? Delia didn't blame her. The job couldn't be very interesting.

"Yes. I'm working on my MBA at the U. I'm in my last semester."

"Nice. What do you—"

The phone in the small office rang. Consuela put a hand to it. "Before I take this, is there anything I can help you with?"

Delia shook her head and backed away. It was silly to

keep the woman from doing her job. Heels tapping on the marble floor, she walked over to the elevator, which opened almost immediately. She looked back at Consuela and waved a thank you. The phone snug between her ear and her shoulder, the concierge was studying her screen and didn't see it.

Entering her apartment, she dropped her bag on the art deco table near the door and made her way to the bedroom that held her wardrobe. Rolling racks of clothing arranged by color lined three walls. The fourth wall was her shoe and boot rack. Methodically, she undressed, carefully hanging up her dress and jacket, stuffing forms into her boots and putting them away. She found and put on a pair of leggings and an oversized cashmere sweater and padded barefoot out to the kitchen. Pouring herself a big glass of wine, she moved over to the large windows overlooking the Seattle waterfront. The giant Ferris wheel glittered as it slowly rotated, carrying groups of people who were out for the evening. Delia had been among the first to ride the wheel on its grand opening. Tonight, that thought, and the view, did nothing to alleviate her mood.

Three months. She had three months to—what was it the smug lawyer had said? Right—be able to support her lifestyle all by herself. She drank deeply, thinking she'd better enjoy the wine, because soon she'd be buying it from the gas station. How would she support herself? She'd never really had a job. She'd answered the phones in her father's office one summer. Once, she'd failed to pass on a message, and a deal didn't go through, so her dad suggested she spend the rest of the summer working on her tan. She'd started businesses and then lost interest. She was happy to snap selfies wearing designer clothes or makeup, but she just wasn't good at detailing the worth of the items. She'd never punched a clock or stood behind a cash register.

That reminded her, and in long steps, she retrieved her tote and settled on the white leather sofa. She pulled out the

Mary Oliver book and smiled. Reaching back into the bag, she frowned. She dumped the contents onto the glass coffee table. Crap. Her planner wasn't there. In it, she documented the details of her day, meticulously recording her workouts, food intake, social activities, and posting history. Today she'd started a list of possible employment opportunities.

Delia pounded the sofa and swore. She'd have to return to that dingy bookstore and confront that rude man again. "Lovely." Sighing, she got up and went for another glass of wine.

❄

With a tap on the door and a wave through the window, the letter carrier slid the mail through the slot on the door of the shop. Cal waved back. Sliding off his stool, he crossed the old wooden floors and stooped to retrieve the pile of flyers and advertisements. He flipped through them on the way back to his stool. One long buff envelope stood out. Recognizing the return address, he thrust it, unopened, into a drawer and dropped the rest of the mail into the recycling.

Resuming his seat, he went back to the outline of the romance novel he was ghostwriting. Stacy Wrigglebottom—sadly, that was both the author's given name and chosen pen name—had stopped authoring her own books long ago. Cal was the third writer she'd engaged since then. Now on their tenth collaboration, they'd established a pattern. Stacy came up with the story ideas, the two would plot and outline the book over a video conference, then he would write it and send it to her for approval. Writing about turgid members and heaving bosoms had gotten monotonous, but it paid the bills, which was more than could be said about Jimmy's Joint, the diner turned used bookstore he'd inherited from his grandfather.

The leather-bound notebook with the big brass rings sat on the counter next to his laptop. Like the woman who owned it, it was expensive and even smelled that way. Cal touched the cover, stroking the buttery soft leather. He imagined Delia Duncan—for that was the name of the woman—would be by to pick it up fairly soon. He flipped open the cover again, staring at her handwritten name in bold block letters. He'd expected flowery cursive with maybe a heart instead of a dot above the i. He'd assumed it was a diary but found calendars and lists and schedules. He applauded himself for not reading it when he wanted to know more about the woman who'd invaded his shop.

He'd been a jerk. He knew it. She'd sought refuge in the shop, and he'd kind of, sort of, barely provided it. He shook his head. As soon as Delia Duncan picked up her notebook, she'd be out of his life, taking her hair and her legs and her scent and her vibrancy out of his shop and back into the city. Closing the book, he pushed it aside and buried himself in the adventures of the haughty duke and his troublesome ward.

The bell tinkled. He looked up, and…there she was. The knee-high boots and leather jacket had been replaced by white high-top sneakers and a blue blazer. Tight-fitting jeans encased her long legs, and she wore a vintage Seattle Sonics T-shirt. Her smile was tentative, as if she was unsure of her welcome.

"You're back," he said.

"I left my planner," she replied.

He pushed it across the counter, and she sighed. Picking it up, she stroked the cover, then shoved it into her tote. "Thank you. My life is in here."

"I noticed," he said, then mentally kicked himself.

Her eyes went big. "You read it?"

"No. I flipped it open to find your contact information and saw your calendar. That's it."

"Oh." She seemed relieved.

"You should have your phone number in there if it's that important to you." God, he sounded like a pompous ass.

She made a face. "You're probably right. I've never left it anywhere before." With that, she sat on a stool, pulled out the planner, and wrote under her name. She beamed, then twirled on the stool, which made a screeching sound.

Cal scowled.

She grinned. "I think it needs some WD-40." She drank from the travel mug she'd brought with her. "Are you Jimmy?"

"That's my last name."

"What's your first? You know mine. It seems only fair you tell me yours."

"Calvin."

"Nice to meet you, Calvin Jimmy. I'm Delia." She held out her hand.

Cal looked at it, then at her expectant smile. He reached across and took her hand. As soft as her skin was, she gripped his hand firmly, then released it. Despite himself, the corners of his lips lifted.

With another screeching twirl on the stool, Delia waved at the books around them. "This is quite the place."

"Sure, we'll go with that." He wondered if she saw the same thing he did. Ancient bookshelves caving under the weight of books no one wanted to read. A bay window for displaying books filled with dust bunnies and dead insects. A few mismatched chairs and rickety tables.

She stood and wandered over to the shelf facing the window. The section was filled with fiction—fantasy, sci-fi, mysteries, action/adventure—all by authors past their prime but still selling well. When Cal did sell a book, it was usually to tourists needing reading material before boarding a cruise ship, and it was usually from this area. He watched Delia sip from her mug and trail a finger over the spines. His throat dry, he rose and went to the coffee maker. Cup refilled, he turned to find her watching him.

"You must have a cast-iron stomach."

Cal snorted. "I'm used to it."

"If this is a bookstore, why is there a diner counter in here?" She stepped close enough she had to tip her head back to meet his gaze. Her eyes were a warm sherry color, filled with interest.

"It's a long story."

She settled on a stool and raised her mug at him. "I've got time."

Cal leaned against the back counter, wondering why her tone had gone flat. *Not my business.* "My great-grandfather opened Jimmy's Joint in the late forties. It was a diner up until sometime in the eighties, when my grandfather took over and removed the tables and added the bookshelves. They kept the counter and stools because it was a bugger to remove them, so they sold my grandmother's pastries and coffee."

"How long have you been here?"

He shrugged. "On and off since high school. I took over a few years ago." No one else in the family was interested, and he didn't want to disappoint his grandfather. It was also a great place to lick his wounds. That part she didn't need to know. He decided to turn the tables.

"What do you do that allows you to swan about the city in the middle of the workday?" Shit, that sounded condescending. If she noticed, Delia had the grace to let it go.

"I'm...between things at the moment."

Code for unemployed. Again, none of his business. He sipped his coffee, not feeling the need to respond other than to nod.

Delia fiddled with the opening of her mug. "Have you had many jobs?"

He nodded again.

"Like what?"

He blew out a gust of air. "Well, here when I was a kid, doing grunt work and whatever my grandparents asked me to do. A couple summers on a fishing boat. Some years for the library, and then back here."

"You're a librarian?" She made it sound like he'd said rock star.

"Was. Now I'm a..." He looked around the small, quiet shop. "A bookseller, I guess." It certainly wasn't what he'd envisioned when he graduated from University of Puget Sound with a degree in creative writing and history. He was going to take down the oral history of his ancestors, the Snohomish and the Duwamish, and combine those stories with his love of fantasy, not write steamy Regency romances. A vibrating in his pocket alerted Cal to an incoming call. Checking the displayed name, he raised the phone and looked at Delia. "I gotta take this." Not waiting for a reply, he settled in front of his computer and accepted the call.

Twenty minutes later, he disconnected and dropped the phone to the counter. Delia's tote still occupied a stool. Looking up at the mirror, he saw her deep in the stacks, books piled around her as she once again removed them from the shelves. "Hey! Stop that." She ignored him, bobbing her head up and down. She pushed her hair back over her shoulder, and he spotted the earbud. With a grunt, he rose from the stool and stomped around the counter and toward her.

"I told you not to do that."

Nothing.

Reaching out, he tapped her on the shoulder, getting close to the scent that had teased him the day before.

She startled and twisted toward him. "Oh! Hi." She pulled the earbuds out and beamed up at him. "You were busy, so I thought I'd get started."

"Get started on what?"

"I'm moving the horror section to the front of the store. Load them on that shelf facing the front window and in the window itself. I'll make a display. I saw you have some tchotchkes lying around. I'll use those for visual interest and some of these larger books for elevation."

"Elevation?"

Rising with the grace of a ballerina, Delia pointed to a stack of hardbound science fiction anthologies from the 1960s. Cal's grandfather had bought them at a yard sale, sure they would sell like hotcakes. Twenty years later, they were still on the shelf, gathering dust.

"Can you grab those please?" Without waiting for an answer, she brushed past him and strode to the front of the store.

Leaving the books on the floor, Cal followed her. She stood, surveying the window display, hands on her hips.

"Have you got window cleaner? Rubber gloves would be nice, too." She stepped forward, picking up a sun-faded poster board. It was an enlarged photo of the cover of the latest John Grisham novel…from four years ago. "When was the last time you changed the display?"

He plucked the poster from her hands and put it back on the window ledge. It wobbled and fell to the floor, sending up a cloud of dust. "Why are you doing this? I don't recall asking you to change things around."

"True. But you brighten this space up and update your shelves, traffic will pick up, driving more sales."

"I don't want that."

"Why ever not?"

He flung an arm out to the side. "Look, lady. This is my store, and how I choose to run it is up to me."

"Running it? Running it into the ground is more like it. Who in their right mind would come in here?"

He opened his mouth to reply, but she held up a hand.

"Don't answer that. Circumstances required my presence here yesterday."

They both looked to the street where the only activity was a crow scavenging in a garbage can.

"What the hell were you doing here anyway? And dressed like…" He waved his hand up and down in front of her.

She crossed her arms and cocked a hip. "Like what? Please, continue."

Opening his mouth was always a stupid idea. Even knowing that, he continued, "It wasn't what you were wearing. It was the fact that you, looking like you do, like a fashion model or a…a socialite, was here. This is not the area for a woman to be walking alone late in the day, especially a woman who looks like a target."

"A target?"

"You draw attention to yourself," he grumbled. Maybe she did it on purpose, because even now, she was a beacon, lighting up his store with her presence. She'd probably glow if she were encased in a burlap sack.

"It's not a bad thing."

"It is when you've got three miscreants intent on mischief following you around."

She snorted. "Miscreants intent on mischief? How old are you?"

He scowled. "You know what I mean. You weren't safe."

Shoulders hunched, she moved to the shelf, running an elegant finger across the raised print of a novel. "I was distracted and not paying attention when I turned down an unfamiliar street."

"Well, you should have been."

"I'm aware of that." She glared at him, then turned back to the bookshelf.

He stared at her stiff posture in the ensuing silence. He'd gotten his point across, so he dropped the subject. "Anyway, I don't need your help to drive more sales."

"Again, why ever not? Do you have another income source? Is this a front for a shady business? Do mobsters come here and make illegal deals in the back room?"

Despite himself, he smiled. "You have an active imagination."

She grinned and flipped her hair back over her shoulder. "I read a lot."

"Look, I appreciate your enthusiasm, but there's no point in changing the display." He pictured the pile of buff envelopes lying in the drawer. "I doubt it would make a difference, and I can't pay you."

Her hand on his forearm stopped him from going back to the counter.

"I have…time on my hands right now, and I love organizing, and I love books. Let me do this for you, and if you don't sell"—she squinted and looked up at the ceiling before gazing back at him—"ten books in the next week, you can say I told you so and I won't bother you again."

"And if I do?" He crossed his arms and glared down at her.

"I get to read ten books for free!"

"You look like you can afford to buy your books."

The light went out of her eyes, and she turned away. Cal kicked himself. "That wasn't fair. I shouldn't judge."

"No, you're right. Up until recently, I've been able to indulge myself."

Hands on his hips, Cal stared around the shop. If he was going to be evicted, he wouldn't be able to take the books with him, and he sure as shit didn't have the energy to deal with the mess.

"Knock yourself out."

Delia squealed and clapped.

CHAPTER 3

"I don't think so."

"Really?"

"Honey, GG doesn't need a social media director. We have a system in place that runs like clockwork. There's not much you can do for us that we're not doing already." Kevin Armstrong's eyes were full of sympathy. A former employee of Duncan Properties, he'd recently bought into Grand Gestures Event Planning. One of his partners, Beth Beckett, was engaged to Delia's brother. The other partner, Jane Beckett, was dating the CFO of Duncan Properties.

"But I have tons of followers. Potential clients for you." Delia pressed a hand down to stop her leg from jiggling.

His brows pinched together, Kevin shook his head. "You are great as an influencer, but we have a waiting list of clients. Sorry."

She knew he meant it. Kevin was a truly kind soul, and they'd been friends for years. She picked up her cup, using it to hide the disappointment on her face. It was empty. She placed it back down on the tiny table in the trendy coffee shop and forced a smile. "That's fine."

"What are your other options?"

Chuck must have told Beth who told Kevin about the trust fund clause, but Delia wasn't going to bring it up. She waved dismissively. "I've got a lot of leads, but you're my first."

Kevin squeezed her hand. "Do you want me to keep my ears to the ground?"

"Sure." She didn't like being in this position, practically groveling to a friend.

"What have you been doing? Your nails look awful." He held her hand up, staring at it.

She snatched it back and tucked it under her thigh. "I was doing some cleaning and didn't have rubber gloves."

"You know better than that. Book yourself a mani before you go out in public."

"Will do."

They made small talk for a few more minutes. When Kevin checked his watch, she knew it was time to go. Delia rose from her chair and planted a kiss on his dark brown cheek.

She left the coffee shop and joined the crowds on the busy sidewalks of downtown Seattle. Stopping at a crosswalk, she inspected her nails. They did look awful.

Yesterday, while Cal had planted himself behind his computer, she had tied her hair up and gotten busy. Finding cleaning products but no gloves under the sink, she'd swept up dead bugs, washed the windows, and dusted the shelves. On the wide window ledge, she'd stacked up large books at varying heights and used them to create a display of horror and thriller novels, all with cover art in a similar color palette. She'd been pleased with her efforts. Cal had grunted. She'd gone home content but tired.

The light changed and she crossed. On the other side of the street, she stepped closer to a wall to look at her phone. She'd missed three calls from her mother. No doubt, she and her father had plans to make everything better. Figure out a way to beat the clause. Delia dashed off a text, making up a nonexistent appointment as an excuse to not meet up, and shoved her phone back into her bag.

Last night, she'd reached out to a few friends, asking them what they thought her best assets were. She should have rephrased the question, because more than one person mentioned her breasts and her butt. Truth be told, she spent a lot of time working out and had a great figure—and the boob job helped as well. Others mentioned her wardrobe, acid wit, and ability to ferret out the best parties. Two friends mentioned her organizational skills. She'd assisted them in purging their wardrobes, rearranging their closets, and building capsule collections for traveling. She smiled in recollection. That had been fun. There was something about creating order out of chaos that resonated with her. The image of the overflowing shelves in the bookshop came to mind, making her itch.

With nothing better to do, her steps turned in the direction of Jimmy's Joint, this time approaching it from a busier street.

Standing across from the shop, she smiled in anticipation of the bright display she'd created, then frowned. What the hell? She jaywalked across the street and pushed open the door.

"What did you do with all the books? The display is empty." She dropped her tote on a stool and glared at Cal.

The big jerk leaned back and planted his hands wide. He nodded at the shelves. "Go help yourself."

"What?"

"Some guy was in here about an hour ago and bought all of them."

"All of them?"

Cal nodded. "He wants them as party favors for a Halloween bash he's throwing."

Delia sank down on a stool. "All of them sold." She said it more to herself than to Cal. Her idea had worked!

"Yep." He rose and stretched, the flannel of his shirt pulling against his broad chest. "He's willing to buy more if we have them. I haven't looked, but aren't there a bunch of other horror books back there?"

Nodding like a bobblehead, Delia jumped up and shucked off her jacket. "Yes. There's a ton of them. But"—she stopped and bit her lip—"I don't know if they're in the same color palette. Do you think that will matter?"

Cal stuck two fingers into his shirt pocket and pulled out a business card. "Call him yourself and find out."

Delia grabbed the card and clutched it to her chest, beaming the whole time.

*C*olor palette. He had no freaking clue what she was talking about.

Cal filled his coffee mug and watched Delia move around the shop, muttering to herself. Today she wore another pair of close-fitting jeans that molded to her backside and disappeared into cowboy boots. She'd rolled up the sleeves of her raspberry-silk blouse and bunched her hair into a messy bun on top of her head. He couldn't take his eyes off her.

He'd been dumbfounded when the guy entered the shop and offered him fifty bucks for the seven old paperbacks on display. No dickering, no nothing. Cal took his money and his business card. Standing by the door, the guy said he'd thought there was a new owner. He'd never seen such a great display in the shop before. Cal was a little pissed, but then realized the guy was right.

When his grandparents owned the shop, his grandmother created a themed display each month, replacing and shifting books around to make them look fresh. After she died, it wasn't quite the same. His grandfather didn't have the heart, and Cal's efforts seemed to upset him, so in the end, Cal stopped.

Nothing seemed to stop Delia. Not only had she dug up the remainder of the horror books, she'd set up more books in the window, these ones all in shades of yellow. Now she was dragging a broken-down armchair upholstered in worn green velvet across the floor.

"Hang on." Cal put his cup down and hustled toward her. "This thing will collapse if someone sits on it. That's why it was back in the corner."

Delia pushed a strand of hair out of her face, leaving a streak of dirt on her cheek. He zeroed in on it, spotting a constellation of tiny freckles under her left eye. That small imperfection in her otherwise flawless complexion made her seem more human. That and the dirt. He lifted a hand and thumbed it away, startling them both.

"You had some…" He stuck his hands in the pockets of his jeans before they could get him into trouble.

Delia colored and cleared her throat. "So the chair. I want to prop it up on books until it's the same height as the ledge. Angle it toward the window, pile more books around it. With the right colors, it will look stunning." She fanned out her fingers and raised her arms as if embracing the shop window.

"Stunning, huh?" Cal rocked back on his heels.

"Yes." If she caught the teasing tone in his voice, she didn't let on. "When I was here the other day and I peeked inside the storage room—"

"You mean when you were hiding?"

She glared at him.

He grinned.

Lips parted, she stared, wide eyes searching his face. Then she blinked and darted past him. "Whatever. In the storage room, I saw some furniture and boxes. Is it okay if I look through them? See if there's anything to use?"

He twisted to follow her, thinking about what was in the back room. Decades of crap, most likely. He followed her to the doorway and opened it. The cool smell of old paper and dust greeted them. He flicked on the light switch, and the big overhead fluorescents flickered, then held steady. He stepped back to allow Delia to enter. "Knock—"

"I know. Knock myself out." She grinned at him and turned back to the piles of stuff.

He hadn't been in the room in ages, so rather than leave her to it, he wandered around, looking at items that were memories of his childhood. His mother worked in the bookstore Saturdays while his grandparents drove around to yard sales. Too young to be left on his own, he was sometimes in the store with his mom or sometimes in the car with his grandparents.

"Seriously? What's the story behind these?" Delia knelt in front of an open box, holding aloft a pair of huge red Converse high-tops.

He snorted. "The one and only time Gram didn't go with Pops to a yard sale, he bought those."

"He must have been bigger than you."

"Hardly. They were a buck, and he couldn't pass them up. Never wore them. Couldn't get rid of them because he didn't know anyone with feet big enough for them. Gram was so pissed."

Delia smiled and tucked them back into the box like they were precious jewels. She opened another box and squealed.

In a flash, Cal was by her side. "You okay?"

"I'll say." She held up a throw pillow in bright orange and yellow colors. "These are perfect!"

"Really?" He scratched his head. "They look kinda gaudy to me."

Tsking, she got to her feet and shoved past him to the doorway. "You have no taste whatsoever. Follow me."

Eyes on her swaying backside, Cal did just that. She placed the pillows on the armchair and fussed with them. Standing back with hands on her hips, she beamed up at him.

"You're right. It's stunning." He wasn't blowing smoke. Out of cast-off books and furniture, she'd made a vignette that was a feast for the eyes.

She nudged his arm. "Go outside and look through the window."

He did as told. The chair looked great. Delia looked even better. She looked pleased and proud and…joyful. He knew nothing about the woman but somehow understood there wasn't much that elicited this response from her.

He walked back into the store to find her bouncing on her toes. "I'll create a shelf with books to replace the ones we sell out of the display and, in two weeks' time, switch it out completely. I'll make a spreadsheet of titles we use and what the theme is. I don't want to repeat a display theme too frequently."

His apprehension increased with the tempo of her excitement. He blurted out, "Stop. I can't hire you."

CHAPTER 4

"I'm not...I'm not looking for a job."

Cal scrubbed a hand over his face. "Isn't that what this is all about? You're out of work and you're looking for a job?"

"Well, yes and no." God, could this get any more embarrassing? While she hoped the floor would open beneath her, Cal was looking everywhere but at her. "I do need to find work, but your shop wouldn't be able to support me." She looked down, her glance taking in his scuffed hiking boots with mismatched laces, and then her own custom-made cowboy boots.

"The thing is, even if I could afford to pay you, there'd be no point in hiring you. This building is scheduled to be demolished, and I need to be out of here in three months."

"Oh." What else was there to say? She wanted to rub his slumped shoulders. Instead, she crossed her arms and tucked her hands in her armpits. "That's hard."

"Yeah. But here." He reached into his pocket and pulled out a fifty-dollar bill. "You earned this, and whatever else that guy buys, you can have."

"Really?"

"If it weren't for you, he wouldn't have come in here."

Delia stared at the money as Cal walked back to his laptop.

Deep in thought, she pulled out her phone and the business card Cal had given her. Her phone dinged with another text from her mother. She ignored it. An idea was niggling at the back of her mind.

Moving into the stacks, she settled into a chair and texted away. A few minutes later, she walked up to the counter, a determined look on her face. She cleared her throat. "Any chance I can buy you a drink?"

Cal's impassive face wasn't inspiring confidence.

She squared her shoulders and flipped her hair back. "I have a business proposition for you, and I'd rather do it where you're not going to frown at me, then stare at your laptop."

"I don't frown at you."

She raised a brow at his lack of self-awareness.

"Well, maybe I do." He glanced at his wristwatch. "It's only three o'clock."

She looked at her smart watch. "No, it's not. It's almost five."

He shook his wrist. "I guess I forgot to wind it." He removed the ancient timepiece and reset the time. "Okay. Give me ten minutes to finish this up. You figure out where you want to go."

If there was one thing Delia was an expert on, it was the location of every high-end bar in Seattle. While he scribbled in a notebook, then shut down his laptop, she studied the notes she'd made in her planner. She knew it was a great idea, but would the crusty guy go for it? She pulled out her makeup bag and sorted through her collection of lipsticks and lip glosses. Which one was best for pitching an idea? She settled on a nude gloss and slicked it on.

"Ready?"

Picking up her jacket and tote, she walked out of the stacks, then stopped in her tracks. Wearing a tan leather jacket, Cal stood next to the front door, backpack slung over his shoulder, jiggling the keys in his hand. The jacket, the flannel, the worn jeans, and the hiking boots were not a look that would normally pique Delia's interest. On Cal, they looked awesome. His jet-black hair curled over the collar, and one lock fell across his forehead. Unlike most men of her acquaintance, he was clean-shaven, which was an odd juxtaposition with his worn and rumpled clothing. "What did you decide?"

His question brought her out of her reverie. He opened the door, and she passed through and waited while he locked the door and pocketed the keys.

"McQuarry's is about six blocks from here. Do you know it?" She tried not to make it obvious as she inhaled the scent of him. Leather and sandalwood were now her two favorite smells.

"Nope. You're gonna have to lead."

He fell into step beside her, occasionally placing a hand on her arm to guide her out of the way of fast-walking pedestrians staring at their phones instead of their surroundings. The streets and sidewalks were busy with people eager to flee the downtown and head home. A drizzle started half a block from the bar, and they hastened to reach it before the skies opened up.

Cal held the door open for her, and Delia stepped inside, shaking the rain off her hair. She turned to find Cal blinking water out of his eyes.

"Oh my God, I'm so sorry!" She reached up and wiped droplets off his cheek.

His dark eyes crinkled at the corners. "I'll be fine. I've been rained on before."

Feeling her cheeks warm, she ducked her head and

moved into the bar, choosing a table in a corner with windows overlooking the terraced garden of a condo below them. She raised her hands to remove her jacket, but Cal's were there already. Over her shoulder, she peered up at him, smiling her thanks. He removed his jacket as well and hung them both on nearby hooks, then waited for her to sit before settling into a chair opposite her. He studied her face with an open expression, as if he had all day. Now that she had his attention, she didn't know where to begin.

"So, umm…you have to vacate your building?"

He nodded slowly. "Demolition starts in three months' time, and the property manager wants me out sooner rather than later. My lease is paid up, and between now and then, I have to offload all those books and find a home for the crap in the back room. It's kind of overwhelming, so I've been keeping the door closed and not thinking about it."

The server came, and Delia ordered a white wine spritzer while Cal asked for an IPA. When the server left, she pulled out her planner and placed it on the table in front of her, fingers interlaced over the cover. "Do you have a plan?"

Again, his eyes crinkled at the corners. "No, but I suspect you do."

She glanced down and then back up. She had the complete attention of an attractive man, a place she'd been many times before. This time, however, it felt different. She ignored the butterflies in her stomach and concentrated on her plan for the bookstore.

"Did you invest in the current inventory?"

"No."

"Are you expecting to make any money off the books?"

Cal leaned back and hooked an arm over the back of his chair. "Maybe if I set fire to them and get an insurance payout."

The server chose that exact moment to bring their drinks.

Wide-eyed, he dropped them off and scurried back to the bar.

"Do you think he's going to call the cops?" Cal looked amused.

"More like film us for a true crime show."

They exchanged smiles and sipped their drinks.

Placing her glass on the table, Delia opened her planner to the talking points she'd written out. "This probably sounds very rude, but you don't seem very interested in running the bookstore."

"That's because I'm not." He shifted to take a drink, then set the glass back down. "The shop has been around for many years. My grandfather expected one of the family to take it over. No one was interested. We all did our time, working there in high school or college, and running a shop in a scuzzy part of town didn't appeal."

"Why do you have it?"

"I'm the family bookworm." He shifted once again to stare out the window.

Delia didn't move. She wanted him to go on. This was the most he'd said at one time. Finally, he turned back to her.

"My grandmother died, and a part of my grandfather died with her. He couldn't handle the store by himself, and he refused to sell it. At the time, I was working at UW, lived the closest to him, and was the obvious choice to be there. He left it to me in his will, and while I don't need the shop, getting out from under it has been more than I've wanted to deal with." He flashed a self-deprecating grin at her. "I'm lazy. Let's leave it at that."

"Delia darling, is that you?" A beautifully made-up man swished his way across the room.

Inwardly, Delia groaned. Normally she'd be delighted to see him, but not today, and not with Cal. Straightening her shoulders, she shook her hair back and flashed her influencer smile. "Why Tommy! How lovely to see you."

❄

The woman was a chameleon. Gone was the funny, friendly, slightly insecure woman who was interested in him. In her place was a beautiful, brittle socialite who should be holding court and a martini as opposed to sitting with him.

Tommy air-kissed Delia and twittered about parties he'd been to, making catty remarks about the people he'd seen. She nodded and gasped and interacted like it was a familiar exchange. Cal felt like he was watching his sisters when they'd been teenagers.

Tommy shifted his attention to Cal, one manicured hand stroking the pearls at his throat while he extended the other. "And who might you be?"

Cal stood from his chair and took the proffered hand in his own. For all his feminine ways, Tommy had a firm handshake. He gripped Cal's hand once and released it in an unspoken warning. Cal looked between him and Delia, realizing that Tommy cared about her. He nodded at the shorter man. "Calvin Jimmy. Would you like to join us? I can get you a chair."

He waved away the offer. "No, darling, but thank you. Just checking on my girl." He turned to Delia and wagged a finger. "Don't be a stranger. Ta ta." With that, he swished back to the bar and seated himself like a queen on her throne.

Eyes on Delia instead of Tommy, Cal sat back down and saw the transformation in reverse. Her face softened, yet her shoulders remained tense and her eyes looked…wary.

He wasn't going to give her the my-best-friend/cousin/roommate-was-gay speech. "He seems protective. Have you known each other long?"

She tucked a strand of hair behind her ear and nodded.

"We had classes together in college. One day we both showed up wearing the same boots and bonded."

"Did they look better on him?"

"Yes!" Her eyes narrowed. "I never wore mine again." She tossed her hair and grinned.

He liked this Delia better and wondered why she'd cultivated the other persona.

Her phone buzzed with an incoming call. With a frown, she retrieved it from her tote, glanced at the caller ID, and shut it off. Immediately, a text came in. She gusted out a sigh. "I've been dodging my mother all day. I have to respond to this. Would you like to look at a menu and order something to eat?"

Most nights he closed up shop, headed to his apartment, heated up something to eat, and then wrote all evening. Dinner with Delia? She'd made it clear this was business, not a date. So yeah, he could do that. "Sure. I'll go get menus."

He stood next to Tommy while the server retrieved menus for them. Tommy eyed him over the rim of his cotton candy–colored drink. "It's not what you think," Cal said.

"Um-hmm," Tommy murmured.

"It's a business dinner."

Tommy looked him up and down. "What kind of business?"

"I need to close down my bookshop. Delia has ideas for me."

Tommy looked over his shoulder. Cal followed his gaze to see Delia speaking animatedly into her phone, looking exasperated.

"It's her mom."

Tommy's face brightened. "Her mother is lovely. Meddles too much, but still lovely."

Cal made a noncommittal sound.

"Delia has great ideas if you need to feng shui the place. Has she shown you her Pinterest board?"

"Ahh, no. We were just getting to her suggestions when her mom called."

They both looked back at Delia. Hair covering her face, both elbows on the table, she cradled her head in her hand while holding the phone. It did not look like a fun phone call.

"I love that girl." Tommy spoke low and fierce. "Something is going on with her, and I'm worried. She's shut me out. If you're the reason…"

Cal raised his hands in surrender. "I met her two days ago when she came into my bookstore. There's nothing between us."

Tommy studied him as if memorizing his features, then turned and went through the messenger bag on the stool beside him. He held out a business card and said, "Call me. If she's in trouble, I want to know."

Cal pocketed the card and picked up the menus. "I will. Got a pen?" When Tommy handed him one, he scrawled on the back of a coaster. "This is me. You can find me at Jimmy's Joint."

He walked back to the table, thinking there must be something about Delia that inspired so much loyalty.

"Your mom okay?"

Dropping her phone back into her bag, she accepted a menu, bright spots coloring her cheekbones. "Yes. I have a… situation, and my parents want to fix it for me."

Giving her a minute, Cal studied his own menu. "Need a body buried?"

Looking both ways, she leaned forward and dropped her voice to a whisper. "Possibly. Got any suggestions?"

He worked hard at maintaining a poker face. "I got a boat. The ocean's that a way."

She opened her mouth, but nothing came out. Sitting back, she shook her head. "I got nothing. But thanks for the offer."

"Can I help?" Where did that come from? He had

enough on his plate without taking on someone else's problems. The words were out, though, and he couldn't take them back. He hoped there really wasn't a dead body involved.

Delia drummed long, slender fingers on the top of her planner. "Oddly enough, we can help each other. I called the guy who bought the books this afternoon, and he wants any and all horror and thriller books you have. He plans to use them for party decorations as well as giveaways, so he doesn't care if they're in great shape. He may gut some books and use pages here and there. Does that bother you?"

The server came and took their orders and the menus while Cal mulled over his response.

"When it comes to things, I'm not a romantic. I'd rather the books be used for something rather than end up in a burn pile or landfill or a recycling center. Because unless I sell them, that's what will happen to most of them. And I'll have to do the work."

Opening her planner, Delia ticked off a box on what looked like a long list. "I know there are people who geek out over pulp novels. I have an uncle with a room dedicated to Doc Savage."

"I've heard that name. He's a character from the 1940s, right? There were comic books as well."

"Actually, the 1930s, but you're right. I think we can contact collector groups and see if there's interest in other pulp novels. We can put items up for online auctions. I can photograph and highlight books on your website."

"I don't have a website."

"Shut the front door! How can you run a business without a website? How do people find you? Wait, how are you able to earn a living?" She gasped and waved her hands in front of her. "Sorry, sorry. You don't have to tell me anything."

Cal huffed out a laugh. "It's fine. I write fiction. Jimmy's

Joint is pretty much my office. It gets me out of my apartment, and sometimes, I actually talk to people."

Fiddling with the stem of her wineglass, Delia appeared to be digesting what he'd said.

"Have I read any of your books?"

"It's possible. I'm a ghostwriter. Authors hire me to write under their name."

"Really? Anyone I might know?"

He shook his head. "I can't tell you. I've signed NDAs forbidding me from disclosing their names."

"Well, that stinks. But you do well enough to keep the shop open? I hope that's not too tacky a question."

"I do all right." It was actually more than all right. He was able to pay off his parents' mortgage and send them on vacation every year. "How will you benefit from selling off the inventory?"

Straightening up, she took a sip of her wine as if needing to fortify herself. "I'll go through the stacks and separate the books into different categories: collector items, decor items, book art, and recycling. Then I'll research values of the collectibles, create vignettes to photograph anything salable, and promote those online, arrange hauling of the recycle/garbage pile. On a spreadsheet, I'll track sales and then, um, I thought we'd um, split the profits fifty-fifty."

He wanted to kiss her feet. Instead, he said, "Seventy-five, twenty-five."

"Oh! Um…okay." She glanced down at the table, her long hair hiding her face.

"You get seventy-five percent of the profits."

Her head shot up. "Seriously?"

"I would never have thought to do any of that, and you're doing the bulk of the work. I'm only providing the inventory and a strong back for heavy lifting."

She blinked, then looked away, blinking some more.

Clearing her throat, she smiled up at him. "Right. We should start with building a website."

Watching her turn to a blank page in her planner and scribble away, Cal hid his own smile behind his raised glass. He'd be happy hauling heavy boxes if it meant spending time with this quick-witted and quick-changing creature.

CHAPTER 5

*J*uggling three boxes, Delia crossed the lobby to the concierge office and dropped them on the counter.

"Good afternoon, Consuela."

"Good afternoon, Ms. Duncan."

"Please, call me Delia."

"Yes, ma'am, umm, Delia."

The younger woman smiled politely, but it didn't quite reach her eyes. For the life of her, Delia couldn't remember meeting her before a few days ago. If Consuela had been on the night shift, and her being a night owl, they must have run into each other.

It came back to her.

She'd closed down a nightclub with a couple girlfriends, but they weren't ready to call it a night. Buying overpriced bottles of champagne from the bar, they'd come back to Delia's place. The car service dropped them off, and while she searched for her key, one friend, Lauren, banged on the glass door to get the attention of the concierge, a young woman. The concierge had rushed across the lobby to open the door. Delia and her friends staggered inside. Then

Lauren dropped the bottle she was carrying. It smashed on the marble floor, sending shards of glass and champagne flying through the air. Mumbling an apology through their laughter, the three women walked through the mess to the elevator. At the time, it had been hysterical.

Now, Delia looked up at Consuela, eyes scrunched up in mortification. "Did I—did I ever say thank you? For when my friend dropped that champagne bottle?"

"Yes, ma'am." Consuela bobbed her head but did not meet Delia's eyes. "You sent a note and a hundred-dollar bill."

"Oh." She wished the floor would open up and swallow her down. "I'm so, so sorry. That must have taken you—"

"Two hours. I spent two hours mopping up the mess, then picking up tiny pieces of glass. Mrs. Tsang in 11B walks her schnauzer every morning at 7 a.m. I had to ensure the dog didn't get a piece of glass in its paw." Consuela cleared her throat. "Now, how can I help you?"

"Umm, I'll come back later." Delia picked up the boxes and scurried back to the elevator.

*E*xcept for a tiny piece of stuck on something, the kitchen sink gleamed. A little more elbow grease should take care of it. Delia pushed back a hank of hair with her forearm and attacked the sink with renewed vigor. After this, she planned to sort through her lipstick drawer. Yesterday, she'd noticed a red got mixed in with a mauve. That wouldn't do.

A knock sounded at the door. It came again before she realized what it was. She never had unannounced visitors.

She stripped off the rubber gloves and tossed them on the counter. At the mirrored table in the hallway, she glanced at her reflection and smoothed back her hair. Through the peephole in the door, she spotted Consuela. Frown lines on her forehead, she scowled down at the carpet.

Crap. Delia hadn't figured out how to face her. She'd been thinking of avoiding the lobby during the late afternoons, perhaps arriving and leaving through the parking garage. Maybe move out of the apartment.

A knock came again.

Taking in and releasing a deep breath, she opened the door.

"Hi!"

Consuela nodded and straightened her shoulders. "Umm, hi, Ms. Duncan—"

"Delia."

"What?"

"Please, call me Delia. Won't you come in?"

"Umm, sure."

Delia held the door open for the clearly unsettled woman, then rushed past her. "I was about to make some tea," she called over her shoulder as she stepped into the kitchen. "Do you have time for some?"

"Ahh, no. I need to get back downstairs." Consuela twisted her hands together.

"Right. Yes. You must be very busy. You're very good at your job." Delia fussed with the kettle, knowing she was blathering away. "All of the concierge staff is excellent. I've been meaning to write—"

"Please don't!"

Consuela's outburst startled both of them. Delia turned off the water and put the kettle down on the counter separating her from the other woman. "I don't understand."

Her spiky hair looked as wilted as Consuela did. "Please don't write a letter to the concierge service. I'm sorry I was rude to you earlier today. I shouldn't have sounded off. It's not like that was the first time I had to clean up after a resident. It's not exactly part of the job, but it's *part of the job*. If you know what I mean. And I'm really sorry."

Delia picked up the kettle, put it on the stove, and turned

on the burner. Buying herself more time to process Consuela's words, she opened a canister of tea and fished out a bag of chamomile. "My drunken friends and I left you with a mess to clean up. What's wrong with me writing to the management and letting them know how thankful I am?"

"That's what you were going to say?"

"Of course. What did you think I'd write?"

Consuela let out a shaky laugh. "A reprimand. For me giving you grief. There's already one in my file, and I'll get fired if I get another."

"Oh. Wow. What for? Wait…no. You don't have to tell me. It's none of my business."

"No. It's fine. Even though The Arches is an adult-only building, we get kids coming to stay with family. There's a couple on the fourteenth floor, whose granddaughters were visiting, twins, I think. Anyway, their grandmother was taking them somewhere, and they just got off the elevator. Grandma forgot something back in her apartment and asked me if I would keep an eye on the girls while she went back. I said yes. Of course, the phone rings at that time, and while I'm dealing with a call, the two of them start racing around. One girl goes behind the big potted Ficus—you know which one I'm talking about?"

Delia nodded. The plant was huge.

"So the little sh—I mean, darling—starts flinging dirt at her sister. That one starts howling and leaps at her. The two of them are behind the Ficus, pulling hair, slapping faces, kicking. Oh my God, it was awful." Consuela took a huge breath. "I pull one of them off the other right as the elevator opens and Grandma steps out. Both of them point at me and start crying, telling her I'd threatened them. I couldn't get a word in edgewise, and the old bat goes up one side of me and down the other."

"Holy shit!"

"Yeah. This happens right at shift change and, fortunately,

it was the supervisor, Yan. He listened to Mrs. Blair insisting I be fired. All the while, the two girls are standing behind their grandmother and out of sight of Yan, high-fiving each other and laughing at me."

The kettle whistled, and Delia took it off the burner and filled the teapot. "You're still working here. What happened next?"

"Fortunately, Yan has been around for a while. After Mrs. Blair and her devil grandspawn left, Yan showed me the video feed from the lobby's security cameras. We watched the whole thing together."

"Did he show the video to Mrs. Blair?"

Consuela rolled her eyes. "Are you kidding? The job of the concierge is to be pleasant and accommodating. We don't make waves."

"But that's…" Delia was at a loss for words. How many times had she walked through the lobby without acknowledging the concierge or left a package on their desk, expecting them to take care of it without even a thank you? Was everyone in the building as self-centered as she was?

"Most of the time, it's a good job. Attached to the written reprimand from Mrs. Blair is a note from Yan about the video tape. But still."

Delia poured two cups of tea and handed one to Consuela.

She wrapped her hands around the mug, as if using it to warm up. "Thanks, but I really should be getting back downstairs. Michel is on the desk and will be wondering where I am."

"Thanks for coming up here. I'm truly sorry for our behavior that night."

"No, it's me who needs to apologize. I was grumpy today and took it out on you. Won't happen again." Consuela put the mug down on the counter and walked to the door, Delia trailing behind, thinking about how incredibly gracious the other woman was.

"Hey," she said as Consuela was about to close the door behind her. "Anytime you want to be grumpy, I'm happy to listen. You don't have to talk to me. Just, you know…"

Consuela's smile took over her entire face. "Thanks, I might take you up on that."

A few hours later, Delia went back down to the lobby with the three boxes and a Tupperware container.

"Hi, Ms. Duncan."

Delia rolled her eyes.

"I mean, Delia."

Delia nodded. "Hi, Consuela."

"If I call you Delia, how about you call me Connie?"

"Deal."

Exchanging shy smiles, the two women nodded in agreement.

Placing the boxes on the counter, Delia handed the container to Connie. "I hope you like snickerdoodles."

"Oh!" Connie looked at the cookies and then up at Delia. "That's so nice. I love snickerdoodles."

Delia smiled. "You said you were grumpy earlier, and cookies make everything better."

"They do, indeed. Thank you." She placed the container under the counter and pointed at the boxes.

"Returning some shoes?" Connie picked up the boxes to relocate them to the corner of her office designated for packages.

Up until recently, it would have been a fair assumption. On a whim, Delia would order a dozen pairs of shoes and then return those that didn't suit her fancy. "Not exactly. I've decided to sell some things online."

Connie returned and folded her hands in front of her on the counter. "Starting up an online boutique for local designers? That's cool."

"Something like that," she murmured. Delia did not want to tell her that the items were things she'd purchased for herself and never worn or had only worn once. She nodded at the open laptop in front of Connie to change the subject. "What are you planning to do when you finish school?"

Grimacing, Connie said, "My long-term goal is to help members of the BIPOC community set up their own businesses. There are a lot of obstacles when you're an immigrant or English isn't your first language."

Having only lived in the moment, Delia had never thought about the long term, and the idea of doing anything altruistic never crossed her mind. She nodded encouragingly as Connie leaned on the counter and propped her chin on her fist.

"For now, I'll be sending out my resume and networking with all the big companies here in Seattle. An accountant with an MBA who happens to be a woman of color is an asset."

"Why not work for a non-profit right off the bat?"

"That would be nice, but most of them can't afford to pay very much, and I have student loans to pay off."

Delia pasted on a sympathetic smile, but it was something she'd never had to face. "Are there lots of hoops to jump through when starting up your own business?" The two failed enterprises she'd had, the interior design store and the vegan clothing boutique, had all been set up—and eventually shut down—by her father and brother.

As far as Delia knew, Connie didn't know any of her history, as she appeared to give her question serious consideration. "It depends on what you're doing. Are you leasing a storefront? Do you have employees? Where is your inventory coming from? What kind of taxes do you need to pay?"

Listening to Connie ramble away about local, state, and other business taxes, Delia stared at the boxes of shoes she was shipping off. She hadn't considered tax implications. She tuned back in as Connie said, "Fortunately, the State of Washington's website for small businesses is comprehensive and pretty easy to follow. Is there something I can help you with?"

For a moment, Delia was tempted to toss her problem in Connie's lap and ask her to set everything up for her. Knowing that would accomplish nothing, and she wouldn't learn anything that way, she shook her head. "No, but thank you. You've given me some great information, and if I need advice, I know where to come."

A smile bloomed on Connie's face. "I'd like that. It would be practical experience for helping businesses in the future."

The tapping of heels on the marble floor alerted them to a woman approaching from the elevator, carrying packages of her own. Delia waved at Connie before heading up to her apartment, feeling like she'd made a friend.

CHAPTER 6

She parked in front of Jimmy's Joint to unload her camera equipment.

"Here, let me." Cal propped open the door and came to her side to grab the tripod and collapsible umbrella lights. "Wow, you're prepared," he said, studying the equipment as she dropped her loaded tote bag on the counter.

"Yeah, well…" She waved at the pile, not wanting to tell him she'd bought it for taking selfies and recording TikTok videos of herself. "I'm going to find a parking spot. I'll be back in a few."

She hustled back to the car to move it to the parking lot two blocks up the street, noticing a street kid loitering by the storefront next door. They were all over the downtown area, and most of the time, she didn't pay them any mind at all. After having been followed into Cal's shop that one day, they now made her wary. She parked her car and walked back to the shop, going through the checklist in her mind of things she wanted to get done that day. The night before, she'd created a document with multiple spreadsheets, one page for each category of books, with columns indicating their quality, perceived value, and potential market. Stuck on what to do with a pile of comic books, she didn't see the kid until he loomed right in front of her.

It wasn't a kid. The man's vacant eyes stared at her, and the smell of unwashed clothing clung to him. She shrieked. "Get away from me!" She shouldered him aside and dashed into the shop, slamming the door behind her.

Cal was beside her in a blink. "What the hell? Are you okay?"

Delia pointed a trembling finger out the window. "He…he…he attacked me."

"Shit!" Pushing Delia to the side, Cal raced out the door and after the retreating back of the man.

Knees weak, she slumped onto a stool to wait for Cal's return and her heart to slow down.

A few minutes later, he returned, hair tousled, color high, lips compressed in a tight line. Stalking toward her, he said, "Tell me exactly what happened."

As clearly as she could, Delia recounted her run-in. "I think he was watching the shop. Planning to steal something, maybe. He was stoned or drunk. Clearly on something."

Hands on his hips, Cal stared off into the distance, listening attentively. "Did he touch you? Threaten you in any way?"

She blinked, having expected words of sympathy or empathy instead of a grilling. "No-o. He…I guess he surprised me—startled me."

Cal grunted and strode over to the window to stare out at the street.

Heart sinking, Delia went over the event in her mind. Had she done something wrong? Not paying close attention to her surroundings was her only crime. "I may have overreacted, but after those guys followed me the other day, I don't think that can be held against me. Hopefully, that"—she flung her arm wide—"person, won't come back here."

"That's what I'm afraid of." Yanking the door open, Cal left the shop again.

She stood in the empty store, listening to the silence, crestfallen. What had she done wrong? And what should she do now? She didn't have keys, didn't know if Cal had his keys with him, and did not want to leave the shop unoccupied and unlocked. She also didn't want to remain in the shop alone. Eyeing the camera equipment and bulging tote bag she'd brought into the store, she made a decision. Walking quickly to the front door, she turned the lever to lock it, then moved about the store, turning on every light in the place.

Putting Cal's insensitivity and her hurt feelings aside, she pulled out her planner to consult her list and set about her first task.

Frustrated and wrung out with fear, Cal stood in front of the coffee shop and scanned the people inside, searching faces, looking for a familiar silhouette, but none of them were Sid. After leaving Delia behind in Jimmy's Joint, he'd spent hours combing the streets for his cousin, because he was positive that was who had bumped into Delia, not attacked her. In his mind, he understood why she would feel that way, but other than himself, Sid wasn't a threat to anyone. Dejected, Cal turned from the window to walk back to the bookstore, then retraced his steps.

Juggling the bag of pastries and two lattes, he shouldered open the door and entered the store to find Delia in an animated conversation with two women.

He nodded, not wanting to interrupt, and rounded the counter to drop his peace offerings on the back counter.

Delia acknowledged his presence with a brittle smile while she listened to one of the women gush about the object in her hand.

"Yes. I agree, Lucille, the craftsmanship is lovely." Delia stepped back and gestured toward him like a gameshow host. "Calvin—he's the proprietor of Jimmy's Joint—can give you more information about its provenance." She stepped back and folded her hands together.

All three women faced Cal, each wearing an expectant and, in Delia's case, challenging smile.

Straightening his shoulders, he entered the fray. "What can I help you with?"

Lucille, a skeletal woman with hair the color of a ripe raspberry, stepped forward and held up her hand. "I saw this in the window. Clearly, it's the work of an Indigenous artist, and I wanted to know if they're local."

Cal smiled politely at the woman before looking closer at the object. It was a chess piece, part of a set made to resemble characters of Coast Salish folklore; the black pieces were local species that dwelled in the sea—whales, salmon, sea lions—and the white pieces were species that lived on the land—foxes, wolves, ravens. Trying not to show his surprise, he cleared his throat. "I haven't seen this in a while. These were carved by my grandfather, Douglas Jimmy."

The birdlike woman cocked her head to the side. "The detail is exquisite. Your grandfather is quite the artist. Has he made many sets? Is each set one of a kind? How much do you want for it?"

Her rapid-fire questions caught him off guard. Staring at the rook piece in Lucille's hand—a tiny totem pole with the head of a raven at the top—memories flooded back of sitting at the counter, doing his homework, while his grandfather carved away. Realizing the women were waiting for his reply, he looked up at Delia, whose expression had softened from frosty disdain to supportive compassion.

Smoothly she took the tiny carving from Lucille and returned it to the window display. "We've recently unearthed the collection and are in the process of evaluating it. If you leave me your contact information, I can get back to you with the story behind the set, the materials used, and the pricing." Smiling brightly, she placed one hand on Lucille's elbow and led her and her companion to the register.

Cal drifted over to the window display. Delia had been busy in his absence. She'd set up a vignette using his grandfather's chess set and arranged it on a small table to mimic a game in progress. Two chairs on either side of the table were pushed back, as if the players had stepped away and would be back momentarily. He tuned out the chatter of the women behind him, wishing they would go away. After a few minutes, goodbyes were said, the door opened and closed, and he got his wish. Silence.

Delia! He whipped around and looked about the quiet shop. Dammit, she'd left. Did he have her contact info? Standing in the light coming in through the window, he racked his brain. They'd never exchanged numbers, but this was the age of the internet and social media. He'd be able to find her. With a plan in mind, he walked toward the counter, his eye on his waiting laptop, and stumbled.

"What the hell?" Looking down, he saw an old jute welcome mat positioned in front of the door. Worn down, the words Jimmy's Joint were still legible. Another blast from the past. Twisting around, his gaze traveled over the interior. The chess set. The welcome mat. What else had Delia dredged up? The place was the same, yet not. It was… warmer, welcoming. Narrowing his eyes, Cal tried to figure out the differences. The list was staggering. When had Delia cleaned the windows, shone the chrome on the bar stools, replaced the dead lightbulbs in the floor lamp, polished the old coffee urn, and swept the floor? The noise of shuffling paper caught his attention, and he looked up to the big mirror in the corner. In the reflection, he saw her sitting at the table she'd turned into a workspace. Neatly, precisely, she wrote on an index card and added it to a pile of similar cards.

For a second, he considered leaving her alone and ignoring his bad behavior. This was a business arrangement, and they weren't friends. However, he did owe her an explanation. She wasn't paying him any attention. Maybe he could put it off...

"Man up, Jimmy," Cal muttered to himself. He picked up the cooling lattes and the pastry bag and went to join her. Standing in front of the table, he waited in silence for her to acknowledge him. Delia didn't look up, her hair hanging around her face like a curtain. He studied the curls and the way the light from the desk lamp she'd set up highlighted the gold and copper strands. Placing his offering on the table, he backed up and shoved his hands into his pockets.

"I screwed up."

Delia's hand jerked, leaving a trail of ink across the pristine white paper. She put the index card aside and replaced it with a blank one.

"The man—the homeless person who startled you—that's my cousin, Sid."

Delia didn't move.

"He's been on the streets for about a year, usually checks in with me once a week or so, but I haven't seen him in a while, and I've been worried. So yeah. That's why I went after him."

Hands clenched together in front of her, Delia finally looked up at him. "He scared the crap out of me. And you blamed me—" She looked away, lips flattened, visibly swallowing. Then she shook her head and looked back down at the table.

Cal pulled out a chair and sank into it. Leaning forward, he said, "Yeah, I was wrong. I handled that badly. I should have looked after you instead of chasing after him."

"I'm not your responsibility," she spoke sharply.

"True." He lapsed into silence and waited.

Palm out, she waved a hand in front of Cal. "You're a big

guy, and I doubt you've ever had someone approach you or follow you…" She sighed. "I like to walk when I have things on my mind, to clear my head. I know a woman walking alone needs to be mindful of her surroundings, but sometimes I get caught up in my thoughts and forget to pay attention. It's my fault—"

Cal walked most places, regardless of daylight or weather conditions, never worrying about being approached on the street. He'd been hit on, more times than he could count, but he was a big guy and could be intimidating without even trying. Delia was gorgeous. No two ways about it. In the city, her looks would attract all kinds of attention, whether she wanted it or not. "No. You should be able to walk the sidewalks in the middle of the day and not be afraid. And you're right. I don't know what it's like to be hassled. I made light of it the other day when those punks followed you in here. I'm sorry about that, and I'm sorry I wasn't sympathetic today."

Delia shot him a grateful look. "Thanks."

It was a start. Cal really wanted to see her smile, that full-wattage, joyous look she'd turned on him once or twice. He pushed the drinks and pastry bags toward her. "One is a chai tea, and the other is a soy latte. Hopefully, you like one of them. Croissants are in the bag. Please tell me you're gluten intolerant so I can have them all."

"Nope. I've never met a carbohydrate I didn't like." She pulled one croissant out of the bag and picked up the chai. "Thank you. But I've kind of gotten used to the motor oil you drink."

Cal laughed. Who knew cleaning the coffee maker would make such an improvement in the coffee itself? Munching away on a croissant, he realized he knew very little about Delia. "When you came in the first time, did you have something on your mind?"

Her smile faltered, and she picked at the label on her drink. "Sort of."

Leaning back in his chair, Cal sipped his own drink, feeling no need to fill the quiet. Over Delia's shoulder, he studied the bookshelves. Despite his protests, she had organized them by color and size within their subject matter. He wondered how she organized items in her home: her closets, socks, underwear. At the last image, his mind skittered back to the present and his gaze back to Delia. She was worrying her bottom lip.

"You know how you have a deadline?"

Cal nodded.

"I have kind of the same thing. Before I've...tapped out my savings."

"So you *are* looking for work."

"Not exactly. I'm an...entrepreneur. I prefer to work for myself." She flicked a glance at him, and then back to her drink cup, where she had carefully removed the sticky label. "Your shop is the perfect venue for me to showcase my abilities to organize items for resale. There are lots of people who have stuff—collectibles, junk—they need to offload, but don't know how to go about it. I can help with that."

"Like an online consignment store. Other than having massive amounts of crap to get rid of, how does Jimmy's Joint play into that?"

Eyes glowing, Delia warmed up to her subject. "I want to document the beginning, the middle, and the end. Show potential clients how I can help them organize and offload while making money for them. One person's trash is another person's treasure." She lifted her hands and gestured at the books. "The shop is a great set to begin with, and you writing me a glowing testimonial will help a great deal. I'm pretty sure I can bring traffic into the store itself as well as sell off a lot of stuff online."

"People coming in here to buy books, huh?" Cal's eyes wandered the shelves again. "That would be a lot better than hauling them off to a burn pile."

"Not just books." Delia cleared her throat. "Your grand-parents have all kinds of items that I think would sell. Like those chess boards."

Cal's eyebrows lowered. "I'll have to think about that." Books, he could part with. His grandfather's carvings, he wasn't so sure about.

Delia held up an index card that she'd folded into a tent card. In lovely script, it read, For Display Only. "That's what I thought. So I made up this."

He was touched by her thoughtfulness. "Thanks."

"How about telling me more about your cousin? And I'll keep my eye out for him."

His eyes clouded, Cal sighed. "Yeah. That's a good idea." He settled back in his chair, thinking about where to start. "Sid's mom was not thrilled to be a mom, so he spent a lot of time here with our grandparents. He took it hard when Pops passed, and I was dealing with my own stuff. Eventually, I realized something was wrong, but when I confronted Sid about it, he told me to piss off, then he took off. Every time someone walks by, I think—I hope, it's him."

CHAPTER 7

Delia sat back on the couch and looked at her laptop, studying the website she'd constructed. It was…good, but was it good enough? With the help of YouTube, building a website wasn't difficult. The hard part was judging its effectiveness. She needed an objective opinion, but who to ask? Cal immediately came to mind. She shook her head; for all intents and purposes, he was her client. When she did show him her website, and the website she was building for Jimmy's Joint, Delia wanted them to be polished and professional. Kevin would definitely be helpful, but he was too close to her brother, and right now, she wasn't prepared to reveal her plans to the family. She wanted them to see her successes instead of her fumbling starts.

Her phone dinged, and she rose from the couch to retrieve it from the kitchen counter. She sidestepped a box of Hermes scarves that needed to be wrapped and sent off to delivery. She made a mental note to take it down to the concierge.

"Connie!" That's who she could ask.

Delia glanced at the text, a reminder from her mother they would be meeting for dinner in a few hours and to drive carefully because it was supposed to rain. Instead of sending an eye roll emoji, Delia sent a thumbs-up and found the contact for the concierge desk.

Connie answered on the second ring. "Good afternoon, Ms. Duncan. How may I help you?"

"Connie, please, call me Delia."

The concierge's voice became obsequious. "Of course, Ms. Duncan. Let me finish with Mr. Abernathy, and I'll be able to assist you."

"Okay... If I come down in about ten minutes, may I pick your brain?"

"I look forward to it, Ms. Duncan."

Delia disconnected and stared at the phone. That was weird. She wrapped up the box of scarves and used the app on her phone to request a pickup from the shipping company. She then sent a payment request to the buyer for the amount of the scarves and the cost of shipping. She'd learned the hard way that shipping was expensive and needed to build that into her prices. Ten minutes was almost up, so she gathered her laptop and the box and made her way down to the foyer.

Connie smiled at her approach and straightened her shoulders. "Hi, Delia."

"So now it's Delia. What was that on the phone?" She placed the box and her laptop on the counter.

Rolling her eyes, Connie picked up the box and added it to the pile of outgoing packages. "It's time for my six-month evaluation. My supervisor was here watching me while Mr. Abernathy from 15A was going on and on about his news-paper not being delivered on time." She returned to the counter and sagged against it. "Sometimes it's hard to care about stuff like that." Then her eyes rounded as her gaze connected with Delia's. "Sorry. I shouldn't be saying that to you. Mr. Abernathy is actually—"

"A lecherous old man with nothing better to do than bitch and moan. Did he stare at your chest the whole time?"

Connie's eyes bugged out. "Yes!"

Delia shuddered in sympathy. "Did everything go okay?"

"Yeah. My supervisor is fairly decent. Which is good because, while I'm in school, this is the perfect job." Connie pointed at Delia's laptop. "What would you like help with?"

"Right!" Delia opened her laptop. "I've been working on a website, and I'm hoping you have time to look it over and maybe give me some feedback?"

"What is the website for? Your online boutique? It seems to be doing well." She pointed at the package Delia had dropped off.

"No. I want to help people value items and sell them, like if they need to downsize or someone passes away and the family needs to clean out the home."

Connie nodded, appearing to be lost in thought.

Thinking the younger woman thought it was a dumb idea, Delia started to babble. "I'm working with this man who needs to vacate a used bookstore and has a huge inventory to offload. He doesn't have the bandwidth to handle it all. I'm going to photograph books that I think would appeal to collectors and put them up on different sites. That will get him top dollar. I've also been going through stuff, figuring out what is salable. I'm using his store as a background to showcase what I can do for people. So could you look over my website as if you wanted to get rid of stuff you think is valuable and you didn't know how to do it or didn't have the time to do it?"

"That's actually a valuable service. I'm sure you'd find tons of clients in this building alone."

Delia nodded but didn't say anything. She did not want Connie to know that shopping used to be her primary pastime and that Delia herself was her own first client.

"I don't have any homework tonight, so if it's a quiet evening, I can look at it today."

Delia clapped her hands. "That would be awesome. I'm supposed to have dinner with my parents. I can leave my laptop with you."

"Or you can give me the link to your website."

"I'm not sure how to do that."

Connie grinned. "I do." She turned the laptop toward her and tapped away on the keyboard. "There. I made myself an editor so I can look at it on my own computer. I promise not to make any changes." She crossed her heart and held up her hand.

The phone on the counter rang, and Delia took that has her signal to leave. "Thanks. I'll check in with you tomorrow, if that's okay."

"Sounds good." Connie lifted the receiver and smiled her goodbye.

*H*er phone dinged with an incoming text. She pressed a button, and the polite disembodied voice from the car's audio system read it aloud. "Connie says, 'Your website looks great. I will have suggestions for you in a few days.' Thumbs up emoji. Do you want to reply?"

Delia responded with a thank you and a kissy face emoji. Traffic was slow on the 520 bridge, and she settled back, feeling lighter. Asking Connie for feedback was the right decision. How could she reciprocate? She didn't want there to be an imbalance, and looking over a website was beyond the duties of a concierge. It was the kind of thing friends did for each other. That stopped her for a moment. Tommy and Kevin were really her only friends. There were women she socialized with, shopped with, and exchanged barbed comments with, but no one to call up when she was feeling down and no one who would understand her current situation. Would Connie? The woman was putting herself through school while putting up with privileged, entitled jerks. Delia realized if they were to become friends, something she'd really like, she'd have to figure out a way to tell Connie. And Tommy. She put the thought out of her mind when traffic sped up and concentrated on driving.

She left her car with the valet and entered the hotel lobby in Bellevue. Finding the elevator, she rose to the nineteenth floor where Persephone's restaurant overlooked Lake Washington. The hostess took her coat and led Delia to her parents' corner table. With a warm smile, her father rose to hug her, and her mother lifted her cheek for a kiss. Both in their mid-sixties, Chuck Sr. and Carol Lee had been together for more than forty years, a number Delia couldn't fathom. She'd never had a relationship that lasted longer than six months. Although he would never truly retire, Chuck Sr. wasn't putting in as many hours in the office as he used to and now spent more time on the golf course. Carol Lee served on the board of many nonprofits and showed no signs of slowing down.

"Hello, sweetheart. We weren't expecting you for another fifteen minutes." Carol Lee beamed at her daughter.

Delia settled into her chair. "Didn't you say the reservation was for 7:30?"

"Yes, but you're never on time," her father said with a chuckle.

About to protest, Delia realized her father was right. She was rarely on time for anything and had never been early in her life, something else she needed to work on. Aloud, she said, "I made good time in traffic."

The server arrived to take their drink orders and then left them alone.

"Is Chuck joining us?" Delia asked.

Her father shook his head. "He's out with Liam."

Delia's brother, Chuck, and Liam Cross, the CFO of

Duncan Properties, were best friends, steered the company, and were dating the Beckett sisters, Beth and Jane of Grand Gestures Event Planning. Chuck and Beth were engaged to be married, and Delia believed that Jane and Liam weren't far behind. Delia had crushed on Liam for years, but he'd never treated her as more than a little sister.

Never one to beat around the bush, Carol Lee got to the point. "We thought we'd discuss the matter of your trust tonight."

Fortunately, the server arrived with their drinks, and Delia took a fortifying swallow of her wine. "I'm on top of it, Mom."

"That may be, but your mother and I have taken steps to ensure you won't lose it."

As parents went, Chuck Sr. and Carol Lee were practically perfect. They loved their children dearly, didn't interfere in their private lives, were good role models for a loving marriage, and active participants in their community. They had been there for Delia on numerous occasions, finding her tutors when school overwhelmed her, setting up the virtual assistant who paid her bills, not batting an eye when she lost interest in the enterprises she started. Now they were prepared to take care of her once again.

Inwardly, she cringed. Almost thirty-five, Delia had been indulged and pampered to the point where she thought it was her due. The meeting in the lawyer's office had been her wake-up call. The rest of the world made their own way. She could, too.

Carol Lee patted her daughter's hand. "We think you would make an excellent fundraiser, and I've arranged a meeting for you with the executive director of Children First. They're an agency here in Bellevue focused on education. I've convinced them you would be perfect for coordinating their annual auction and meeting with donors. They'll tailor the position just for you."

"Won't there be more experienced people applying for the job?"

"Oh, the job doesn't exist yet." Her father chuckled. "With a word in the right ear and a generous donation, it will, though."

"You'd be paying me."

"Well, not exactly." Carol Lee glanced at her husband.

"Yes, exactly. You'd be giving them money to give to me because you don't think I can fend for myself." Mindful of the other diners around her, Delia kept her voice low.

"Now, dear, we simply want—"

"I know what you want, Mom, and I appreciate it. But I have a plan, and it's a good one." Delia flipped her hair back and reached for her wineglass as if it were a lifeline.

"Are you ready to order?"

The server's presence allowed Delia to collect her thoughts. Her parents had cleaned up after her multiple times, and they deserved to know it wasn't going to happen again. After returning their menus to the server, she turned to her father.

"Remember when my interior design studio shut down and we had all that furniture to get rid of?"

"I remember." He rolled his eyes. "There are still pieces in the storage unit."

"Sorry about that," Delia said. She'd walked away from the business with no thought about who would take care of the cleanup. "I'm currently helping a business owner liquidate." She explained the work she was doing for Cal, the combination of in-store and online sales.

"And you're getting seventy-five percent? Do you have that in writing?"

"Yes." She crossed her fingers under the table. She didn't have a contract with Cal but would rectify that shortly, although, honestly, she didn't think he'd renege on her.

"Send me the contract tomorrow and let me look it over."

"Yes, Dad."

"Your idea is actually a good one."

Delia smiled at her mother, knowing that she didn't mean to sound condescending.

Her mother sipped her martini before going on. "You are a very organized individual. Are you sure you wouldn't want to help women curate their closets? I have a number of friends who could use your services. Why, just the other day, Josie—"

"Thank you, Mom. I have thought about that and may branch out into it in the future. Right now, I want to concentrate on refining my skills on this one shop."

"Your mother is on to something, Delia. Starting small, with individuals who we know, may be the best way to go. That way, you won't get in over your head."

Wanting to scream, instead Delia smiled and drank her wine. It was her own damn fault her parents didn't believe in her. She didn't have a reputation for following through. She started things and then walked away when she was bored. The storage unit full of furniture came to mind. She hadn't been to it since she'd staged the storefront for Grand Gestures using pieces from her former design studio. If Cal was agreeable, she could use Jimmy's Joint as a place to sell off the extra items. Feeling a bit better, she tuned in to her parents' conversation.

"I will think about that, Mom. You can tell Josie to give me a call."

Her father wasn't quite ready to let things go. "How did this business owner find out about you? At a social event?"

Delia bit the inside of her cheek as the image of rumpled flannel and scuffed hiking boots came to mind. She couldn't imagine Cal at any social event. Then again, she really didn't know much about the big, dark, quiet man. She also didn't want to tell her parents how she'd found the shop.

"I wandered into his bookstore to...get out of the rain,

and we started talking about rare books. He has a number of them on his shelves and no time to find the right buyers for him."

"A rare book dealer, then." Her mother sounded impressed.

Thinking of some of the books she'd dug up, Delia nodded. "Among other things, yes."

"It does sound promising. Again, send that contract over for me." Her father looked like he was about to say more, but the arrival of their meal put an end to the conversation, and she sighed with relief.

CHAPTER 8

Delia sat back on her haunches, examining the contents of the chest in front of her. If she'd counted accurately, there were twelve complete chess sets. She hadn't studied the intricately carved Indigenous art closely yet, but from what she'd seen, no two pieces were the same. If Cal agreed to sell them, they would be worth a small fortune. She would be able to—she shook her head. The chess sets were not junk that had been picked up at a yard sale. They were family heirlooms, probably carved by Cal's grandfather. As such, she didn't think she should profit from them.

The chessboards themselves hinged in the middle and, when folded, became boxes to contain the chess pieces. She picked one up and walked from the back room into the bookshop itself.

Hunched over his laptop, Cal frowned at the screen, muttering to himself, "Another stupid duke. Why can't she write pirate romances?"

"I'm sorry?"

Blinking, Cal looked up at her and leaned back, rolling his shoulders. "This is the fifth straight story idea with a duke the author has sent me this year. I'm getting bored. But it pays the bills, so what am I going to do?"

Knowing it was a rhetorical question, Delia answered anyway. "Why can't the duke be a pirate? Or be kidnapped by a pirate queen and held for ransom?"

"Not bad. I'll suggest that to her." He pointed at the boxed chess set. "What have you got there?"

She placed the chessboard on the counter and opened it, revealing the small chess pieces for him to see. He reached out and gently touched a tiny pawn shaped like a field mouse where it lay in its velvet lined box. His gaze seemed to turn inward, as if with each piece, he was looking at a memory. He didn't smile. He didn't frown. He showed no emotion at all, except for the bobbing of his Adam's apple. Leaving him alone with his thoughts, she returned to the back room.

Out of a wobbly end table and an overturned crate, she'd created a workspace where she could set up her laptop and planner. Meticulously, she photographed and recorded the items she found in the myriad boxes. Like the chess sets, there were many things she would need to consult with Cal about: handwritten recipes, photo albums, ledgers—things she couldn't simply dispose of. Then there were old kitchen utensils from the time Jimmy's Joint was a diner. She'd set aside a couple pieces that looked like they may have some value, but the rest could go to a recycling center. Standing in the center of the room, surrounded by the boxes and crates and piles of furniture, it was easy to understand why Cal didn't want to deal with it and why he was willing to let her take so much of the profit.

She added a box of well-worn bar towels to the recycling pile. Some of them were practically see-through and should have been tossed years ago. The walls of the windowless room closing in on her, she picked up her laptop and planner, intending to work on a display of mystery novels she'd unearthed. Old Hardy Boys and Nancy Drew books sold well, and Delia doubted she'd have to put much effort into the display. The door opened as she reached for the knob.

"Oh!"

She blinked up at Cal. He met her gaze, then looked beyond her.

Twisting around, she extended an arm. "There is a method to my madness. Do you have time for me to explain it?"

"Yeah."

Divesting herself of the laptop and planner, Delia walked over to one stack of boxes. "These are books that can be resold. I've boxed and labeled them according to value. That stack over there has tchotchkes and furnishings that can be resold. That area is stuff for recycling—there's a place in SoDo that accepts metal goods, and theses boxes here"—she walked over to another pile of boxes—"have business and personal items. That's where I put the other chess sets."

She opened the flaps of one box and stood back for him to see. "I found twelve of them."

Hands stuffed in his pockets, Cal peered into the box, then stepped back and looked around the room. "Did you find any carving tools?"

"Not yet, but there's still a lot to go through. Did your grandfather carve them all?"

Cal picked up the box and headed for the door. "I don't think so. I need to look at these in better light."

Grabbing her stuff, Delia followed behind and joined him at the counter, where Cal was setting out each chess set. "I'm not sure who taught my grandfather to carve, but he taught all of us cousins, or he tried."

"How many of them are there?"

"I have two sisters and six cousins." Having emptied the box, he placed it on the floor behind him and looked at Delia. "Can you help me set these up?"

"I was hoping you'd ask."

Standing on opposite sides of the counter, they opened the chess sets and pulled out the pieces. Once emptied, they turned the boxes over and placed the pieces on the chessboard. Neither moved quickly, handling each chess piece with great care. Delia finished first, and while she waited for Cal, she stood back and studied the collection. Now that she looked at them more closely, it was clear the sets were not all carved by the same person. All were beautifully crafted, but some were bold and stark, while others were delicate and intricate.

"Did you carve any of these?"

Cal gave a derisive snort. "Hell no. In one of those boxes back there, you'll find my one and only attempt at wood carving. I didn't have the patience for it."

"What was it?"

"It's supposed to be a raven in flight, but it looks more like a walrus."

Hiding her smile, she murmured, "I'll be on the lookout for it."

"Sid had the most interest and aptitude for carving. Most of these are his." Cal pointed to the sets with edgier pieces. Picking up a rook from one set and a rook from another, he displayed them to Delia. They were both totem poles, both crowned by a wolf, but there the similarity ended. One piece was calm and quiet. The other restless, almost angry. "Pops encouraged Sid to channel his energy into the wood."

"And his anger?"

Cal nodded. "Sid had a lot of anger. Messed up parents. Crappy home life. He spent a lot of time here with our grandparents. It helped a lot. Carving was a great way for him to express himself."

Delia thought about the young man she'd encountered. He'd looked like a hollow shell, with nothing in him to express, and not like he had the focus to carve anything with detail. "If Sid sees the chess boards, what do you think he would do?"

"Try to take them. Pawn them probably."

"I can sell them for you. Galleries would pay top dollar—"

Cal shook his head. "I don't want—"

"Let me finish." She shifted to look up at him. "I don't want a cut. Take the money and use it to buy food, clothing, whatever Sid needs."

"I do that already. Why do you think I'm down here in this place?" Cal's voice rose with frustration. "I could lock the door and work somewhere else. I'm here in case Sid shows up and needs me."

Delia took a step back, shaken by his unexpected vehemence. Had she ever shown that much concern for someone else's welfare? She didn't think so.

"Me scaring him off that day didn't help, did it?"

"If it wasn't you, it could have been someone else. He's… he's not himself."

Drugs, alcohol, mental illness. It could have been one of the above or *all* of the above. Sid was not the first wounded soul to wander the streets of Seattle. Concern for his cousin was clearly getting to Cal.

Delia walked over to the window and stared out at the street. Two people stood on the other side of the glass, pointing at items in the window and talking. Seeing her, they smiled, waved, and moved on. Her displays were clearly attracting attention and some business. An idea came to her, and she strode back to the counter.

"What if—"

"The chess boards aren't mine to sell. So stop thinking about it."

"Give me a break here. I'm trying to help."

"I don't need your help!"

Delia covered his mouth with her hand. Cal's eyes bugged out. Much bigger than her, he could easily have removed her hand or moved away. Instead, he glared at her, one eyebrow raised.

"Will you let me tell you my idea before shooting it down?"

Cal nodded, and she removed her hand.

"Okay. So this was the place Sid came to when things were bad at home. I'm assuming it felt warm and bright and homey to him?"

He nodded again.

She took a breath. This was the part where he could really get upset with her. "And after your grandparents passed, and you took over, you didn't have the heart to keep up the appearance of the shop."

Cal stared at her, a muscle ticking in his jaw. Then he looked around at the shop and back at Delia. "I'm an idiot," he muttered.

She placed a hand on his arm and gave it a gentle squeeze. "You're not an idiot. I think you were grieving, and it was just plain hard." She could only imagine what it had been like to come into the shop day after day, without the presence of his grandparents. The responsibility of running the place must have weighed on him.

The big man in front of her blew out a breath, then gently placed the rooks back onto the chessboards. "The rest of the family, my parents, aunts, and uncles, wanted to close down the shop a long time ago. They didn't know how important it was to Sid. I kept it open, but I haven't done a good job. Now, I have to be out of here in three months. If Jimmy's Joint isn't here, I don't know how I'm going to be able to keep an eye on him."

Delia wanted to wrap her arms around Cal and tell him it would be okay. She wanted to make him feel better and take away his pain. Instead, she walked around the counter to pour him a cup of coffee. "Sit," she said. "Let me tell you my plan."

With a finger wave and a sympathetic smile, Delia stood at the door, ready to leave.

"Wait!" Cal jumped up and walked toward her. He dug through his pocket and came up with his keys. "I forgot to give you this. If you go through the back room, there's a door leading out to the alley, with a parking spot for the shop. Here's a key for you."

Delia's eyes widened as she held out her hand to accept the key, like it was a precious object. "Thank you!"

"No, thank you. You're helping me out a lot. Giving you a key and a parking space is the least I can do."

"And seventy-five percent of the profits."

He grinned. He'd been impressed with the contract she'd presented today; putting their agreement on paper would protect them both. Delia's energy and enthusiasm was giving him impetus to take care of things. Having her in the shop day after day wasn't a hardship, either.

Standing in the entry way and smiling at her, Cal searched his brain for a reason to keep her longer. Her phone rang before he could speak. She pulled it out of her bag and looked at the name on the screen. With another wave, she turned and was out the door.

Not allowing the door to close, he stood on the sidewalk, watching her walk away, telling himself he was concerned about her safety.

She stopped two stores down to dig through her bag while answering the phone. He couldn't see her face, but from her posture, she looked annoyed. She spoke with the same voice she'd used while speaking to her friend in McQuarry's. "I haven't forgotten. I'm an *absolute* mess, so give me a couple hours and I'll meet you there. What's that? Fine. Tell Tommy I won't be at dinner, but I'll meet you all at The Cave. Right. Love ya." With that, she crossed the street and headed to her car, hair tossed back and hips swaying. Cal watched until she was out of sight.

The woman on the dance floor was not the same Delia who had been digging through years of his family's junk for the past few days. This Delia wore a dress that, while not revealing, managed to show off her curves and legs and everything. It must have cost a mint, and if it hadn't been custom-made for her, it sure looked like it. Cal wondered how she was able to dance in shoes with pencil-thin heels while not spilling a drop of the drink she held.

Thanks to the internet, he discovered that The Cave was a nightclub on Capitol Hill with a cover charge steep enough to keep most people under the age of thirty out. At ten o'clock that evening, he stood at the bar, holding a beer and wondering what the hell he was doing. Everyone on the dance floor appeared to be Delia's friend. It might have had something to do with the fact she'd just bought a round of drinks for the house.

Except for the well-lit dance floor, the rest of the club was dark. Lights set into the floor itself allowed servers to walk about without stumbling into customers, while dimly illuminated wall sconces shone above booths set against the wall. In one corner, accessed by three steps, was a roped-off VIP section complete with a surly bouncer. That was where Delia's group had taken up residence. At that moment, Tommy descended the steps and tapped the bouncer on the shoulder. Impassively, the big man detached the rope, allowing Tommy to pass. Tommy skirted the dance floor and made his way to the bar.

Tommy stopped next to Cal and raised an eyebrow. "Is that the same flannel shirt?"

He looked Tommy over, taking in the snug black slacks and open-necked paisley shirt. His hair looked freshly cut, short above the ears, with carefully tousled curls on top. His makeup was flawless, and he'd swapped diamond stud earrings for glittery hoops. "Is that the same pearl necklace?"

Snorting, Tommy arched his neck, showing off the three-strand necklace that fit him like a choker. "Do you like it? I can find you a matching one."

It was Cal's turn to snort. "I'll get back to you."

While Tommy ordered a drink, Cal continued to watch Delia. Light gleamed off her hair, and while she wasn't in the center of the dance floor, the activity revolved around her. She was fluid and graceful and sexy as hell. Like every other man in the room, he couldn't take his eyes off her.

Two young women approached the bar, and Cal shifted to the side to get out of their way. One of them gave him the once-over and a sly smile. At his bland stare, she tossed her hair and turned back to her friend. The bartender brought their drinks and waved off a proffered credit card.

"Don't we have to pay for them?" one girl asked.

The bartender shook her head and pointed to Delia. "Nope. She's buying for everyone tonight."

The two women cheered and went back to their friends.

"Why is Delia paying for everyone's drinks tonight?" Cal asked Tommy when he returned to his side.

"I have no idea. I haven't talked to her in ages, and then out of the blue, I get a text telling me to meet her here." Tommy shook his head, then placed his drink on the bar. "Oh shit. This isn't good. Come on."

"What?"

Tommy plucked Cal's beer out of his hand and slammed it down on the bar. "Things are about to get ugly. Come on."

The smaller man pushed his way through the crowd to the dance floor, Cal following in his wake. Getting closer, he saw that most of the dancers had fallen back, creating a ring around Delia, another woman, and a man. Delia swayed on her feet, a confused expression on her face. A tiny Asian woman stood in front of her, waving a finger between Delia and the man, who was clearly loving the attention.

"Get away from my man!"

"Babe, it's all right. We were just dancing."

"Dancing?" The woman rounded on the man. "You were grinding against her."

The man waved at Delia. "Well, yeah. Look at that ass."

The music still played, but no one was dancing, the crowd focused on the drama in front of them. Delia's so-called friends hung over the balcony of the VIP section, cameras pointed her way.

She raised a hand, looking surprised to find it empty. "Is someone bringing me a drink?" she slurred.

Cal stepped in front of Tommy, arms extended to shove people out of his way. When she spotted him, Delia's eyes lit up, and she staggered his way.

"Ooh! You're here. Dance with me." She grabbed his hips and shimmied in front of him, undulating like she was a stripper and he was her pole.

"Okay, honey, it's time to take you home." Tommy appeared behind her and caught Cal's eye with a nod toward the exit.

Cal wrapped his arms around her, trying to guide her that way, but Delia wasn't having any of it. "Dance with me, big guy. I know you can shake this ass." For emphasis, she squeezed his butt cheeks to a roar of approval from the crowd.

Tommy threw his hands up in the air, and Cal called out to him over Delia's bobbing head, "You lead the way. I've got her." He scooped her up and held her tight as they trailed after Tommy to a hallway next to the bar.

She looped her arms around Cal's neck and nestled against him. "I knew you were strong, but oh my," she murmured.

Tommy reappeared, holding what Cal assumed was

Delia's purse, and motioned him toward the exit sign at the end of the hallway. "I've settled up with the bartender and called a car. You okay?"

"I'm fine. Not so sure about Delia." Cal looked down to study her. Her eyes were closed, but her lips were turned up, and she appeared to be having a conversation with herself. He jiggled her softly. "Hey, you with me?"

"I like flannel," she said, rubbing her nose against his shirt.

He groaned. If she remembered this tomorrow, things were going to be awkward.

After the noise and the heat of the club, the damp night air felt good against his heated skin. Shifting Delia's weight, he leaned up against the rough brick exterior of the building.

Tommy stood in front of him, regarding her with a mixture of exasperation and concern. "The car will be here in about five minutes. You can put her down, and I'll support her."

"It's fine. I wouldn't want your shirt to get wrinkled."

Lips twitching, Tommy rolled his eyes at Cal, then reached out a hand to stroke Delia's hair back. "She doesn't talk about you."

"There's nothing to talk about. She's doing some work for me. That's all."

"You watched her all night, rescued her from a cat fight, and are now refusing to put her down. You're either completely smitten or intending to hold her for ransom. If it's the latter, you're doing a lousy job. Kidnappers don't take Uber."

Cal grinned. "It's neither the former nor the latter. I just feel kind of...protective of her." The right word was eluding him. He was interested, attracted, curious, and had many other feelings he did not want to share about the woman in his arms, but protective worked for right now.

Head cocked to the side, Tommy tapped his lip with an elegant, manicured finger. "That works for now." A horn honked, and Tommy looked over his shoulder. "That's the car. I'm going to take her home. Are you coming with us?"

This was not how he'd thought his evening would go. Most nights, it was him, reheated takeout, a mystery novel, and Jimmy Kimmel. He could place Delia in the car with Tommy, knowing her friend would take care of her, but he knew that wasn't enough. He wanted to be sure she was all right. "Yeah. Grab the door."

Smiling, Tommy held the door, and Cal slid in, cradling Delia like she was precious cargo. Tommy climbed in after them, and they headed off into the night.

CHAPTER 9

The car pulled into a parking circle in front of an elaborate building with large ceramic pots containing beautifully sculptured trees that were taller than Cal. A uniformed doorman came out of the building to hold open the car door. Tommy exited first, then moved aside so Cal could slide out, still holding Delia. The car took off as another person in a uniform, a small woman, hurried out of the building as well, concern on her face.

"Is Ms. Duncan all right?" she asked.

Tommy turned to her with a reassuring smile. "She will be after a good night's sleep. Can you help us get her up to her apartment?"

The woman said sure but was overridden by the man.

"We can't let people up without the resident's approval." The man wore a name tag that identified him as Michel, with the title "Concierge" under it in smaller font.

The woman, Consuela, according to her name tag, rolled her eyes at the guy. "Ms. Duncan needs assistance to her apartment. I think we can relax the rules under the circumstances."

Michel barely managed to control a sneer as he studied

Cal and Tommy, clearly memorizing their faces. "Fine, but I'm going to take photos of their ID and enter this into the logbook. This is clearly unorthodox."

"Don't be a dick, Michel." Consuela shouldered past him and opened the door to the lobby. "I'll accompany them upstairs and take photos of their ID."

Michel huffed and glared at her, then jerked his head at the men to enter the building.

"Thank you, Michel." Tommy strolled past him, gliding a hand down the concierge's arm.

Cal bit the inside of his cheek to control his smile and followed the others to the gleaming doors of the elevators.

The doors opened at Consuela's touch of a button. She entered after the others, and when the doors closed and the elevator started its ascent, she turned to the men. "I'm Connie, one of the concierges here."

Tommy extended his hand. "Tommy Federov. Delia and I have been friends since college."

"Calvin Jimmy." He looked down at Delia. "I've hired Delia to do some work for me."

Tommy quirked an eyebrow but didn't say anything.

Connie nodded. "I'm so sorry about Michel. He's a stickler for following the rules. Is Delia okay?" Her eyes big with worry, she looked up at Cal, who leaned against the wall, still carrying the sleeping woman.

"I think so." He looked at Tommy for confirmation.

"She's normally better at holding her liquor. I don't want to leave her alone. Will there be hell to catch if I stay with her?"

Connie extended her hand, wiggling it back and forth. "It would be better if I stayed with her. I'm going to give your information to Michel, but no offense, you two are strangers, and I can't let you spend the night without Delia's consent. I'm off shift right now, so I can stay with her."

The elevator dinged, and the doors opened. Connie led

them down a hall covered in thick carpet and illuminated by intricate sconces. They passed a few doorways before she stopped at one entrance and used a key to open the door. She led the way, turning on lights as she went. Spotting a couch, Cal walked toward it and propped Delia in a corner.

Her eyes opened, and she smiled up at him. "Thank you," she murmured, then closed her eyes with a sigh.

"That makes me feel better." He grabbed a soft lightweight afghan off the back of the couch and tucked it around her, then stepped back to look at the others. They looked relieved as well. He pulled his wallet out of his pocket and handed his driver's license to Connie. Tommy did the same.

The concierge took the licenses over to a round glass dining table to photograph them and email them to Michel. Cal accepted his back and gazed around him at Delia's home. It was a corner unit with a view encompassing Elliott Bay and Lake Union. White was the predominant color in the room. The large couch, club chairs, and fluffy rug anchoring the conversation area were white, with pillows and throws in varying shades of yellow, orange, brown, and red. Six chairs upholstered in grey velvet surrounded the dining table, and beyond the counter separating the living area and the kitchen, he could see white painted cupboards and counter-tops. The place was warm and inviting and expensive. His apartment contained the same cast-off furniture his parents had given him when he finished college.

Rubbing the back of his neck, Cal's gaze bounced off Delia, to the furniture, to piles of open boxes filled with clothes, shoes, purses, and jewelry, then to Tommy and Connie. "Obviously, I don't know anything about the person I hired in my bookshop."

"I thought she was running a consulting business." Connie frowned.

"Delia has a job?" Tommy blinked.

All three of them stared at the woman in question, who sighed and snuggled deeper into the couch.

"I need coffee," Cal said.

"I second that." Connie nodded.

"I'll make it." Tommy headed into the kitchen to take care of business.

Minutes later, the three gathered around the big granite island in the kitchen, mindful of the sleeping woman on the couch.

"Delia lives here, so why is she working in your bookshop?" Connie had removed the jacket and tie of her uniform and sat on a stool in a white button-down shirt.

"I don't know exactly. It sounded to me like she was out of work and had only a few months left before her savings ran out. I have to close down my shop—the building is being torn down—and she offered to sell off my inventory for me. We struck a deal, and that's what she's doing for me." He lifted his chin toward Tommy. "You seemed surprised that she was working."

Tommy blew a raspberry. "Delia Duncan doesn't need to work. She has a hefty trust fund." At the look of surprise on Cal's face, he continued, "She's part of the Duncan family of Duncan Properties. They own this building and probably half of Seattle."

Connie leaned forward. "She's never worked?"

"I didn't say that. She's started a few businesses over the years, but none of them panned out."

It seemed to Cal that Tommy was choosing his words carefully.

"She told me what she's doing for you and had me look at her website." Connie shrugged when Tommy looked at her with raised eyebrows, and she explained the conversations she'd had with Delia. "I assumed she was going to be doing the same for other people. But this"—she waved at the boxes around her—"makes me think she's selling off her own things."

"Delia does love to shop," Tommy murmured.

Surveying the apartment, Cal wondered what the hell was going on. What more didn't he know about the woman he wanted to get closer to? And why had she got so drunk she needed to be carried home? He thought about Sid. He didn't have the capacity to deal with more than one alcoholic.

*D*elia turned over and immediately regretted the action. Her head felt like a drumline was practicing inside it. She cracked one eye open, taking stock of her surroundings. That was her coffee table. Good. Under it were her shoes, standing side by side. On it was a glass of water and a bottle of ibuprofen. Okay…

A murmur of voices and the aroma of fresh-brewed coffee drifted toward her. A rustle of sound alerted her to someone—make that multiple *someones* nearby. This time, she cracked both eyes open and was met with the faces of Tommy, Connie, and Cal. She slammed her eyes shut. *Shit shit shit! Why was he here?*

"Good, you're awake." Tommy was using his no-bullshit voice.

"Here's some coffee. Can I make you some breakfast?" Connie's voice was sympathetic.

Cal didn't say a word.

Delia came up to a sitting position, one hand braced against her head. She hoped it wouldn't fall off. Connie sat beside her while Tommy and Cal occupied the chairs opposite the couch. All three stared at her expectantly. "So last night was fun." She tried to smile without wincing.

Tommy crossed his arms and crossed his legs, one foot tapping the air. "Not for the people who carried your drunken ass home and stayed up all night watching over you."

Reaching for the pain meds and the water, Delia rolled her eyes at her friend. "Like I haven't stuffed you into a cab before."

"He"—Tommy pointed at Cal—"literally carried you home. In his arms. Through the club, in the car, in the elevator, down the hall. In his arms."

She had no memory of this. Cringing inwardly, she wanted to crawl under the furniture and hide for the rest of the day. Instead, she tossed back her hair and winked at Tommy. "Wanted to switch places, didn't you?"

Soundlessly, Cal rose from his chair. He spoke first to Tommy. "Thanks for the information." Turning to Connie, he said, "Your proposal sounds good. Let me know if I can help. I doubt that I know anyone, but I can look it over for you."

Connie glanced between Cal and Delia, who held the full water glass, hoping she wouldn't spill it. Looking embarrassed, Connie rose from the couch and walked with Cal to the door, speaking in a soft voice. Cal rumbled out a reply too low for Delia to hear, and then he was gone. Delia and Tommy were in a stare down when she returned. Chewing on her bottom lip, Connie stuffed her laptop into her backpack and picked up her jacket. Facing the other two, she said, "I'm not working today, but if you need anything, give me a call. I wrote my number down on the pad in the kitchen. I can help with…" She waved her arm at the boxes.

Staring at Delia, Tommy addressed Connie. "Thank you for staying up all night as well. Get some sleep, and good luck on your exam tonight."

Delia winced. "You have an exam tonight?"

Tommy answered, "Yes, she does. But instead of studying, she spent the night watching over a drunken tenant so she wouldn't drown in her own vomit. Fortunately, her new *friends,* who know what it's like to work hard, spelled her so she could study, and she will do awesome." With that, he stood and approached Connie. Wrapping her in a hug, he rocked her side to side, whispering something in her ear, that when Connie stood back, she was blinking back tears. Connie waved at Delia then made her exit.

Head pounding, Delia shrank back on the couch and stared at Tommy's very unhappy face. Makeup free, he'd removed his jewelry and was wearing—

"Is that my sweater?"

Tommy examined a sleeve of the ivory cashmere roll neck sweater. On Delia, it was loose and slouchy. On Tommy, it fit well. He sniffed. "You have one in six different colors."

"I know. You were with me when I bought them. You encouraged me to buy them in a larger size. Now I know why."

Not a hint of guilt showed in Tommy's eyes. "I'll have it dry-cleaned before I return it."

Delia waved away the offer. "That's fine. Keep it."

"Are you sure? You don't want to sell it off on your online boutique?" He pointed at the boxes lined up against the dining room wall. "What the hell is going on?"

"I'm going Marie Kondo on my closet."

"Bullshit. I looked at your website, and that is not what you're doing."

Delia gaped. "You went into my computer?"

"I didn't have to. You gave the URL to Connie. She showed it to us. That is not a link for buying used books."

Us. Great. Now Cal knew as well.

"I'm selling Cal's books. There's a catalog and photos and—"

"Yeah, yeah. We saw that." He pointed beyond Delia to the hallway leading to the bedrooms. "We also saw the website for Delia's Closet. The videos for the clothing you're selling. Your clothing." Tommy stood and paced around the room.

"I've known you for fifteen years. I've been on countless shopping trips with you. And I've been with you when you've cleaned out your closet. You always donate. Always. So why are you selling things now? What's changed?"

Delia pulled the afghan around her, looking everywhere but at Tommy. "I feel like crap, and I have a lot to do today. Can we talk about this some other time?"

"Nope."

"Don't you have work?"

He looked down his nose at her. "I've already emailed my staff telling them I'll be in late. They'll be fine."

Tommy had the job of Delia's high school dreams: a senior clothing buyer for Nordstrom. He traveled the world, attending fashion shows and meeting with designers. Mindful of who the clients were, he was always looking for clothing for those on the cutting edge and those who wanted timeless classics.

A few years ago, he'd arranged an interview for Delia as a buyer and even coached her on what to say during the interview. By the time the day arrived, Delia was so wound up she took a shot of vodka to calm her nerves and then got drunk. She never made it to the interview. She and Tommy never spoke about it, and their friendship cooled. Yet he was here.

One hand to her head, Delia rose from the couch. "Let me get changed, and then I'll tell you."

"Everything. Promise?"

At Delia's nod of agreement, Tommy rose as well. "Fine. I'll see what I can make us for breakfast."

A half an hour later, the two friends faced each other across the dining room table, a stack of paper between them. Feeling embarrassed, Delia told him about the stipulation in her trust fund. Good friend that he was, Tommy didn't bat an eye. Then she told him about winding up in Cal's bookstore.

"I figured I could use the same system to offload some of my wardrobe. The experience I gain from that, I can use when I meet with individual clients who need to downsize or want to refresh their closets." She picked at her nails and looked up at him. "I can't afford to donate it all, but I intend to donate some of the money I bring in."

"It sounds like you're on the right track. Cal seems happy with the arrangement, and I can see you've made some sales." He nodded at the pile of invoices in front of him. "So what happened last night? Why buy drinks for strangers and get shit-faced?"

Delia winced at the description, wanting to make light of the situation. The presence of Tommy at her table and the evidence that two almost-strangers had spent the night out of concern for her meant she had to be honest.

"It was just supposed to be drinks and dancing...until I checked my email."

Tommy tsked. "Honey, how many times have I told you never to read emails when you've been drinking?"

"I know. But I was waiting for confirmation on a sale."

"I get it." He pointed at her phone. "Show me the email."

While Tommy read the email, Delia stood and picked up their breakfast dishes. She took them into the kitchen and placed them in the sink. She'd deal with them later. Returning to the table, she watched Tommy pluck at his bottom lip while reading the email again.

"Your lawyer sounds heartless."

"Right? I think that's what set me off. Not so much the reminder that I now have two months, but her conde-scending tone. And then Briana said something bitchy to me about being a lady of leisure, and I thought, 'Screw 'em all.'" She'd then marched over to the bar, slapped down her AMEX card, and declared she'd be buying the drinks for the rest of the night. She didn't remember much after that. "I didn't see Cal at the bar. Did he really carry me out of there?"

Tommy smirked at her. "Oh yeah. Refused to put you

down. Sat in that chair over there most of the night and watched you sleep. What's that about?"

A warm, squishy feeling took up residence in her belly. Embarrassment as well. What did he think of her now? "I don't know. He's my client, and a good guy, and I think we might be friends." She chewed on her lip and considered the implications of Cal's presence. "Did he…um, say anything about me?"

"The man would make an excellent poker player. He had no idea about your family's business. And believed you were between jobs. I did not monitor his movements—except to note he has an exceptional ass—so he may have gone through your medicine cabinet and underwear drawer, but he didn't pry." Tommy gave her a sly look. "He's the one who took off your shoes and covered you with the afghan and laid out the water and ibuprofen."

Delia's cheeks pinked up. "He doesn't talk a lot."

"Oh, I didn't say that. He and Connie got along like a house on fire. He was very much interested in her plans when she finishes school."

A shaft of jealousy shot through her. Connie was everything Delia wasn't: Smart, goal-oriented, hardworking, kind, and caring, and very pretty under that awful uniform. How was Delia going to face her now?

"I owe some apologies, don't I?"

"Yep."

Delia didn't move. She stared off into the distance, hoping she could rewind the last twenty-four hours. She shouldn't have answered her phone. She should've made up an excuse to not go out and stayed home with a book instead. Thinking of books made her think of Cal. Maybe she could work from home for the foreseeable future. Tommy smacked the tabletop, startling her out of her reverie. "You are going to take me to Cal's bookstore and show me what you've been doing there."

"I don't think—"

"Stop thinking and go get ready. There's no time like the present."

Scowling, Delia headed to her bedroom, wondering what to wear when groveling for forgiveness.

CHAPTER 10

The blinking cursor mocked him. Cal had been staring at the blank page on his screen for half an hour. He was supposed to be writing about a duke seducing an heiress while dancing at a ball, but all he could think about was Delia swaying on the dance floor. He shouldn't have been there. It was none of his business why she'd gotten drunk and thrown money around like she was a trust fund baby. And she was. Delia Duncan came from privilege and lived a privileged life.

His eyes gritty from lack of sleep, Cal reached for his coffee cup, then put it back down on the counter. More caffeine was the last thing he needed. First Tommy, then Connie, had made pots of the stuff in Delia's tricked-out kitchen. He glanced over at the ancient commercial coffeemaker that she'd cleaned and polished a few days ago. Next to it stood three ceramic canisters she'd found among his grandparents' stuff. She'd cleaned those up and then filled them with teas she'd brought with her.

It was close to eleven, two hours past the time Delia normally showed up. Would she do so today? Wearing the vestiges of last night's makeup and clearly hungover, she'd still been beautiful this morning. Her attitude, not so much. She'd been bitchy. For the umpteenth time, Cal wondered who the real Delia Duncan was. He knew she was bright and energetic, well organized, and had an eye for style. She understood the power of social media, how to employ it to sell a product. The website she'd constructed for Jimmy's Joint was great, and wherever she was posting about items to sell was working, because sales had been good the past week or so. Delia's Closet, the name of her other business, seemed to be designed the same way, with beautifully photographed images of women's clothing and accessories and a few videos of Delia herself modeling an item and giving its history. Cal had no doubt she would do well with it. The mystery remained, though: why was Delia doing what she was doing?

Most of the night, he'd sat in the chair, watching over her, worried she'd throw up and choke on her own vomit. He'd tune in to the conversation between Connie and Tommy now and then. Without denigrating the residents in the building, Connie told amusing stories of her work as a concierge, including the first time she'd met Tommy.

"I don't know what the celebration was, but I opened the door of the car, and the two of you practically fell out of it. You were both in tiaras and feather boas and matching dresses and wearing heels so high I worried one of you would break your neck."

Tommy had laughed and touched the back of Connie's hand. "Sweetie, I've been wearing heels since I came out of the womb. I have yet to fall off them. I remember that night. It was a surprise wedding shower. The bride and groom wanted a small, intimate wedding and weren't going to have any attendants. Delia organized the shower, paid for all of us to wear the same dresses and accessories." He looked regretful. "I don't remember seeing you. I hope we weren't awful to you."

Connie reassured him. "You weren't. Delia always comes

home from parties in a good mood." Then her eyes widened as if realizing what she'd said. "She's not. I mean—"

"Sweetie, I've known her for many years. I know she doesn't do that a lot. She's really not much of a drinker."

Tommy's words reassured Cal, though he still wondered if she came home alone or brought company. Not that it was any of his business.

At one point, he'd needed the bathroom. He took his time walking down the hallway and looking into the rooms he passed along the way. One room was set up as an office/photo studio. He recognized the same lights and camera equipment Delia had brought into the shop. They looked expensive, and she apparently owned two sets of them. Another room was set up as a closet or wardrobe. Cal didn't know what to call it, knowing only he'd never seen more women's clothes in one room in his life. He'd shaken his head, found the guest bathroom, and done his business, then returned to the main living area. Restless, he prowled around, staring out the windows at the bay, then decided to be social. He settled into a chair at the glass-topped dining table where Tommy and Connie were sitting. The two smiled a welcome. Connie had opened up a battered laptop and was typing away at something, while Tommy perused the pages of a fashion magazine, now and then typing a note into his phone.

Cal cleared his throat, thinking about the room full of clothes. "Does Delia style women? Like a personal shopper."

"No," Tommy replied. "But she tried it. Her mother introduced her to some friends, and it went okay for a while, but then it didn't. I believe a husband made a pass at her, and the wife blamed Delia. Didn't want to believe that her husband had a wandering eye and wandering hands. The Duncan family didn't want Delia to make a fuss, so they closed the business down."

"They didn't believe her?" Connie asked.

"Oh, they believed her. They didn't want the Duncan name to be dragged through the mud." Tommy sat back and crossed his arms. "She hasn't been the same since."

Cal had wondered what it was like to have a family that cared more for their image than their daughter.

The door to the shop opened, and Delia entered, closely followed by Tommy. Carrying a bakery bag, Tommy walked to the counter and smiled at Cal. "This place is fabulous." He dropped the bag on the counter and moved toward the window, reaching out to touch the worn velvet of the old chair.

Cal looked at Delia, who stood next to the door. Her hair pulled back in a ponytail, her fresh makeup couldn't completely hide the ravages of the night before. Twisting the straps of her tote bag, she glanced his way, then moved to stand next to Tommy, her steps tentative.

Tommy wrapped an arm around her shoulders. "Sweetie, you've outdone yourself. You found all of this on site?" At her nod, he continued to gush. "You are going to make a buttload for Mr. Tall, Dark, and Stoic over there. You set up for online sales yet?"

Delia straightened and started digging through her tote bag. Cal knew she was looking for her planner to consult and check off one of her innumerable lists. "That's what I'm working on today. I need to pick up packing supplies and figure out delivery, but it should be ready in a few days."

Tommy touched one of the tiny pawns in the window display. "It's a shame these chess sets aren't for sale. They're exquisite."

Delia flicked a glance back at Cal before replying, "We need permission from the artist before we can do that, although I may start up a list for people who are interested."

He hadn't thought of that. If Sid had future customers, a source of income, it might motivate him to do more carving. Maybe here in the shop, so Cal could keep an eye on him.

When it was time to move out, they could find a small studio for him. Cal shook his head at his wayward thoughts. He'd have to find Sid first and help him get sober. He tuned in to the conversation between Delia and Tommy.

"For now, how about I take some photos for my Insta?" Tommy held up his camera, looking between Delia and Cal. Cal shrugged. Delia nodded. Tommy rolled his eyes. "Such enthusiasm." He went out the door and stood on the sidewalk, taking pictures of the display.

Her cheeks pink, Delia approached the counter where Cal remained sitting on his stool. The bitchy socialite had disappeared, and the vulnerable woman stood in her place. He waited. He wanted to chastise her for her dismissal of Connie's and Tommy's concern. He wanted to rail at her for scaring the shit out of him. Instead, he waited.

Her knuckles whitening on the strap of her tote bag, Delia cleared her throat. "Thank you for looking after me last night. I um…something was on my mind, and it…got out of control."

No shit. Words stuck in his throat. They were barely more than work acquaintances, and if she did stupid shit on her own time, it was none of his concern. At least, that's what he told himself.

At his silence, Delia sighed. She reached into her bag, and bringing out a stack of business cards, she placed them on the counter next to his laptop. "I'm going to be working from home today. If someone has a question you can't answer, give them one of these." She walked toward the door, then halted and retraced her steps. "I almost forgot. I found this yesterday." She pulled out a crumpled paper bag and dropped it on the counter before hastening back to the door.

Through the window, he watched Tommy speaking to Delia. She was alternately nodding and shaking her head at his questions. Tommy threw up his hands, then peered through the window. Catching Cal's eyes, he waved, then put his hand to his ear and mouthed the words, *I'll call you.*

Cal waved back, then watched them walk up the street until they were out of sight. His attention returned to the items before him. He dismissed the business cards and the bakery bag and drew the crumpled bag toward him. He tipped it upside down, and a lumpy bundle fell into his hand. The soft old deer hide looked familiar. Placing it on the counter, he untied the deer hide lace that held it together and unrolled the soft material. Inside was a collection of much used, much loved carving tools. A lump formed in his throat. She knew it was important to him and took the time to search for it. And he'd been a jerk to her.

The bell jingled over the door. Cal blinked back his tears before turning to greet the customer.

A familiar voice said, "She's pretty."

Cal whipped his head around to meet the shy smile of his cousin Sid.

CHAPTER 11

The bedraggled young man huddled in the doorway. Almost ten years younger than Cal's thirty-seven years, Sid looked much older. Cal could smell him from across the room. At least he looked lucid, if not completely sober.

He acknowledged Sid's presence with a lift of his chin. He moved to retrieve the small duffel from under the counter and placed it on the surface. It contained a complete change of clothes, including shoes and a rain jacket. Not new, but clean and in good repair. A zipped plastic bag held toothpaste, toothbrush, shampoo, soap, hand towel, deodorant, washcloth, nail clippers, hand sanitizer, and condoms. Another bag held a notebook, pens, a cheap cell phone and charger, and Starbucks gift cards. No cash.

For whatever reason, about five years ago, their grandparents had renovated the bathroom to include a shower as well as a washer and dryer. A cupboard above the washer contained more clothing and cold weather supplies. He was thankful for its presence when Sid made his infrequent visits. The room was stocked with other hygiene supplies, including disposable razors, condoms, pads, and tampons.

Once in a while, a woman would show up with Sid, and one had requested the pads. Not knowing what to buy, Cal had her write down suggestions and shopped from the list. Despite his level of intoxication, Sid always cleaned up the bathroom. He, and whoever he brought with him, would clean up, stock up, warm up, eat up, and then leave.

Sid picked up the duffel and headed for the bathroom, mumbling a thank you.

"Do you want coffee or tea?"

That caught Sid's attention. He'd never been given a choice before. "You've got tea?"

"Yeah. Tetley." At Sid's look of surprise, Cal continued, "Delia was cleaning up and found Gram's teapot. She asked me what kind of tea to buy, and I remembered you and Gram drinking Tetley. So…"

Sid continued to stare at him, as if lost in a memory. Then he turned back toward the bathroom. "Tea would be good."

Cal gusted out a sigh and leaned against the back counter, thankful for Sid's appearance after six long weeks. As much as he wanted to fuss over his cousin, he'd learned the hard way that would only drive him away. He'd been in and out of facilities, and sometimes jail, multiple times, preferring the insecurities of the street to rules and confinement. Once, Cal had locked up the store and followed Sid from a distance. He'd made his way down to the waterfront and joined a group of men sitting around a blanket with carvings for tourists to buy. Sid had opened up the duffel and distributed the contents like he was Santa giving out toys on Christmas morning. Cal had been pissed at Sid for giving away the supplies Cal had bought for him. About to storm over, he checked himself when one of the other men opened up a battered backpack and gave something to Sid. Cal squinted, watching as Sid's eyes lit up at the paperback novel. Shit. He was a librarian, a writer, and ran a used bookstore, and had never thought to offer a book to his cousin. Cal had settled back against a wall and watched Sid and his friends share among themselves. For better or worse, Sid had found a community.

While waiting for Sid to have his shower, Cal made tea in the big old Brown Betty teapot. In the small fridge beneath the coffeemaker, he found the milk Delia had bought. He retrieved the sugar bowl and a large mug from the shelf above the coffeemaker. He spotted the bakery bag from Tommy and the carving tools and hesitated. Rightfully, the carving tools belonged to Sid. They'd been gifted to him from their grandfather, who had received them from *his* grandfather. Cal picked up the deerskin bundle and tucked it under the counter. Hopefully, Sid hadn't seen it and recognized it.

Sid emerged from the bathroom looking much better. He'd shaved, pulled his long dark hair back into a ponytail, and dressed in clean jeans, a T-shirt, and hoodie. He wore new socks and carried a newish pair of sneakers. The first time Cal bought clothes for Sid, he'd gone to Target and bought everything new. The next time he'd seen Sid, he wasn't wearing any of those clothes; someone had beaten him and rolled him for the new sneakers and jacket. From then on, Cal frequented Goodwill, choosing items that were durable but wouldn't attract attention.

Settling onto a stool, Sid accepted the mug of hot tea Cal set in front of him. He doctored it with milk and sugar and drank deeply, then sat back with a sigh. He waved a hand toward the washing machine that was visible through the open door. "Most of the clothes are still good, so they're in the washer. I threw away the shoes, though."

Cal nodded. If the clothes were still usable, that meant Sid wasn't living too rough. Cal pointed at the bakery bag. "Not sure what's in there. Help yourself."

Sid opened the bag and pulled out each item, placing them, one by one, on the plate in front of him. It was a mixture of savory pastries—sausage rolls, ham and cheese croissants, egg wraps, with a couple of plain doughnuts as well. Tommy may have been carrying the bakery bag, but the selection was pure Delia.

After devouring the first sausage roll in four bites, Sid took a swallow of tea and looked about the shop. "It looks good. Your friend, the pretty girl, is doing a good job."

"She's not my friend. I hired her to offload the inventory."

"Looks like it's working. You haven't sold any chess sets, though. No one wants them?"

Cal shook his head and met Sid's curious glance. "They aren't mine to sell. They belong to you."

Sid studied Cal before getting up to walk to the window. He reached out a hand to one of the boards, then stopped. "May I?" he asked over his shoulder.

"Of course." Cal joined him. This was the most interest Sid had shown in anything in a long while.

Sid picked up a knight, fashioned in the shape of an otter, and held it up to the light. "This was the first set I made. The work is rough."

"You were thirteen. Give yourself a break." Cal pointed at another chess set, this one with clams as the pawns. "Look at the grooves you carved into these. You got better with age."

"I did." Sid placed the knight back in its spot and went back to the counter, Cal following behind him.

"Are you doing any carving these days?"

Sid shrugged. "A bit. Sometimes I make cheese boards out of cedar for Ivan. Whatever the hell a cheese board is. I carve the handles for him."

"Does Ivan have a shop at the market?"

Sid shook his head. "Nah. He sells to someone there. A woman who sells to tourists looking for native art." He emphasized the word *native* with an eye roll.

Cal laughed softly. He grabbed a doughnut and took a

healthy bite, using the time to chew to think. "Does he pay you fair?"

"Not cash. I'd just piss it away. I get credit at a hotel with a coffee shop."

"Like room and board?" There were a number of hostels and places in Seattle for people with addiction issues, provided they were willing to adhere to the rules of the place. Some were more reputable than others.

"Sort of." Sid fidgeted under Cal's watchful eye. "I, umm, fell off the wagon last week and lost my privileges for a few days. I was locked out until I sobered up."

Cal schooled his features not to give away his emotions. Sid working a program—because that was what it sounded like—was a good thing. Sid being locked out because he was drunk or stoned scared the shit out of Cal. He thought about the timeline. "Was that the day you bumped into Delia?"

"Yeah. Didn't mean to scare her." With fairly steady hands, he poured himself another cup of tea. "So you started going through Gram's stuff. Find anything good?"

Cal blinked. Maybe this Ivan was really helping him. Most times, Sid would show up, barely saying a word. He'd respond to questions with monosyllabic answers. If Cal pressed too hard, Sid would take off, sometimes not returning for weeks. Cal learned not to press. He pointed at the chipped teapot on the counter. "I guess that depends on what you consider good." That earned him a smile, emboldening Cal. "This room you have, do you have space to keep stuff? If so, you want to take the teapot with you?"

Sid cupped the rounded belly of the teapot in both hands, which was clearly no longer hot. "Nah. If I can stay straight for four weeks in a row, then I can have a room to myself. Right now, I share with three other guys. You keep the pot here. For now."

Cal smiled slightly. For now sounded promising, like Sid had a goal. "Where is this place at?"

"Near Seattle Center. It used to be a hotel. Now a nonprofit agency runs it. Hang on." Sid reached into his back pocket and pulled out a worn leather wallet. It was nearly empty, with a few cards and a bus pass. Sid extracted a card and gave it to Cal. "I've been there off and on now for a month or so."

Cal studied the card. On the front it said, ODAAT House, and it gave an address and a website. "Can I keep this?"

"Sure. I, umm, thought you'd like that."

"What does ODAAT stand for?"

Sid met his eyes, his own gaze steady. "One Day At A Time."

The doorbell jingled, and both men turned to see Delia enter in a hurry.

"I forgot I'm supposed to make a delivery. I'll just grab the books and go." Shoulders hunched, she darted over to the stacks.

Cal held up a hand. "No. Wait."

Delia stopped in her tracks and twisted to look at him.

"Delia Duncan, this is my cousin, Sid. You bumped into him a while ago."

Sid stood to greet her. "Hi. I'm sorry I scared you that day. I wasn't at my best."

Eyes wide, Delia moved closer with her hand extended, her glance darting between Sid and Cal. "I wasn't paying attention, and you startled me. It's okay." A warm smile took over her face, and Cal watched its impact on his cousin. He looked like a high school kid who'd earned the prom queen's attention. Cal wondered if she knew she had that effect when she dropped the artifice and allowed her true self to shine through. Sid took Delia's hand in his, and she covered it with her other hand. "You look like you're doing better."

Sid raised and lowered one shoulder. "I am."

"I'm glad." Delia's warm gaze dimmed when she looked at Cal. "I'll get the books and get out of your hair."

"I'm making a fresh pot of tea. Want to join us? We ate all the pastries, but I can go and get more. Whatever you like." Now who was acting like a bedazzled high school boy?

"I've got time. Thanks."

Sid made big eyes at Cal as she removed her jacket and went to drop it and her tote bag off at the table she used as a desk.

Cal pointed at him. "Make the tea." He followed her, ignoring Sid's grin. She turned, and he grabbed her upper arms to prevent a collision.

"Oh!" She raised both hands and placed them on his chest, staring into his eyes.

He wondered if she remembered any of the words she'd said to him last night. Her cheeks pinked up, and she dropped her hands. It looked like maybe she did.

Cal gave her arms a gentle squeeze, then released her and stepped back. A glint of something that looked like disappointment flickered in her eyes.

"I'd like to know more about what set you off last night."

She looked embarrassed, and he thought she might deflect, but her shoulders slumped and she pressed her lips together. "Yeah. I owe you an explanation."

He waited for her to tilt her head back to meet his eyes. She'd done a good job, but he could see her exhaustion under the makeup. "Later will be fine. Thanks for finding the tools. That means a lot to me."

Her eyes softened, and her lips tilted up.

"I tucked them under the counter. When I think he's ready and won't give them away, I'll return them to Sid."

"That's a good idea. I won't say anything." Eyes dancing, she mimed zipping her lips.

Cal chuckled low, pleased she was looking better.

"Tea's ready when you are," Sid called out.

Cal turned to acknowledge his cousin and saw him waggle his eyebrows. His heart felt lighter to see Sid being animated and goofy. It had been a long time since he'd shown any life at all.

Delia pushed past Cal and plopped down on a stool in front of Sid. "So you're the one who carved those awesome chess sets. I hope you don't mind I put them in the window display."

"Nothing I've ever done has been on display before."

"Not true." Instead of going to his usual stool behind the counter, Cal took a spot next to Delia. "Pops put your nesting dolls on display one time."

Sid laughed. "I'd forgotten about that."

At Delia's look of interest, Cal continued, "Gram had a set of nesting dolls she put out at Christmas. Mary, Joseph, the three wise men, and Jesus. Sid played with them all the time when he was little. As his carving got better, Pops showed him more challenging techniques. So, one Christmas, Sid gave Gram a set depicting the local food chain. The largest was an orca, but I can't remember what the smallest one was."

Sid stared up at the ceiling and scratched the underside of his chin, a distant smile on his face. "A snail."

Elbows on the counter, Delia propped her chin on her folded hands. "That sounds awesome. Maybe I'll find it in one of the boxes."

The smile left Sid's face, and he shook his head. "No, you won't. I took it and traded it for a bottle of whiskey."

An awkward silence fell. Cal was not going to break it. He nudged Delia, and she turned to see him shaking his head. She pressed her lips together and nodded. She poured tea into the three mugs on the counter and passed two to the men. Cal picked up the mug and sipped, eyes on his cousin.

Sid's gaze returned to Cal. "It was one of the shitty things I've done that I need to atone for."

Again, Cal did not say anything. Sid's actions had hurt a

lot of people, and he did need to make amends. Letting him off easy wouldn't be helpful for anyone.

Delia picked up the card Sid had given Cal earlier. "What's this?"

"ODAAT is where I'm staying," Sid said.

Her brow furrowed as she turned the card over and read the print on the back. "Duncan Properties owns the building. ODAAT is one of the nonprofits we support."

Cal watched her cheeks pink up as she flicked a glance at him. This was the first time she'd mentioned her connection to her wealthy family. He waited to see what she would say next.

She took a big breath and glanced between Cal and Sid. "Duncan Properties is my family's business. They own a bunch of buildings in Seattle. I don't work for them, though. Being stuck in an office looking at numbers isn't my thing."

Sid nodded. "Not mine, either. I'd rather work with my hands." He pointed at Cal. "He likes to scribble stories."

"So I've heard. He won't let me read any, though," Delia said.

"Really? There's a bunch of them on one of the shelves, written under the name of Stacy Wrigglebottom."

Delia twisted to stare at Cal. "You're Stacy Wrigglebottom?"

Oh shit.

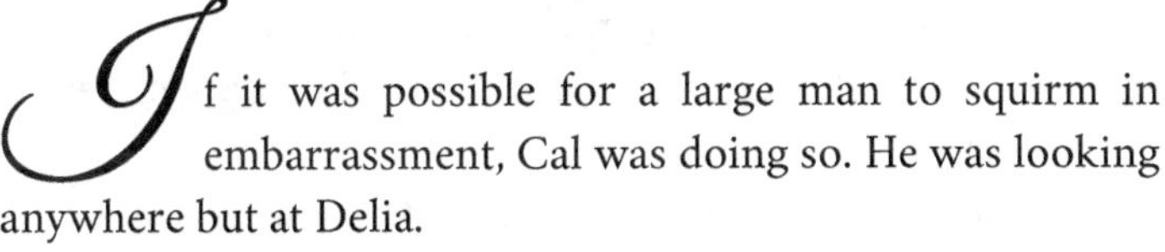

If it was possible for a large man to squirm in embarrassment, Cal was doing so. He was looking anywhere but at Delia.

"I love those books!" she said.

"I know, right?" Sid raised his mug in agreement.

Delia couldn't believe she was sitting next to one of her favorite authors. Although…

"Hang on for a second. I've seen the writer on talk shows. A woman with a Texas accent and bright red hair. That's who you ghostwrite for?"

Cal mumbled, ears pink, "It pays the bills."

Sid grinned ear to ear, clearly enjoying his cousin's discomfort. "Have you read all of her books?"

She nodded.

Sid walked around the counter and went into the stacks, beckoning her to join him. He knelt next to a shelf of paperback novels, all with bare-chested men embracing swooning women on the covers. She had spotted them a while ago and was in a quandary about selling them, trying to figure out a way to keep them for herself. Sid picked two books off the shelf, one she'd read a number of years ago and one that had been published fairly recently.

"The guys and I noticed that the stories have improved since Cal started writing for her," Sid said, putting the books into Delia's hands.

"You and your, umm, friends talk about books?"

Sid gave her a frank look. "What do you talk about when you're drinking? Or do you not drink?"

Her hangover was still making its presence known. "I do. I don't know that we really talk about anything." She was not going to tell Sid—and have Cal overhear it—that they tended to trash talk when they got together. Other than Tommy, her friends weren't really friends. She put that out of her mind. "I'll have to go back and re-read these." Carrying the books with her, she went back to the counter where Cal sat, glowering at them. "How did you get started doing this?"

A flash of something that looked like pain moved across his handsome face. She sensed that now was not the time to talk about it, so she faked a stumble. Before she could catch herself, gravity got the upper hand, and she fell forward. Cal opened his arms and drew her into his chest. It was more of a distraction than she anticipated, and for a moment, she and Cal stared into each other's eyes.

"You okay?" Cal's gaze searched her face before landing on her mouth.

Delia had the urge to lick her lips to see his reaction. Instead, she huffed out a laugh. "Just a little clumsy today." She pushed herself away from Cal, catching Sid's smirk over Cal's shoulder. She'd managed to make the situation even worse. Unfortunately, no customers entered the store to save the day. Her gaze landed on the ODAAT card lying on the counter. "I hear they're having a fundraiser next week."

The men looked at each other and then back at Delia. "My mother serves on the board for a number of nonprofits and drags me with her to luncheons and dinners when my dad can't make it. The one next week is hosted by a sorority. Each year, they choose a local nonprofit to highlight and raise money for. ODAAT is the recipient this year."

Sid nodded. "Right. Ivan asked me to carve some things for the silent auction."

That got Cal's attention. "What did you make?"

"A couple of cheese boards. I carved the handles on the small knives that go with them. He wanted me to make tiny bowls for holding olives or stuff like that, but I didn't have the tools to do the job right."

Delia shot a side-eyed glance at Cal. His lips quirked up, and he gave her the smallest of winks. Rising from his stool, he passed behind her with the lightest of shoulder bumps. Walking around the counter, he said, "Well, you're in luck, 'cause Delia found these yesterday." He pulled the deerskin package out from under the counter and placed it on top, then pushed it toward Sid.

A look of wonder crossed Sid's face. He stared at the package as if seeing a ghost. With fumbling fingers, he untied the lacing and spread out the soft hide, revealing the tools. His face crumpled, and he leaned both hands on the counter and sobbed. Delia and Cal exchanged frantic looks, then Cal wrapped his arms around his cousin and rocked him side to side. Not knowing what else to do, Delia reached over and placed her hands over Sid's, squeezing gently. She looked up at Cal to see him smile and mouth the words, *Thank you.* After a minute or two, Sid sniffed and wiped his eyes on his sleeve. Watery-eyed, he smiled at Delia, then over his shoulder at Cal. "I'm good," he said.

They let him go, and Sid turned to grab a piece of paper towel and blew his nose. Turning back, he said, "Sorry, that brought back a lot of memories. Where did you find them?"

"Cal asked me to look for them after I found the chess sets. The tools were in a box filled with salt and pepper shakers."

Cal huffed out a laugh. "Only Gram would do that."

Watching the two men bond over a shared memory, she decided to take the plunge. "Sid, your carving is very good. Ivan wouldn't have asked you to make pieces for the auction if he didn't think so as well."

Sid shrugged. "It's been a while, but I've done better."

"If you donated one of your chess sets, it would go for a pretty penny at the auction."

Both men frowned at her, Sid as if he were in thought and Cal as if he wanted to take her head off.

She ignored him. "You have a skill that could earn you a regular income. And there is a market for what you do." She looked at Sid while directing her next statement at Cal. "Perhaps if you had a place to create, a place where you could keep your tools and your works in progress, it would help in your recovery. We could make that happen here in Jimmy's Joint." She walked over to the front window and pointed to the chair and lamp arranged next to the window display. "What would you need? A chair? A table? Good light? Why not do it here?"

Cal crossed his arms but didn't say anything, his face

totally blank. Sid shoved his hands into his pockets and rocked back on his heels. "That's, umm, that's a lot to think about. Do you really think they'd sell?"

"Absolutely," she said.

"Can I think about it?" Sid glanced between Delia and Cal.

"Of course," Cal said. "You want to carve here in the shop, go for it."

"'Kay. I got a meeting this afternoon. Can I come back tomorrow?"

Cal's features softened, and he jerked his chin up. "Absolutely."

Delia went into the stacks to find the books she needed to ship off while Sid and Cal said their goodbyes. She heard the bell tinkle, and then Cal's firm steps headed her way. She was tempted to duck into the bathroom or out the back door, but she remained in place, ready to receive Cal's lecture. Instead, she was wrapped in a flannel bear hug.

"That was bloody brilliant!"

She peered up at him. "You're not mad?"

"Yes and no. Yes, that you brought up the auction without talking to me first, but no, because Sid seems to be on the road to recovery."

She pushed back from Cal's embrace. "Sid staying at ODAAT and the fundraiser being next week was too good of an opportunity to pass up. He could secure requests for future work, which would give him purpose and—"

Cal pressed a finger against her lips. "It's all good. You put the chess sets in the window to bring Sid here, and that worked. And you found the tools. He's relapsed before, so it's too soon to get excited." He removed his finger, continuing to smile down at her. "He's coming back tomorrow, and we'll talk more about it then. I can't tell you how much this means to me."

Bobbing her head, Delia rubbed her lips together, wishing

he would hold her again. Knowing now was not the time for that, she asked, "Do you want me to follow up on donating to the silent auction? I think my mom is on the organizing committee, and if she's not, she can certainly point me in the right direction."

Crossing his arms, Cal grinned down at her. "Even with a hangover, you are quite the energizer bunny."

"Don't remind me of that."

His grin turning into a soft smile, he leaned against a bookcase and watched her. To no avail, she prayed a customer would enter and she could put off the conversation they needed to have.

She focused on the bright binding of a book over Cal's shoulder. "My great-great-great-grandmother set up trust funds for her descendants, and I've been living off mine for years. Unless I can demonstrate that I can support myself without it by my thirty-fifth birthday, the trust fund goes away. Yesterday, I received an email from the lawyer who administers the trust, reminding me about the deadline. I read that after I'd had a few drinks, and her tone was conde-scending, and I kind of..."

"Went off the rails?"

At his quiet tone, she looked up at him.

"You did it in a spectacular fashion," he said.

She winced. "Right after reading the email, one of my friends said something snide and I...I don't know, wanted to show her up, I guess."

Cal continued to study her, not saying a word. He now knew her big secret, and it was mortifying that he had seen her so drunk she needed to be carried home. Then it hit her. "Why were you there? Not that I think you were following me. The Cave doesn't seem like your kind of bar. So, umm..."

"I don't know why I went there. I heard your phone conversation." He colored slightly. "You didn't look excited to be going out, and I just...had this feeling."

"What, umm, what kind of feeling?"

"I'm not sure I can describe it." He shuffled his feet.

She smirked. "You're the writer. Surely you can do better than that. Or were you off the clock?"

"Exactly. My powers of description go dormant after 6 p.m."

"Well, I'm glad you were there."

The air thickened as they stared at each other. Whatever this was, it was awkward as hell.

Delia picked up the books and brushed past him. "I think Tommy is as well. He'd never be able to carry me home."

CHAPTER 12

With one more apology to make, Delia looked longingly at the elevator but took the stairs from the parking garage to the lobby instead. The headache had subsided, but she was exhausted.

Connie walked over from the concierge's desk. "How are you feeling? You look okay."

Waving off her concern, Delia said, "Never mind me. How did your exam go?"

Connie seesawed a hand. "Eh. We'll see."

At that, a wave of guilt hit Delia. Instead of studying, Connie had spent the night watching over her. She had no idea how to make it up to her. "Do you get a break any time soon? Would you like to come up for something to eat?"

Connie looked at her watch. "Yeah. I'm only working a half shift today, so I can come up in about an hour and a half."

"Great. I'll make dinner."

"Do you want me to pick up a bottle of wine?" Connie asked with an evil grin.

"God no!"

Connie laughed and walked back to her desk. "I'll see you in a bit."

Inside her apartment, Delia switched out her shoes for slippers and hung up her jacket. Walking into the kitchen, she thought about what to make for Connie. The rare times she had friends over, it was for a drink before going out. Delia could count on one hand the number of times she'd cooked for someone else. Coffee and a bagel for a man who'd spent the night didn't count. Finding all she needed for a pasta dish with a smoked salmon cream sauce, she left the ingredients on the counter and settled on the couch with her laptop and cell phone. It was time to face the music.

She opened up her AMEX account to find the charge from last night's escapade and winced. Paying for all those drinks was roughly equivalent to the total sales Delia's Closet had made over the last three weeks. Delia threw the phone down and rubbed her forehead. She was her own worst enemy.

To torture herself further, she opened up Instagram and was bombarded with images of herself weaving on the dance floor. Lovely. Her parents would be thrilled. Then she found a video of Cal scooping her up and carrying her out of the club. She watched it over and over again. She had a blurry memory of him holding her and feeling the rumble of his voice, but that was all. She'd love to press rewind and not make a fool of herself in public—and not spend a large amount of money while doing so. However, she wouldn't have the knowledge that he was interested in her and cared for her enough to look after her when she was at her worst. What did that mean?

She'd been in love. Had her heart broken. Had learned to keep things light. Too afraid that men were attracted to her name and her family's money, she'd never accepted a proposal. She knew she worried her parents. They believed she needed someone to look after her. In their eyes, her thirty-fifth birthday loomed like an expiration date. She snorted. They probably worried she'd have to move back in with them. That was not going to happen. Yes, last night was a financial setback, but it was also a discovery. She'd found out who she could depend on.

By the time Connie arrived—carrying a bottle of sparkling water—Delia had cleaned up her apartment, prepped three packages for delivery, and studied the website for Jimmy's Joint. The shop was more than a used bookstore, so packaging its products was not cut and dried. Cal had given her the okay to offload a variety of the things she'd found in the back room. It would be easy to simply drop the stuff off at Goodwill. Cal was fine with that. Delia wasn't. With the right photos and good stories for each item, she knew she could find buyers for many of the old items. It would take patience, but her AMEX bill dictated she do the work. Unfortunately, time was against her; the building needed to be vacated, and Cal couldn't take the inventory with him.

The two women ate their meal at the island. Delia watched as Connie finished the pasta and steamed vegetables, then laid her cutlery across her empty plate and sighed.

"Thank you," she said. "You saved me from eating takeout again."

"I thought you lived at home and your mom cooked for you."

Folding her napkin and placing it atop the plate, Connie nodded. "I do and she does. She made a bunch of meals and put them in the freezer while she and Dad went on vacation. I keep forgetting to take them out to thaw, so I stop at a food truck on my way home." She rose from the table and, picking up their dirty dishes, took them into the kitchen and put them into the sink.

"You don't have to do that."

Connie waved off Delia's protest. "You cooked. It's only

fair. While I do this, why don't you go over my suggestions for your website? I emailed them to you."

"Umm. Sure." Retrieving her laptop, Delia resumed her seat at the table and opened up Connie's list. Her heart sank at the length of it. There were two columns with multiple headings and many bullet points beneath them. She had her work cut out for her. She hit print and retrieved the three-page document from her office. Connie was setting two mugs on the table when she returned.

"Don't freak out," Connie said. "One column is for Jimmy's Joint, and the other is for Delia's Closet. I figured it made sense to look at them both because they're similar businesses and a lot of the fixes will be the same for each. We'll go through each one, and I'll explain the what, the why, and the how."

"I have no clue what you're talking about, but okay."

Connie settled at the table, where she'd laid out a folder with her own copy of the document. "We'll look at what is wrong, why it's wrong, and how we can fix it."

What was it about herself that people assumed she was a damsel in distress? Being carried home by Cal probably didn't help the matter. She studied the earnest expression on Connie's face.

"You keep saying we."

Connie wrinkled her nose. "I do, don't I? I mean how you can fix it, but I'll be available to help you if you want."

"Kind of like tech support?"

"Yes! And you would be helping me out as well. I can use this experience to figure out if I'm providing clear, concise feedback."

Delia digested this while looking over the document. Knowing it was for both websites made it less intimidating. "Before we go any further, I need to tell you why I'm doing this." Seeing the concern on Connie's face, she hastened to say, "It's not bad. I've just been..." How does a grown woman describe the fact she'd never thought about the future, about where her money came from, about looking after herself? She settled for the word, "Foolish." Then she went on to explain the circumstances of her trust fund.

Alternating between jotting down notes and nodding in places, Connie didn't say a word. When Delia finished, Connie rose and went to the kitchen, coming back with the teapot. She refilled both their mugs and returned the pot to the counter. She sat back down and cupped her jaw with a hand. "I'm having a hard time wrapping my head around this. I started earning money when I was thirteen. I've babysat, walked dogs, worked retail, been a barista and a bartender. I'm holding down two jobs while going to school, and you—you're worried that your trust fund will be rescinded." Her gaze was frank as it flicked from Delia to the room surrounding them and back to Delia.

Delia squirmed. Connie's flat, even tone hurt more than if she'd yelled at her.

"If the trust fund was rescinded, what is the worst that would happen to you? Have to sell this place? Downsize?"

Delia squirmed some more. "My parents own the apartment. They'd probably support me."

Connie's lips thinned, and the hairs on her closely shorn head appeared to bristle. "I'm in the same bedroom I had when I was a kid. For my tenth birthday, I asked for unicorn wallpaper. My parents nearly divorced putting it up, it was such a pain in the ass—and expensive. My mom won't let me take it down. I wake up to it every morning. When I can afford a place of my own, I'm going to paint all the walls white."

Unsure if a response was required, Delia kept quiet. Her mother redecorated frequently. She herself had redone her entire apartment three times in the ten plus years she'd been there.

A beeping sounded, and Connie pulled her phone out of her pocket to turn it off. "I gotta go."

Delia pushed her chair back and stood to collect the mugs. "Is that, umm, your second job?"

Connie grimaced. "Yeah. I'm tutoring kids to prep for college entrance exams. At least it's online." She walked to the chair holding her battered messenger bag and jacket. Turning back to Delia, she tilted her head toward the kitchen. "Thanks for dinner. Look over the suggestions and let me know if you don't understand and I need to clarify."

Delia nodded and hastened to the door to hold it open for Connie. The younger woman murmured a goodbye and strode down the hallway, her footsteps muffled by the deep carpeting. Closing the door, Delia sniffed back tears. This was why she didn't open up to people. She shuffled back into the living room, the headache that had dogged her all day coming back to throb painfully in her temples. The words *pampered, selfish, privileged* pulsed in time.

Determined not to wallow in self-pity, she headed to the bathroom for ibuprofen, stopping when she heard a knock at the door. Hurrying over, she yanked it open. Connie stood, arms crossed, tapping her foot.

"I'll work for you on a contract basis," she said. Brushing past Delia, she spoke over her shoulder as she moved toward the table. "We'll put together terms that are satisfactory to both of us, and you will write glowing references for me in the future."

"Absolutely."

"Good." Connie nodded. "For now, you need to figure out what you want to get out of this."

Delia trailed behind her. "I don't know what you mean?"

"Do you want a short-term fix to maintain your trust fund, or do you want a viable business that can support you even if you didn't have a trust fund?"

"I hadn't thought about that."

Connie leaned against a chair and gestured at the stack of boxes against the wall. "What you've got going with Jimmy's Joint helps you out in the present. Once the inventory is offloaded, you're done there. You've got a similar issue with Delia's Closet. Eventually you'll run out of items to sell."

"I intend to help other people curate collections and find buyers."

"I know. But how hard are you willing to work at that?"

The blunt words caught her off guard. "As hard as I need to?" The response sounded like a question to her own ears.

"Need or want? There's a difference."

There was indeed a difference. Her trust fund was the security blanket, safety net, and training wheels she'd never lived without. About to turn thirty-five, it was time for her to live without it. "This is something that excites me and something I can be good at. I'm willing to work as hard as I need to."

Connie dropped her bag and settled into a chair. "Good answer. Now pour us some more tea, please."

"What about your tutoring?"

Connie grinned. "I resigned."

CHAPTER 13

The small boat was afloat. Barely. Using her hands, her shift, anything that would hold water, Luna bailed as fast as she could. She could see shore, she'd almost made it. Suddenly a—

Cal's fingers hovered over the keyboard, then hit the backspace key and watched the words disappear. Delia's offhand comment about pirates had prodded him to start a story of his own. Whether it would float or sink—he snickered at his own thoughts—would remain to be seen. For now, it was fun to write about something other than dukes and parlor maids.

Stretching his arms out to the sides, he sat back, feeling each vertebra in his spine groan with relief. He really needed a proper chair and a desk. Pushing the stool back, he rounded the counter and went into the back room, coming out a few minutes later with a box. He placed it on the counter, put his laptop on top of the box, and stood back. He grunted in satisfaction at the makeshift standing desk. The jingle of the door heralded a visitor, and his gaze moved to the wall clock. 10:30 a.m. Since Delia had spiffed up the place, especially the windows, browsers and buyers were more frequent and came in earlier in the day.

Turning to greet the potential customers, he met the shy yet eager smile of Sid and another man.

Sid made the introductions. "Ivan Thompson, this is my cousin, Calvin Jimmy."

At Cal's hello, Ivan smiled, then looked around the shop. He stepped over to the window display. "Sid, you're too modest. These chess sets are remarkable. Yes, I think we should include one in the silent auction. Maybe two."

Cal winked at his cousin, then walked around the counter ostensibly to fiddle with his new workspace but, in truth, to give Sid and his friend a little space. Sid glowed as Ivan heaped praise on his work. Compared to Sid's wrinkled but clean clothes, Ivan looked like a model for an outdoor company—jeans, rugged shoes, checked button-up shirt, down vest on a frame that was taller than Cal's yet less bulky. His sharp jaw line, flat belly, and visible biceps made Cal think he spent a lot of time in the gym. Unlike Sid, Ivan did not look like he'd spent time on the streets, but Cal suspected the fit, well-groomed man before him had pulled himself out of a bottle. Perhaps working out was how he'd fought his own personal demons.

"I'm so glad you told me about that parking spot. It will save me both time and money. I—" Delia's quick steps sounded as she came through the back door. She stopped speaking when she spotted the two other men. Making big eyes at Cal, she pressed her lips together.

He grinned. "It's fine." Lifting his chin toward the box she carried, he asked, "Got more? Do you need some help?"

Placing the carton on a stool, she dropped her tote bag on top of it and shook her head. "This is it." Her honey-colored hair glowed in the lights, and she looked energized. Today she wore a fuzzy green turtleneck sweater over a short gray leather skirt. Black tights encased her long legs, and she wore short low-heeled boots. Ivan gravitated toward Delia like he'd been drawn by a magnet.

Obviously too smart to let his gaze travel overtly over Delia's figure, his smile was far too appreciative for Cal's liking. "You must be Delia. Sid's mentioned you."

"I am. And you?"

Cal watched bright spots of color appear on her cheeks. Her debutante smile was missing. In its place was a look of polite caution and possibly…interest. Delia shifted on her feet, her gaze darting from Cal to Sid and back to Ivan.

"Ivan Thompson." He extended his hand. "I'm with ODAAT."

"Oh!" She relaxed and accepted his hand. "Your organization does great work."

"We're trying our best."

His self-deprecating grin annoyed Cal. It was working on Delia, though. She was smiling up at Ivan. Cal wanted to leap over the counter, remove her hand from his grip, and claim her as his own. He must have made a noise because three heads turned his way. "Tea?" To his annoyance, Sid and Delia looked at Ivan, who shook his head.

"Thanks, but no. I have to be back at the center soon." He turned his attention back to Delia. "Sid says you suggested he set up a place to carve here in the shop."

"Yes!"

Cal watched Delia lead Ivan over to a seating area close to the front window. She moved her hands with sweeping gestures as she described her ideas. Ivan nodded and said something that made her laugh and flip her hair over her shoulder. She looked back at Cal and grinned, clearly pleased. He shoved his hands in his pockets and returned her smile, although not as brightly. He looked at Sid. He'd shoved his own hands in his pockets and stood, shoulders hunched, rocking back and forth on his heels.

"Is this something you want to do?" Cal asked.

"I think so."

"You don't sound excited."

Sid took a stool at the counter and idly picked at the flap of the box Delia had brought in. "I'll kind of be on display."

"Aren't you on display when you're carving at the market?"

Sid shrugged. "I had friends with me, and most of the time, I was drinking."

Cal nodded, looking at Sid, then looking to where Delia and Ivan were standing. "We can move things around and make room for your friends if you want them here. No booze, though."

"Yeah?"

"Yeah."

Sid grinned. "I'll see what Ivan says."

Cal schooled his expression to remain blank. Inwardly he bristled at Sid's deferral to Ivan. If the suave guy was helping keep his cousin sober, he wouldn't interfere—unless he was hitting on Delia. Then all bets were off. He jerked his chin toward the taller man, who was pointing at something, the light catching on the metal of a bracelet he wore. "He's not local."

"No. Métis, from across the border. The Tulalip brought him down."

Cal nodded. The Tulalip tribes were well known for using the proceeds from their hotel and casino for funding community services well beyond the boundaries of their own reservation. So Ivan Thompson was of mixed blood and Canadian. Not surprising. Many Indigenous people in the Northwest had family on both sides of the forty-ninth parallel. The Jimmys, Cal's family, originated in the Chilliwack area. His great-grandfather moved to Seattle to enlist with the US Army in the Second World War. On his return, he'd married a Duwamish girl and opened Jimmy's Joint when he mustered out.

"He's been sober for seven years and…knows the struggle." There was a hint of hero worship in Sid's voice.

Cal decided to tread lightly when speaking of Ivan. "You don't have to sit in the window. Maybe at the counter, to get used to being here, for a while."

"Close to the teapot. I like that." Sid grinned. He reached into the pocket of his hoodie and brought out a fist-sized lump of wood. Cedar, from the scent of it.

Reaching under the counter, Cal pulled out the wrapped bundle of tools. "What are you going to make?"

"I don't know yet. Right now, I'm letting the wood talk to me. It will tell me what it wants to be."

"I hope it doesn't want to be a canoe. Too damn small."

Sid laughed, looking relaxed and happy. The noise drew the attention of Delia and Ivan, who wandered over.

"That smells wonderful," Delia said, bending over Sid's shoulder to inhale.

Sid smiled shyly up at her. Cal wondered if he looked like that when Delia paid attention to him. He remembered inhaling her scent while carrying her out of the club. Under better circumstances, he'd like to hold her again. He halted that thought train and focused on the box Delia had brought in.

"What's in there?"

"These are books I had at home. It makes more sense to sell them here."

Brow furrowed, Cal asked, "Won't that be hard, tracking the sales to Jimmy's Joint or Delia's Closet?"

Before Delia could answer, Ivan raised a hand. "I'm going to take off. Cal, it was nice meeting you. Sid, see you later. Delia, I'll give you a call." He waved and sauntered to the door.

To Cal's great relief, Delia didn't watch him leave. She murmured a goodbye while opening the flaps of the box. "I don't want anything in exchange for these books. You're putting a lot of faith in me, so whatever you make off these is for you." Flipping her hair over her shoulder, her gaze bounced from the books to Cal to the counter. "And it's a thank you for the other day."

A skein of hair slipped back over her shoulder. If Sid hadn't been avidly watching the exchange, Cal would have tucked the hair back behind her ear. He scowled at Sid, who grinned back, making no attempt to pretend he wasn't paying attention.

"Anytime." The words came out low and gruff. He cleared his throat. "Until this one figures out what he's going to make, he can help you."

Sid jumped up. "Happy to. Where do you want the books?"

Pointing at a rolling book cart near the cash register, Cal said, "Over there. I have to enter them into the POS."

"Great. Then, Sid, let's figure out where you want to work."

Sid looked at Delia. "I thought you wanted me to sit near the window."

She shook her head. "If you're comfortable there, sure. We can also move the shelves around and give you a spot farther back in the store. You'd be visible from the window but not on display."

Cal watched Sid's shoulders relax.

"I like that," Sid said. He hefted the box and took it to the book cart to unpack it.

Reaching across the counter, Cal took Delia's hand and squeezed it gently. "Thank you. That was really thoughtful."

She smiled up at him, squeezing his hand back.

With Cal's help, they offloaded bookshelves and shifted them around, creating a nook for Sid to sit and carve. Delia clearly had a plan in mind because she gave the men clear directions as to where to place what. Now, while Cal stared at the blinking cursor on his blank screen, Delia and Sid were restocking the bookshelves—arranged by color—and chatting about authors.

"What time is it?" Sid asked.

"1:30. Do you have to go?"

Sid rose from the floor and dusted off his knees. "Yeah. Got a meeting at two."

"'Kay. Help me up." Sid grasped Delia's extended hand and hauled her to her feet. "Take care." She waved and walked toward the restroom.

Cal stared after her and turned back to see Sid's smirk. "What?"

"Did you drool all over the keyboard? Is your laptop still working?"

"Bugger off." He leaned back against the counter behind him and crossed his arms.

Sid laughed and grabbed the hoodie he'd left on a stool. "I'll see you later."

The front door closed behind Sid as Delia emerged from the restroom and walked toward Cal. "How's the writing going?"

"Don't ask."

She sank down on a stool, propped her elbows on the counter, and rested her chin on her intertwined hands. "Do you ever get tired of being Stacy Wrigglebottom?"

About to say something snarky and dismissive, he hesitated, then shrugged. "Yeah. There's not a lot of scope for the imagination."

Delia cocked her head. "Did you just paraphrase Anne Shirley?"

"Maybe I did."

"I loved the *Anne of Green Gables* books."

"Me too." He picked up his mug and went to the coffee station for a refill. "Want something?"

"No, thanks." When he returned, she said, "Why don't you do something different? You clearly are a great writer."

"It's kind of a long story."

"I've got time." She raised an expectant eyebrow.

"When I was working in the library at the U, I had a coworker named Julie."

"There's always a girl."

"Do you want to hear the story or not?" Delia mimed zipping her lips, and he continued, "We were both writers, and after work, we would meet up and write together. We got close, eventually moving in together. And it was…good."

Delia held up a hand. "You don't have to give me the details. I figure we both have stories that don't need to see the full light of day."

He tipped his chin up. "Fair enough." In his mind, he sorted through the memories, figuring out which ones he was willing to share. "We were together for a couple years. She met my family, charmed my grandfather and Dad. She knew I wanted to fictionalize our people's myths, bring the stories of the raven and the wolf to life. We bounced ideas off each other. I helped her outline her novel, she helped me do mine—a paranormal fantasy incorporating native traditions and folklore."

"Wait." Delia frowned at him. "Isn't that a series by…hang on, the name will come to me."

He waited.

"J.S. Talltree!" She snapped her fingers. "The first book was great, and then the series kind of petered out. That was your idea?"

"Yeah. I wrote the first few chapters, then put it aside. I'd taken on a big research project at the library right around the time Pops got sick, and I didn't have the time or the energy to write."

"Is that why you broke up?"

"Part of it. She entered a PhD program back east and wanted me to go with her. The timing was bad. I was committed to my family and committed to my work, so I told Julie I would follow her after things settled down. They didn't settle the way I thought they would. Pops got worse, so I started working here with him. And then he died." He cleared his throat.

Delia's eyes were warm and sympathetic.

"Julie came back for the funeral and was really helpful, because I was shell-shocked. She stayed for a week and fussed over me, cleaning up my apartment, organizing my desk. One day I heard her on the phone, talking to a commercial realtor about valuing Jimmy's Joint. She didn't understand why I couldn't leave, and we fought. It was too fresh, and I couldn't let it go. She gave me an ultimatum."

"And you chose your family."

"I chose the bookstore."

Delia extended her arms, looking side to side. "This place is full of your family's history. Your history, your childhood. Your grandfather."

Cal met her direct gaze, then shifted it to focus on the chessboards in the window. "I guess you're right. I did choose family."

"How did she wind up with your book?"

"We shared our work. She had my complete outline and the first few chapters. She made enough tweaks to avoid plagiarism and finished the book. I don't know if she found an agent or queried directly to publishers, but you know the rest."

Delia nodded. "I saw her interviewed on TV. She wove together the supernatural with Northwest Indigenous folklore into contemporary fiction. What tribe is she with?"

Cal leveled a look at her. "She's not. Her family immigrated from Holland after WWII. She has no native blood at all."

"Seriously?"

"She's smart. She cultivates the look but has never

claimed to be Indigenous, and she was born here. Her family name is Dyck."

Delia giggled. "That seems appropriate. When the book came out, did you challenge her?"

"No. The publisher sent me a letter offering me money to sign over rights to the story and included an NDA. I didn't have the energy and couldn't see any upside in fighting it, so I signed. I donated the money to the hospice that cared for Pops. I quit the library and spent the next year here, drinking bad coffee and re-reading old favorites."

"And watching over Sid."

Cal bobbed his head. "That too." He'd never examined those gray days closely. They were a swirling bucket of misery. The books in Jimmy's Joint were both a comfort and a reminder of what he'd lost.

"It must have been painful, seeing the woman you loved succeed based upon your work."

Cal tilted his head back and forth. "I'm not sure that it was love. We kind of fell into it. We were young and…" He looked up to see the same color climbing Delia's cheeks as he felt on his own.

"How did you become Stacy Wrigglebottom?"

"Drunken fan fiction."

"Seriously."

He shifted his weight and caught Delia's eyes following the movement. He just stopped himself from flexing. "I'd finished her book, *The Duke and the Doxie*, and thought the ending was unsatisfying. It really bugged me. So, one night, after a long conversation with Don Julio, I wrote my own ending and sent it to her. I mean, I don't think I even proof-read it before hitting send. Then I forgot about it. A few months later, I got a letter from her publisher asking for a meeting, the same company that published Julie's books."

"Oh, wow."

"Yeah. That could have gone all kinds of sideways. The

publisher made the connection, but Stacy, God bless her stubborn Texas soul, liked my writing and wanted to hire me. My parents insisted I talk to an intellectual property lawyer and have them go over any contract before I signed, which I did. For three years, up until the end of last December, I was bound from not writing anything featuring mythical, paranormal, or Indigenous folklore. I wasn't writing anything anyway, so that wasn't a hardship." He sipped his coffee. "Ghostwriting wasn't how I wanted to be published, but it's been good to me."

"Wait, if you signed an NDA, how did Sid find out?"

He rolled his eyes. "I left a manuscript open on my laptop one day, and he saw it. He gave me so much shit. To shut him up and swear him to secrecy, I promised to give him an advanced reader copy for each book."

When Delia stopped laughing, she asked, "What's stopping you from writing your own stuff? You said that the contract ended in December. There's nothing to stop you from picking up those stories again. Is there?"

Cal blinked. "The day came and went, and I didn't even think about it."

Delia rose from her stool and reached over to tap on the back of his laptop. "There's nothing stopping you now." She smiled and headed back into the stacks.

*S*itting on the floor was awkward in a short skirt. Delia shifted around from her position next to a shelf of memoirs. She studied the title of one of them: *The Man Who Chose Liberty Over Marriage*. She shoved it back in its place. No wonder it was on the bottom shelf. A kick stool appeared beside her, atop it a steaming cup of fragrant tea. She looked up to see Cal's big frame rising above her.

She lifted the cup and took a tentative sip, mindful of the heat. "Thank you."

"I thought the stool would be more comfortable than the floor. Cleaner, too."

Grinning up at him, she handed Cal the cup before standing and dusting herself off. "You're right about that."

"So, umm, what do you need to talk to Ivan about?"

"I told him I knew someone who would be able to value the chess set for the auction." The endless number of art openings and cocktail parties at the homes of her parents' rich friends were coming into use. Her address book was full of names and numbers (and occupations) of the people she'd met over the years. Networking really was everything.

"Oh. That's good."

She was beginning to be able to read Cal's expressions. That one looked like relief. Despite his admiring glances, Ivan had not asked her out. A month ago, his good looks would have caught her attention and she would have angled for a date or asked him out directly. Not now. She had hazy memories of Cal holding her, rubbing her face against his chest, and she wanted a repeat. Maybe, after they'd finished up with Jimmy's Joint and were on an equal footing, she'd ask him out. There was too much to do right now to get caught up in a romance, or fling, or relationship. Whatever it might turn out to be.

Delia's phone dinged with an incoming text. She looked at it. "That's my mom." She rolled her eyes. "She thinks texts are limiting and prefers phone calls. I need to call her back."

Cal straightened. "I'll let you get to it."

"She can wait." Cocooned between the bookshelves and Cal's big body, Delia felt warm and safe. Being close to him, talking to him, even if it was just about what to do with old books, was nice. "These memoirs, are you okay if I give them to an artist? I'm not sure I'll be able to sell them."

"Whatever you think best. I trust you."

His words settled her. He trusted her. She hoped it wasn't misplaced. Before doubt could trample all over her, he went on.

"I went over the books last night and compared last month to this time last year. Revenue is up seventy percent. Thank you for that. When it comes to dealing with the inventory, feel free to do as you think best." He pointed at the back room with his thumb. "I like what you're doing with my grandparents' stuff as well. Sid can help you with that, too. Just separating it for me is a great help. I can make decisions instead of ignoring it."

Delia smiled. "I used to watch those TV shows where professional organizers would go into someone's home to help them get rid of things, sorting things into salable items, keepsakes, and crap. When it's done by an outsider who doesn't have any sentimental attachments, it makes it easier."

"I'll say."

Delia's phone dinged again.

She sighed.

Cal chuckled. "You talk to your mom. I'll get you another cup of tea."

Feeling squishy inside, she watched him walk off. He was one of the good ones.

She dialed her mother and, putting the phone on speaker, set it on a bookshelf. Carol Lee Duncan tended to ramble, and Delia would cull the books while they talked.

"Hi, Mom."

"Hello, sweetheart. Why do you want a dealer in native art?"

"There are some chess sets here in Jimmy's Joint done by a Duwamish carver. One or more of them will be silent auction items for the ODAAT fundraiser, and they need to be valued."

"I didn't know you were working on the auction."

"I'm not." Delia went on to give the short version of meeting Sid and Ivan and the connection to ODAAT.

"I see. I'm working on the event committee and could use some help with—"

"I'm sorry, Mom. My hands are full right now, and I won't be able to do that." Delia studied the books she was currently holding. She was not lying. If she agreed to help her mother, the event would take over her life for the next week or so.

"Oh. Well, how about if you—"

"Really, Mom. For the next few months, I have to focus on my work. The bookstore has a deadline, and I have mine."

Carol Lee huffed. "Can I put you down for two tickets at least? Bring Tommy. I haven't seen him in forever."

"Yes. I'll buy two tickets." *And stay away from the bar.* Alcohol and auctions were a bad combination. Delia regularly brought home items she'd paid too much for and had no use for.

"Oh good. Now I know you said your hands are full, but don't forget about the commemoration."

Delia sat back on the stool, searching her memory. "Remind me please."

"It's the 150th anniversary of the founding of Duncan Properties, and the city will be commemorating Gweneth Duncan. We need to come up with a video presentation about her."

"Right. When is it again?"

Mentally, Delia compared the date to her calendar. It was after she'd be done with Jimmy's Joint. Not a problem.

Her mother went on, "I was going to hire someone to do the video and remembered the one you made for your brother's last birthday. Will you do something similar? Paid, of course."

"Seriously?" Delia was used to being volun-told by her mother.

"Yes. Duncan Properties has the budget for it, and you certainly have the skill set."

"Thanks, Mom."

"Sweetheart, you're good at a lot of things. Now, I must go. I'll email the contact info for the art dealers. Love you lots!"

CHAPTER 14

$\mathcal{D}$elia looked at the unfamiliar phone number and let the call go to voicemail. After crawling around on the floor of Jimmy's Joint, she'd headed home for a much-deserved shower. Now in yoga pants and a burgundy cashmere hoodie, she scowled at her computer, determined to make headway on the list Connie had given her.

One of the tasks was giving her a headache. She wasn't sure if the instructions for the inventory management software weren't clear or if she was too dense to understand them. The tutorial videos were equally incomprehensible, so she opened a tab on her computer for YouTube. She found a video she could understand and used it to guide her while working on the inventory system. Finally, success. She'd managed to align inventory, sales, invoices, and shipping. To celebrate, she walked over to the large windows in her apartment and went through some yoga poses to get the kinks out of her back. Refilling her water bottle in the kitchen, she listened to the voicemail.

"Hi Delia, this is Ivan Thompson from ODAAT. Not sure if you remember me, but we met the other day at Jimmy's Joint."

Oh, she remembered him. He was a snack and a half. Not only that, he talked to her like she was an intelligent being.

"We're in a bind for the fundraiser. The person who was supposed to arrange the displays for the auctions backed out. I was impressed with the display you'd done at the bookstore and thought of you."

As flattering as that was, she didn't have time to take on a volunteer job, regardless of how good the cause was.

"It's a paid position, and your business would receive credit in the program."

That got her attention. He went on to name a figure that made her jaw drop. For a moment, she wondered if her mother had bent Ivan's ear. Did she care? A little, but if she was actually going to go somewhere with this business, the auction was a good place to start.

"I know it's last minute, but I'd appreciate it if you would give it some consideration and get back to me. Thanks, and take care."

Delia replayed the message twice. Someone wanted to pay her to set up displays. The money wasn't enough to cover the bar bill from her drunken escapade, but it would put a nice dent in her AMEX bill. Could she do it? Absolutely. But did she have the time? Delia's Closet could be put on hold for a couple of weeks, but Jimmy's Joint? She needed to talk to Cal. Blowing him off was not an option. She dashed off a text to Ivan, letting him know she would get back to him by the next day. She found Cal's contact info and gave him a call. It rang four times before he picked up.

"Hey, what's up?" Traffic noises came through in the background.

"Do you have time to chat?"

"I will in a few minutes. I'm going to pick up something to eat. Okay if I call you after that?"

Delia's stomach growled at the idea of food. "Umm, do you want to meet somewhere?"

Cal was silent. If it weren't for the blare of a car horn, she would have thought they'd been disconnected.

"Cal? You there?"

"Yeah, sorry. Damn bicycles. I can do that. I'm about four blocks away from McQuarry's. Will that do?"

"It'll take me about fifteen minutes to get there if you don't mind waiting." She was on the move already, trying to remove her pants while walking and holding the phone. About to fall over, she propped herself against the wall and got one leg out.

"Not a problem. I'll have a beer."

"Great. Bye." She tossed her phone onto the floor and grabbed a pair of jeans. She intended to walk the dozen blocks, but she was not going to a bar in yoga pants. Shimmying into the jeans, she pulled on a pair of socks, thrust her feet into low-heeled boots, and hurried to the bathroom. The hoodie was fine. Her makeup was fine. She released her hair from its tie and shook it out. She was almost out the door when she remembered her phone. Grabbing it, her keys, and a tube of lip gloss, she stuffed them into the pockets of a thinly padded white vest and left the apartment. She took the stairs down to the lobby, threw a smile and a wave at the concierge on duty, and speed walked down the street. She'd never moved so fast in her life.

Outside the bar, she stopped to catch her breath. Sixteen minutes from the time she'd hung up the phone. Not bad. Using her phone as a mirror, she fluffed up her hair and touched up her lip gloss. Breathing out a big sigh, she pulled open the door and stepped to one side to look around. In a quiet corner, a familiar flannel-covered back caught her eye. Delia stopped at the bar and ordered a glass of white wine. While she waited, she watched Cal. A full glass of beer sat in front of him, and he was bent over a book, idly playing with a coaster. She chuckled. The man ran a bookstore, wrote for a living, and still read in his downtime. Would it be a Regency romance or a psychological thriller? Delia paid for her drink and threaded her way through the early evening crowd to Cal's table. He looked up, blinked, then aimed a warm smile that reached his eyes in her direction. She practically skipped the last few feet.

"Hi."

"Hi yourself." He stood and pulled a chair out for her.

She sat, and he pushed it in, leaving behind the scent of leather and sandalwood.

"I was starved, so I ordered some appetizers for us." He nodded at her glass of wine as he resumed his chair. "I wasn't sure what you'd want to drink, so I figured I'd wait for you to order."

"White wine is always a safe bet for me."

"Even in dive bars?"

"I don't know that I've been to a dive bar."

His eyes crinkled. "So noted."

Two servers approached their table, loaded down with plates of food. Delia picked up her glass to make room for the mountain of appetizers.

"You weren't kidding about being hungry."

"I'm a big guy, and I didn't know what you'd like." His lips quirked up. "You first."

She served herself a generous amount of food, and they ate companionably for a few minutes.

"Thanks for meeting me. I hope I'm not intruding on your evening."

"No problem. It would have been me and takeout and Miss Beverly Jenkins." He patted the book by his side. "I'm happy to join you. What's up?"

She wriggled in her seat with nerves and excitement. "Ivan called me today and asked if I would help out with the fundraiser. They need someone to curate the auction items and oversee the setup and display of the items."

"I heard you tell your mom that you didn't have time to volunteer."

"That's the thing. This is a paying job, and my name would be in the auction literature. It would be good advertising."

"When do you start?"

"Umm…I don't know. I haven't said yes yet."

"Why not?" He was looking everywhere but at her.

Delia reached across the table to touch the back of his hand. His eyes came up to meet hers. "Because I needed to talk to you first. The event is two weeks away. I can back off on Delia's Closet, but working on the fundraiser might impact the time I spend on Jimmy's Joint. I will make your deadline. If necessary, I'll hire some assistants to haul stuff away and put it in storage units. I can—"

"Hey." He turned his hand and engulfed hers in his, squeezing gently. "Slow down. Take a breath." He released her hand and drank deeply from his beer. "Give me a to-do list, and I can work on clearing out the back room. I'm good at following orders."

"You're okay if I take the job?"

"Delia, you're phenomenal. If you gave me a detailed job list, dusted your hands off, and never came back, I'd be able to clear out the inventory and the back room way before the deadline. I wouldn't do it with your flair, but the job would get done. So yeah. You take a few weeks to deal with the fundraiser. I'm good with that."

Phenomenal. The man was good with words. Relaxing her shoulders, warmth filled her. "Okay, I'll write you a detailed job list."

"You going to be working closely with Ivan?"

She hid her smile behind her wineglass. "I doubt it. I'm pretty sure I'll be working with the organizing committee, and I don't think he gets involved with minutia. My preference is to work out of Jimmy's Joint as much as I can."

He flicked a glance at her, then back down at his food. "Good. If I have questions, I can reach you easily."

She was pretty sure his ears were turning pink. For a man who wrote alpha men, he was sweet and incredibly cute.

"This is a pretty big deal for you, eh?"

She bobbed her head and finished swallowing before answering. "Yes, for a few reasons. I've tried a bunch of things, and this—what I'm doing for you, organizing and offloading stuff, and what I will do at the event—is something I enjoy. I can see myself doing this long term. And I made this happen on my own, without help from my parents."

"There's nothing wrong with parents helping out their kids. I mean, Jimmy's Joint was given to me."

Delia waved a hand in front of her. "Totally. But your family doesn't write those books and didn't find the contracts for you. Your success is not because of Jimmy's Joint." She shifted in her seat, trying to figure out how to explain. "Whenever I've expressed interest in something, my parents have been right there, serving it up to me on a silver platter. I loved opening up the two businesses, the planning, the excitement of throwing ideas around. But I didn't have any skin in the game. So after they were open, and it was the same thing every day, I got bored." She drank her wine. "I know I'm privileged and sound entitled. I treated people like I was entitled..."

"Sounds like having your trust fund taken away was a wake-up call for you."

"I'll say. For the first time, I feel like I have a purpose when I get up in the morning. You're counting on me." She buried her nose in her wineglass, embarrassed that she'd said too much.

"I am. And you've delivered in spades. I had a bit of writer's block that day you came into the shop. Planned on closing early because the walls were closing in. Then I figured out the scene. Good thing. Otherwise, Jimmy's Joint wouldn't have been open."

"And I wouldn't have walked into a flannel wall."

They'd finished their meal and haggled over the bill. Cal paid, feeling victorious, then insisted on sharing an Uber with her and paying for that. He considered it a double win. It prolonged the evening, and he would know she arrived home safely. The car idled in the driveway of the luxury apartment building while Cal watched Delia get into the elevator. He then paid off the driver and started walking toward his own apartment. The three-mile hike through the dark streets allowed him to process his thoughts.

He had a job he was good at and brought in a comfortable income. His relationship with his family was good. The underlying worry about Sid was diminishing, and offloading Jimmy's Joint was progressing better than he ever imagined. Even with seventy-five percent of the proceeds going to Delia, Cal's bank account was getting fat. So why did he feel unsettled?

He wasn't raised with a trust fund but had never had to scrape. Raised up near Everett, his father was a commercial fisherman while his mother owned her own insurance agency. He took advantage of the educational opportunities available to Indigenous students and had done well at University of Puget Sound on a scholarship. After completing the library science program at UW, he'd been hired on to work in the archives, specifically with maintaining Indigenous historical records. If that had continued, if Pops hadn't died, would he and Julie still be together? Would he have continued to write, maybe publish under his own name? Where would he be now? Certainly not walking home after dinner with Delia Duncan.

Standing at a crosswalk, waiting for the light to change, a couple across the street caught his eye. The man had his arm slung around the woman. He casually kissed the side of her head, and the woman smiled up at him. Could Cal have that? With Delia?

If her business took off, no doubt there would be a lot of socializing and attending events in her future. Was that something he wanted to do? Not all the time. He was a man who appreciated quiet, but he could compromise. When the door closed on Jimmy's Joint for the final time, Delia would no longer be in his employ, and he would see if she were interested in a relationship—with him. There were seven weeks left. He could wait. In the meantime, he would assist her in any way he could. He wanted her to succeed on her own.

The next morning, a laminated sheet of paper landed on the counter beside him. "Here you go."

Cal looked up at Delia. "Here I go, what?"

"Your to-do list. Please tell me you haven't forgotten."

"No, no. I wasn't expecting it to be this detailed and certainly not laminated." He looked over the extensive list and grumbled. "I don't remember agreeing to all this."

Delia picked up the list and held it like a parent would a storybook to a child. She pointed to the bottom of the page. "This is the legend. Our names are in different colors. Mine is pink. Yours is blue, and Sid's is green. Each task is in a different colored font to indicate who is responsible for its completion."

He took the list from her hand and studied it again. Now that she'd explained it, it wasn't nearly as daunting. "Sid's agreed to this?"

"Yes. We negotiated a wage, and I have a signed agreement from him." She poked him in the shoulder. "He was adamant that you don't go near the coffeemaker."

Cal grinned. "I can agree to that. Do you need me to sign something?"

For a moment, doubt crossed her face, and she banded her arms around her waist. "Umm. No. Are you sure you're okay with this? I haven't signed anything with the event committee yet, so if you've changed your mind—"

He wanted to hug her, take away her self-doubt. Instead, he held out his hand. Wide-eyed, she looked at it and then up to his face. Slowly, she placed her own hand in his, and they shook. "We have a deal. I promise to uphold my end and complete the tasks assigned to me."

"Thank you."

He released her hand and teased, "Do I have to do them in order? Can I swap out some with Sid?"

"Smart ass."

Cal grinned, watching her go back to her table.

CHAPTER 15

The two weeks passed in a blur.

After signing the contract with the event planner, she'd been bombarded with phone calls from her mother. Carol Lee was giddy with excitement and had all kinds of suggestions for displaying the auction items—most having to do with balloons. Delia tactfully but firmly asked her mother to back off, promising to reach out if she needed help.

Cal and Sid did swap out tasks, but things got taken care of, maybe not exactly the way she would have done them, but for the most part, she was satisfied. The back room was empty to the point that Delia's steps rang against the concrete as she crossed the floor. Opening the door from the back room to the store, she caught Cal waving to the retreating back of the mail carrier. He smiled her way.

"Hey. Something got delivered for you."

Delia approached the counter, a finger tapping her chin. "Something's different today. What can it be? I know. You aren't muttering at the laptop like a goblin over its gold."

Cal narrowed his eyes at her, the corner of his lips

twitching up at the same time. "Har, har. I sent in the manuscript last night."

"Glad to hear it. Does that mean you'll stop glaring at me?"

"If you wouldn't stomp around like a clog dancer, I wouldn't glare."

Cal had been working on last-minute changes for a book and was none too happy with his editor. He took his frustrations out by slinging crap into the large dumpster in the alley. One more reason why the back room was getting cleaned up so fast.

Reaching for the large envelope, she grinned. She tore it open and withdrew two large tickets. She groaned.

"Crap!"

"What's wrong?"

She waved the tickets as she sank onto a stool. "I promised my mother I'd sit with her at the event and that I'd bring somebody. Tommy is busy, and it's way too late to ask someone else, and Mom will be seriously put out."

"Won't you be working at it?"

"No. If all goes well, I should be done with my work by noonish." She pulled her phone out of her bag. "Maybe I can find someone."

Cal plucked the phone out of her hand.

"Hey!"

"I'll go."

About to cuss him out, Delia blinked. "What?"

Cal shrugged. "I said I'll go."

"You mean that? It's…kind of formal."

"I can do that. I *do* own a suit." Cal put Delia's phone on the counter and pushed it toward her with one long finger. "Unless you don't want me to." There was a hint of vulnerability in the tightness of his jaw.

"I would *really* like you to come with me. Are you sure?

You do realize you will be meeting my parents, and it's possible I may have to help out with something."

"I can carry on a conversation when required, and I want to see the work you've done."

"Yeah?" At his nod, she smiled. It was going to be awesome, and she would really like him to see what she'd done. "Excellent."

Retreating to the stacks, she texted her mother that Cal would be her plus-one. Carol Lee replied with an offer of a pampering session. She'd send a team to Delia's apartment to do her hair, makeup, and nails the afternoon of the event. Tempted to accept the offer, Delia demurred. She could use the time better, and while Carol Lee would pay for the service, she would be expected to tip—generously. She shoved her phone into her back pocket and went back to work, mentally patting herself on the back for making the decision.

Twelve dresses lay in a heap on the floor, with an equal number of shoes piled next to them. She'd finally decided on a knee-length, bottle green, wrap jersey dress cut to display a minute amount of cleavage. This was not a fun evening for drinking and shopping for a cause. She stuffed business cards into her clutch along with lip gloss, keys, and phone. Grabbing a gray pashmina, she gave herself a final inspection in the floor-length mirror, fluffing up her hair, and apologized to her clothing. Tomorrow, she would give them the proper treatment they deserved. Tonight, she didn't want to keep Cal waiting.

The elevator door opened into the lobby, and Delia saw Cal standing in the foyer, talking to Connie. In a dark suit, he was heart-stoppingly handsome. He wore a burgundy shirt, unbuttoned, revealing the smooth column of his throat. His dark hair was smoothed back, curling slightly over the collar, and his strong jaw was clean-shaven. He turned at her approach, his gaze traveling from the top of her head to the tips of her toes and back up again.

"Wow," he said.

That one word was vindication for leaving her dressing room looking like a tornado had gone through it. She wanted to strut. Strike a pose. Maybe twirl like a majorette tossing a baton.

"Right back at you. You clean up pretty good as well."

Behind and to the side of Cal, Connie waggled her eyebrows, grinning like a loon. Delia gave her an imperceptible nod.

"You ready to go?" Cal asked, unaware of the silent conversation going on between the two women. "It's cold out. Let me help you with that." He took the wrap from Delia's hands and draped it around her shoulders.

Bouncing on her toes, Connie said, "You kids have a good time."

Following Cal's broad back as he led the way to the door, Delia whispered to Connie, "It's not a date."

"Uh-huh. You tell yourself that."

The jacket fit comfortably even if it felt unfamiliar. He'd had it custom-made after receiving his first check from collaborating with Stacy Wrigglebottom. The suit didn't get a lot of wear, but he was glad he'd made the investment. The tailor had suggested which shirts to purchase as well. Cal did own a few ties but hated the damn things, so he'd stuffed one in his pocket instead of putting it on.

He opened the door to his Jeep and held out a hand to Delia. She didn't need his assistance climbing into the SUV, but this was a perfect opportunity to touch her. She smiled her thanks, and he closed the door before hustling around to the driver's side. The last time he'd driven it was on a camping trip with his dad and it had been covered in mud. This morning, before work, he'd dropped it off at a garage close to Jimmy's Joint, where they'd detailed it for an exorbitant amount. He hadn't blinked while signing the receipt. What good was money if you didn't use it?

Keenly aware of Delia's lavender scent, Cal tried not to inhale too deeply, lest he hyperventilate. Distance wise, the venue was not far away, but Seattle traffic on a Friday night was its usual slow-moving jam. During the drive, conversation was light and easy. Delia told him about working with the committee members and how the ladies swooned when Ivan was around.

Cal made a noise that drew a look from Delia.

"The man is good at what he does."

That didn't make Cal feel any better. Then he thought about the fact Delia was beside *him*, in *his* car. That made him feel smug.

After leaving the car with a valet, they ascended the escalator with others dressed for the occasion. They moved over to a table to check in and get their table assignment. The last auction he'd been to was held in the gym of his old high school. It was far less glamorous, definitely not as well organized, and drew a much smaller crowd. Cal followed Delia's lead, as she appeared to know exactly what she was doing. With the exception of large bid cards for the live auction, everything else was digital and available from an app on their phones.

"Where do we start?"

Wearing four-inch heels that made her legs look awesome, Delia met his gaze almost on the level. "We'll drop the bid cards and my wrap at our table, then circulate through the silent auction tables."

"Got it." Cal headed in the direction of the open doors to

the ballroom. Perhaps fifty tables, each with twelve place settings, filled the room. Waitstaff and other attendees circled the room.

"There." Delia threaded her way through the tables, Cal following closely behind, watching her hair bounce with each step instead of staring at the sway of her hips.

Putting the bid cards and her wrap on a chair, Delia pursed her lips and studied the place cards. "I hope you don't hate me tomorrow because we're sitting at my parents' table."

"Are they awful?"

Delia huffed out a soft breath. "No. Just…inquisitive."

"I have nothing to hide."

"Really, Stacy Wrigglebottom? My mom's read all your books."

Cal scratched the underside of his chin. "Well, maybe some things." He watched her brows knit together and placed a hand on her shoulder. "It'll be fine. Let's get a drink."

They exited the ballroom into a mezzanine milling with people. Long tables were set up around the perimeter, and a bar was at either end. A server approached with a tray of beverages and stopped in front of Cal and Delia.

"I have sparkling water and nonalcoholic sparkling cider." She then pointed to the bars. "We have mocktails, nonalcoholic wine, and nonalcoholic beer, as well as alcoholic beverages."

At Delia's nod, Cal picked up two sparkling waters and thanked the server.

"This is the first time I've been offered a nonalcoholic drink at an auction." Delia lifted up her glass.

"Well, they are benefiting a sobriety program."

"Yes, but alcohol fuels a lot of the purchases at these events."

Cal smirked. "Are you speaking from experience?"

"Yes. Part of your job tonight is to keep me from spending money foolishly."

"Haven't you got the entire catalog memorized? You did set out all the items."

"Nope. I decided where each of the items would go. The volunteers did the actual placement. That's why I was a bit late this afternoon. Someone put a vegan leather handbag next to a pair of crocodile cowboy boots."

"And that would be bad?"

She grinned. "You have no idea."

"I think I can curtail your spending spree. What else am I supposed to do?"

"Sing my praises to anyone who asks what I'm doing." There was an edge of nervousness to her voice.

"That's easy." He took her hand and tucked it into the crook of his elbow. "Let's go see how the chess set is doing."

They went up and down the tables, looking over the offerings for the silent auction. There were weekend stays at hotels, restaurant meals, golf packages, gift baskets, and handcrafted items. He watched Delia's reactions to each of the items up for bid. Interestingly enough, it was the golf packages that piqued her attention. He tucked that bit of information away. To Cal's relief, bidding for the chess set was active. It was valued at $800, and the latest bid was for $920.

He let out a low whistle. "I didn't think it would go for so much."

Delia pointed at one of the pawns. "I'm not surprised. The workmanship is exquisite. Sid really is quite skilled."

Pride for his cousin filled Cal, replacing an anxiousness he'd been carrying since they entered. He took Delia by the hand and led her to a quiet corner. She looked up at him in silent question.

"Thank you," he said. "This is going to go a long way to help with Sid's recovery."

"I didn't do—"

Cal placed a finger against her lips. "Yes, you did. If you

hadn't offered to clean out Jimmy's Joint, those chess sets would still be sitting in a box, and Sid and I wouldn't have reconnected." He removed his finger and engulfed her in a hug. "Thank you."

❄

Standing in the circle of Cal's embrace was the best place in the world. Delia breathed in his scent, wanting to bury her nose in the notch of his throat. Instead, she hugged him back.

"Oh my God, he does own something other than flannel."

Delia reluctantly released Cal and stepped back. "Hello, Tommy."

He waved a hand at her while staring at Cal. "Not bad. Definitely not Men's Wearhouse. Who made this for you? It's not off the rack."

"A tailor down in SoDo. He was a friend of my grandfather."

"You must give me his name. That suit fits you like a glove, but dear boy, do you not own a tie?"

Cal tipped his chin at Tommy. "You're not wearing one."

Tommy preened as he fingered his pearls. "Pearls go with everything, darling." He'd paired his black wool suit with a white tuxedo shirt, open at the collar to expose a strand of pink pearls. Pink pearl earrings completed the ensemble.

"You didn't say you were coming." Delia pointed an accusing finger at him.

"You asked if I was busy, not what I was doing." He winked and sipped from his fluted glass. "These mocktails aren't bad, but it feels weird being sober at one of these things."

"I know, right?"

"Well, it will be good for my pocketbook. And it will save you from buying stupid stuff you don't need."

Delia glared at Tommy. "I don't—"

"Oh, yes, you do. Remember buying four hours of yard work from the firefighters? You don't have a yard."

"I gave that to my parents. And if I remember correctly, you showed up with a lawn chair and mimosas to watch them." Delia poked him in the shoulder.

"You joined me." Tommy poked her right back.

"Do I need to separate you two?" Cal mock-scowled at them.

"We're fine." She gestured at the tables covered with auction items. "I like shopping with a purpose. Supporting worthy causes."

"I agree," Tommy said. "But you can do so without buying something. Make a donation. I did that before I left the house."

"I didn't think about that." Delia had attended many fundraising events and worked a few with her mother, but this one meant more to her than the others. "Will you hold this please?"

Cal took her glass. "Sure. Why?"

Taking her phone out of her clutch, her fingers danced over the keyboard. "I'm making a donation right now." She looked up in time to catch a look passing between Cal and Tommy. "It's generous without being foolish."

"Are you making amends for the other night?" Tommy inquired.

"Maybe," she mumbled.

A big hand settled between her shoulder blades. She smiled up at Cal.

A kiss landed on her cheek. She rolled her eyes at Tommy.

"You guys." Their affection was soothing.

While Cal went off to get a beer for himself and wine for them, Delia and Tommy found a small couch in an alcove and sat to watch the crowds. She couldn't tell if Tommy was checking out what people were wearing or looking for someone in particular.

"Obviously, he accepted your apology. Did you tell him everything?"

"Yes."

Tommy smirked. "Including the part where you wanted to reenact being carried through a crowd in his arms?"

She fiddled with the hem of her dress. "Did I say anything awful to him? I mean, I know I embarrassed myself but—"

"Sweetheart, it's fine. I doubt he would be here with you if he didn't want to be."

She craned her neck and looked through the throng to find him. His broad frame was so familiar, it was easy to pick him out. Talking to someone she couldn't see, he seemed relaxed. She reminded herself that *he* had asked her. Why? She'd think about that later.

"Who did you come with?" She waved her glass at the people milling around them.

"Myself."

"Who are you sitting with?"

"You."

Delia frowned. "I didn't see your name at our table?"

He waved a negligent hand. "I spoke to your mother. I'm now sitting between you and her. You can thank me later."

He stiffened beside her, and she followed his gaze to see what had caught his attention. A slender man turned around, and Delia recognized Kevin Armstrong. She raised her hand and called out his name. Tommy hissed.

"What? I thought you two were friends." Delia distinctly remembered seeing them laughing together at a party.

"We were," Tommy said between gritted teeth.

Kevin spotted Tommy, and his smile moved from warm to pasted on. Oh dear. She'd introduced them to each other a year ago, hoping they'd make a connection. Somehow, that connection had gone sideways.

"What did you do?" She gave Tommy a look.

"Nothing."

She grasped his arm in a tight hold.

"Ow! Let go before you wrinkle the fabric."

"Don't even think of leaving. He'll be here in three seconds. Tell me what you did."

"I ghosted him." Tommy's tone was flat.

She released his arm and rose to her feet. Twisting to place her glass on the table beside them, she leaned into Tommy. "I expect the whole story."

Kevin walked up to Delia, arms extended. She stepped into his hug, feeling the tension in his body, and rubbed her hands across his back. Pulling back, she studied his expression. His eyes looked guarded, his smile tight. Dressed in a plum velvet jacket, the soft blush of his shirt set off his smooth ebony complexion. He looked directly at Delia, as if Tommy didn't exist.

"That color suits you," he said.

Feeling the need to lighten the moment, Delia did a pirouette, shaking back her hair.

"Thank you, darling. You aren't working this evening?"

Kevin teetered a hand back and forth. "I'm on a recon mission."

"Probably looking for a rich sugar daddy." Tommy's comment was barely audible. If Kevin heard, he ignored it.

"Grand Gestures is considering bidding on the contract for this event next year." He moved to stand on Delia's other side and gestured at the room full of people. "This is a larger scale than what we're used to, but I think we can handle it."

"I have complete faith in you." Delia had been both dismissive and jealous when Kevin jumped ship from Duncan Properties to Grand Gestures. However, Kevin's talents had been wasted working as a personal assistant to Liam Cross, and he was now in his element as an event planner with the two Beckett sisters. She couldn't begrudge him his happiness. "Don't you, Tommy?"

Tommy's nod was polite. "Of course."

Both men made appreciative noises about the auction items and the work Delia had done, but it was hard to keep the conversation going when they wouldn't speak directly to each other.

Where was Cal? She finally spotted him with hands full of drinks, talking to a woman. Delia narrowed her eyes. There was something familiar about her, but she couldn't quite place where she'd seen the dark-haired woman pressing her bosom against Cal's arm. He gestured toward Delia. The woman turned her head to follow the direction of his hand, then stiffened and stepped back. Cal said something to her and headed toward Delia, looking relaxed. He must have picked up on the posture of the two men bracketing her, because he looked them over and shot her an inquiring glance. She rolled her eyes. The corner of his mouth tucked up in a tiny smile.

"Hey," he said, handing drinks to Tommy and Delia, then focused on Kevin, hand outstretched. "I'm Calvin Jimmy."

"Nice to meet you." Kevin took his hand, turning the full wattage of his smile up at Cal, then over to Delia. "I'm Kevin Armstrong."

A woman approached, holding up a camera. "Can I get a group photo?"

The foursome murmured assent, arranging themselves with Delia standing in front of Cal, her arms around Kevin and Tommy.

"I can take pictures of each couple and email them to you?"

Tommy shook his head.

Kevin said, "We're not—"

Cal snagged Delia's hand and pulled her to him. "Sounds good. Where would you like us?"

While the photographer snapped away, Tommy and Kevin stood off to the side, Tommy staring at his phone, Kevin alternately looking at Tommy and watching the proceedings around them. The woman took down contact info and drifted off.

"What's going on?" Cal's voice near her ear gave Delia shivers.

"I'm not sure. I think Tommy may have broken Kevin's heart. Hurt his feelings at least." She sighed and turned a troubled face up to Cal. "I need to find out. They're both great guys and would make a cute couple."

"Not the way things look now. Are you planning on getting involved?"

Delia chewed her lip. Good question. She'd known Tommy since forever. He went through men like Kleenex, rarely anyone serious. While Kevin was just as much a flirt, he'd said some things lately that made Delia think he was looking for a forever person. She'd hoped Tommy could be that person. Looking at the two men now, backs stiff, attention focused in opposite directions, perhaps she was wrong. She twisted to look up at Cal. He wasn't giving advice or making suggestions, simply waiting patiently. The thought that *he* could be *her* forever person skittered through her mind. "I'll let them figure it out. They're both adults. Most of the time."

"Yes!"

Kevin's exclamation drew their attention. A satisfied smile on his face, he walked toward them, holding up his phone. "I got the hand-carved chess set."

"Oh, wow." Delia gestured at Cal. "Cal's cousin made it."

"He did beautiful work. My mom is going to love it." He stuffed his phone into his pocket, looking like a kid at Christmas.

"You bought the chess set for your mother?"

Still smiling, Kevin answered Tommy's question. "When

my dad was alive, my parents played chess almost every night. She just started playing again with a group from her church. Sometimes, I play with her, but she usually beats the pants off me. This is a birthday present for her. Do you play chess?"

"Yeah. But I'm more of a Scrabble guy."

Kevin's eyebrows went up. "Do you play Words With Friends?"

"I do." Tommy fingered his pearls. "Would you like to try a game sometime?"

"I can do that."

The two men reached for their cell phones, then huddled together, smiling and laughing.

"Looks like they sorted things out."

"Let's hope so." Delia clinked her glass happily with Cal's.

CHAPTER 16

God bless Tommy. Seated next to Carol Lee, he kept Delia's mother occupied and her attention away from Cal. Delia knew a grilling was inevitable. She just wanted to put it off for a while.

Twelve people sat at the large table: Cal and Delia, Tommy, Carol Lee and Chuck Sr., a distant cousin who spent most of her time representing Duncan Properties at one fundraiser or another, two couples who played bridge with her parents, and two junior employees who looked both scared and excited to be at the grand affair. They were also casting appreciative glances Cal's way. Delia didn't blame them. In a flannel shirt and jeans, with his dark hair, thick dark brows, and coppery skin, he was head-turningly good-looking. In his suit, he was drool-worthy. In front of the two young women, she wanted to stake her claim on Cal. But he wasn't hers. Instead, she sent the women pointed looks.

The person on Cal's other side got up to chat with someone. Delia tensed up when Chuck Sr. lowered himself into the temporarily vacant chair. Cal shot her an amused glance before turning his attention to her father.

"Remind me where your shop is again."

Cal gave him the address.

"Right." Chuck Sr. snapped his fingers and pointed at Cal. "The old Clark building. It's slated to come down soon."

"That's why I hired Delia. I have inventory to shift and seventy years of family junk to deal with."

"Is it possible to preserve the building, Dad?" Delia leaned around Cal to ask. Her father lived and breathed commercial real estate in Seattle.

He shook his head. "It was slapped together in the 1930s with bubblegum and baling wire. Architecturally speaking, it's nothing to look at. They didn't spend any time trying to make it pretty. They've done a retrofit on it many times to bring it up to code, and it's now at the point where it's not cost-effective to keep patching it up."

"My grandfather told me he'd known for years it would be coming down. I've just been putting off dealing with emptying the place," Cal said. "Delia is a godsend. She has an eye for design and detail that's brought in more customers than I've seen in months, both physically and through online sales. She's made emptying out the shop pretty painless."

A proud expression bloomed on her father's face. He puffed out his chest. "My daughter is very talented."

Delia wasn't sure what made her feel better, Cal's words of praise or her dad's expression of pride. Finding something she enjoyed doing, using a personality trait that she'd never thought of as a skill set, which was useful to others, filled her with joy. On her other side, Tommy nudged her, winking, then rose from the table, murmuring an excuse. The chair was then filled by Ivan Thompson, who looked dapper in a dark suit, sporting a red and black tie printed with Indigenous designs.

"I was hoping to see you here." Ivan smiled easily, his admiring gaze fixed on Delia.

With a soft grunt, Cal draped his arm over the back of her

chair. She bit the inside of her cheek to keep from smiling, amused by his possessive gesture.

"Nice to see you as well." She sat back and gestured between her parents and Ivan, making introductions.

"We're so glad Delia was able to jump in at the last minute and do the displays for the auction items. She has quite the eye," Ivan said.

Blushing, Delia wriggled in her chair. It was nice to get the validation after so many years of disappointing her parents.

Ivan went on, "Mr. and Mrs. Duncan, I don't know if Delia has told you, but she's been beneficial in aiding the residents at ODAAT." Ivan twisted and leaned into the table, capturing her parents' attention. He described the setup she'd created for Sid to carve at Jimmy's Joint. "Being able to work in a space that's been historically occupied by Indigenous peoples"—he tilted his chin at Cal—"makes some of our residents more comfortable."

Delia smiled up at Cal. Sid and two of his friends had been coming to Jimmy's Joint regularly. The first day, while drinking endless pots of dark tea, they looked over Delia's arrangements, then moved things around to their own satisfaction. The second day, Sid and one of the men, named Sam, sat and carved while the other man, Gary, crocheted. With deft fingers, he wielded the slim hook, making an intricate scarf from fine wool. The men were more comfortable with Cal than they were with Delia, and she hadn't spent much time with them. Now that the event was done, she hoped to help them in some way.

Ivan went on, "I'm hoping we can create something similar after Jimmy's Joint closes, maybe find a space for an artist's co-op."

"We can set aside the furniture the guys are using. It's not worth much, but taking that with them, having the connection, might be helpful." Delia looked between Ivan and Cal. "Too bad we can't move the counter and barstools."

"Actually, you probably can," Carol Lee interjected. "If they have historic value, the Museum of History and Industry might be interested, or the Tulalip Cultural Center. They may want to create a display of the interior of Jimmy's Joint when it first opened."

Delia looked up at Cal. He squeezed her shoulder and looked between her and her mother.

"Great idea. I'll run it past my parents. Mom has connections and should be able to help with that."

Ivan pushed back from the table and stood. "It's time for the speeches. Nice to meet you all." He nodded and smiled at everyone and made his way to the raised dais where the female auctioneer and the male emcee stood. Ivan was introduced and took the microphone. He thanked the sponsors and those attending, spoke about the successes of ODAAT and the challenges facing the group. He was smooth and polished, obviously not a stranger to public speaking. The auctioneer and master of ceremonies took over, and the bidding got under way for the live auction. Within an hour, more than $300,000 was raised. Ivan spoke again, this time thanking the organizers, then singled out Delia's parents as representatives of Duncan Properties, which owned the building housing ODAAT.

Carol Lee leaned across Tommy and grabbed her daughter's hand. "That's $40,000 higher than the target. Honey, you did great!"

"Mom, I just set out the items—"

Her cousin interrupted, "Don't sell yourself short. I've been to a lot of these and, hands down, your displays made the items enticing. Whatever they paid you, it was well worth it."

Tommy nudged her on one side, and Cal beamed at her from the other. She had done good. Around her, people rose from their tables and chattered on the way to the exits. Her parents said their goodbyes and took off, Tommy kissed her on the forehead and joined some friends, and she and Cal were the last ones at the table.

"What would you like to do now?" Cal's voice rumbled low. At some point in the evening, he'd removed his jacket and rolled up his shirtsleeves, exposing well-muscled forearms. Twisted toward her, he had one arm on the back of her chair and the other on the table in front of her.

There was an after-party at one of the bars in the hotel. She pictured herself walking into it with Cal on her arm, making the other women drool with envy. Then she pictured being alone with Cal. That held more appeal.

"I think I'm done. Can you take me home?"

"Absolutely." His smile was all for her, his gaze fixed on her mouth.

Frozen in her chair, she watched him lick his bottom lip and felt his hand move from the back of her chair to the back of her neck. She shivered. He pulled her close, his dark heavy-lidded eyes studying her. He pressed his lips against hers softly, then with more pressure, licking the seam of her lips, asking for permission. Her tongue met his as she opened to let him in. He twined one hand in her hair, the other coming up to cup her jaw as he deepened the kiss, thrusting his tongue into her mouth to tangle with hers. She whimpered when he pulled back with an air of reluctance. She became aware of the activity around them, as hotel staff dismantled the stage while waiters cleared the tables.

Breathily, she laughed. "I guess we should go."

"Yeah." With one last stroke of his finger down her cheek, he sat back.

"Let me"—she gestured over her shoulder—"stop at the restroom, and I'll meet you at the escalators."

"Got it." Cal rose, pulled her chair back, and helped her to stand.

She wove her way through the tables, smiling at people she knew but not stopping to chat. She wouldn't be able to carry on a conversation anyway. She took care of business in the empty restroom and stood washing her hands, smiling at her flushed face, when the door burst open. Startled, Delia met the gaze of a slightly disheveled woman. Her hair askew, she listed to the side.

"You," she said.

Delia didn't know who she was, but it was the woman who'd been speaking to Cal earlier in the evening. She smiled politely. "Have we met?"

"Oh, yes. I guess I didn't make much of an impression." The woman approached and leaned against the counter, glaring at Delia through the mirror. "I work for the law firm handling your trust."

"Right!" The uptight woman in the office looked nothing like the siren standing next to her, breasts spilling out of a snug red wrap dress. "Ms...?"

"Sanchez. Naomi Sanchez," she said. "You're here with Calvin Jimmy."

It sounded like an accusation. "Yes, he's a good friend."

"Yeah? You two looked cozier than friends."

The woman was drunk and not a friendly drunk. Delia didn't rise to the bait. She put her lip gloss back into her clutch and moved toward the door, but Naomi wasn't done with her yet.

"It's funny you'd be with Cal, what with your families' history."

"Excuse me?"

"Right. I forgot how clueless you are. Here's a little history lesson for you. All that land that Gweneth Duncan built her fortune on, where do you think she got it from?"

Delia's heart raced. "She purchased it through land grants." Her great-great-great-grandmother was legendary for her shrewd business practices and lauded for being a woman ahead of her time. In her parents' home was a biography that Delia had leafed through, looking at the pictures, but never read.

"Land grants. Right. It was appropriated from the local tribes." Naomi turned and poked Delia in the shoulder. "Calvin Jimmy's ancestors were kicked off that land, and your ancestors profited from it."

"That's not…that's not true." The Seattle waterfront had been originally occupied by the Duwamish when white settlers came to the Pacific Northwest. "They were compensated. There's a treaty."

"Look it up, princess. The treaty was signed but never upheld. The Duwamish were told to leave. A law was passed, not allowing native people to live in Seattle."

"That's not true. I've been to the longhouse." It was an outing her mother had taken her on when the longhouse was open.

"Less than an acre. That's all they have left of their ancestral home. They can't get recognition from the federal government because there isn't enough evidence of their existence." Naomi gave Delia a derisive smirk. "No wonder your parents donate heavily to ODAAT. The Duncan family has so much to be proud of, building their empire on the backs of displaced people."

Delia stared after her as she lurched out of the restroom. How much of that was true? She knew Seattle was named after a Duwamish chief. That was about the limit of her understanding of the city's original inhabitants. Staring into the mirror, the reflection of the glowing woman anticipating a night with a wonderful man was replaced by an unsmiling woman uncertain about who she was. The shine was off her evening.

Cal stood by the escalator, looking content and handsome. Walking toward him, Delia studied his features. Raven-black hair brushed back from a high forehead, coppery skin, and dark eyes that crinkled at the corners when he saw her. She pasted on a smile, not wanting to cast a pall over the time they'd had together but sure that she needed some time alone.

He'd retrieved her wrap and placed it around her shoulders, then stroked one hand down her arm to take her hand. "You ready?"

That was a loaded question. She was ready to go home, and ten minutes ago, she'd been ready for a whole lot more. Now, not so much. She darted a smile at him and nodded. They rode the escalator down to the lobby and waited outside for the valet to bring Cal's Jeep around. She shivered, and he put his arm around her, drawing her into his side. She smiled up at him, seeing the warmth as well as the question in his eyes. The car came, and he made sure she was seated before climbing behind the wheel. They joined the queue of vehicles leaving the hotel and moved slowly through the downtown streets.

"You good?" He took her hand and held it loosely on the console between them. She wondered if he could feel how cold she was inside.

Another loaded question. No, she was not. "Yeah, just tired," she said.

"It was a good night for both you and ODAAT. Lots of people singing your praises."

"Thanks for that. I appreciate you coming with me tonight."

"Happy to. It wasn't a hardship. Although, if I do this again, I need to buy new shoes. These hurt like a bugger."

She laughed. "Normally it's the woman who complains about her shoes. Maybe Tommy can find you some black patent hiking boots."

Cal grinned at her. "Do you think he and Kevin patched things up?"

"I hope so. I think they're both headed to the same party

right now. So fingers crossed." Looking at the crowded streets, she realized it would be a while and decided to do some fishing. "I saw you talking to Naomi Sanchez."

"Yeah. Almost didn't recognize her. Normally she's all buttoned-up."

Delia flashed to Naomi's ample cleavage pressed against Cal's arm. "Same here. How do you know her?"

"Her firm has done work with the tribes. She's a real advocate for Indigenous rights. Quite the pit bull. How do you know her?"

Pit bull was an accurate description. Delia hoped she'd never have to see her again. "Her firm does work with Duncan Properties."

Cal nodded while switching lanes. Delia wondered if he'd made the connection between Duncan Properties and Indigenous land rights. Now was not the time to get into it, though. She was tired and confused and, as Naomi had told her, needed to do some research.

They lapsed into silence for the rest of the trip. Leaning against the window, Delia could see Cal's reflection. Every now and then, he looked over at her but maintained the silence.

He pulled into the drive and stopped in front of the doors to her building. "Wait there," he said. Putting the car in park, he left the keys in the ignition and came around to open her door.

Delia exited the car and looked up at him, knowing this was an opportunity too good to waste. They were both sober, and she could ask him up and see where that kiss would lead. She knew he would comply with whatever she decided. It was clear he desired her, and the Delia from two months ago would have happily taken him upstairs without a second thought. But this Delia had to work with him, had to see him every day, and *wanted* to see him every day. This Delia cared what Cal thought about her and had no desire to hurt him, however good it would feel to spend the night in his arms. She reached up and smoothed her hands over the lapels of his jacket. Their lips were so close. He waited, that question again in his eyes. When she stepped aside, his eyes dimmed, but he squeezed her hand, clearly disappointed but accepting of her decision.

"Thank you for everything tonight. I'll see you on Monday."

Shoving his hands in his pockets, Cal raised his chin and watched her walk into the building.

CHAPTER 17

Sunday morning, Cal pointed his Jeep north, getting out of the city before most people were out of bed. He settled into the center lane for the drive up I-5, the volume turned low on a talk radio station. Something changed last night, and he couldn't quite put his finger on it. As far as he could tell, the evening had been a success. Delia shone, received accolades, and was visibly pleased to be with him. She'd responded to his kiss like she'd wanted more. He replayed the aftermath. He'd watched Delia walk off to the restroom. Strutting, more like, as if pleased with herself and the world. When she met him at the top of the escalator, her step was slow, almost hesitant. She didn't object when he took her hand, didn't move away when he put his arm around her, but didn't invite more contact.

Delia's scent clung to the car's interior, and he pictured her leaning against the window looking forlorn. Why? Was she not interested in him? Had he embarrassed her? Did she think he didn't fit into her world? He rolled his shoulders. "Give your head a shake. Maybe it's not about you at all." If that was the case, what was it?

He cranked up the radio volume, letting an interview with a prominent author distract him from restless thoughts.

It wasn't fishing season, but he knew his dad would be on his boat, puttering, cleaning, studying maps, drinking coffee, and eating the doughnuts his mother had declared contraband. Not quite as tall as Cal, Dan Jimmy was broad-shouldered and big bellied. His wife, Angie, worried that diabetes was in Dan's future and watched his diet like a hawk.

The docks of the Tulalip Marina were filled with other like-minded souls, men and women who lived to be on the water, drawn by the smell of saltwater and seaweed. Most of the boats were well used and well loved, not flashy but functional. Clomping along the wooden boards, Cal scanned the marina, spotting gulls and cormorants and the odd heron. The *Angie Baby* hove into sight, nestled between two cabin cruisers. Why his father chose to name his boat after a bad 70s song was beyond Cal. Some kind of inside joke between his parents that made his father grin and his mother scowl.

"Permission to come aboard?"

His father poked his head up from the galley. "Depends. What have you got?"

Cal lifted the paper bag. "Old-fashioned doughnuts."

"With chocolate frosting and sprinkles?"

"Uh, no. Plain."

Dan screwed up his face in distaste. "What's the point of that?"

"If you don't want them, the gulls will be happy to eat them for breakfast."

"No, no. Give 'em here. I'll dunk 'em in coffee."

Cal grinned and climbed aboard the Boston whaler fishing boat. He looked around. Shoving aside a pile of life jackets, he sat on the bench by the motor. "What are you up to today?"

"Checking emergency supplies. Some of this shit's outdated

and probably useless." Dan had bought the boat secondhand from an older tribal member who hadn't bothered to clean it out before handing it over. He poured a mug of coffee, handed it to Cal, and settled beside him. They dunked their doughnuts and drank their coffee, turning their faces up to the sun.

Dan wiped crumbs off his belly and deposited them in the water. "Your gal looks pretty."

"How do you know? And she's not my gal."

Dan smirked and pulled out his phone. "Your mom showed me." He showed Cal the photo of him and Delia with Kevin and Tommy. "Maybe one of these guys was my date. Did you think of that?"

Dan scrolled to the photo of him and Delia alone, and then sitting together at the table. In both, he was gazing down at her with a shit-eating grin.

"Fine. But she's still not my girl."

"Did you screw it up?"

"I don't know." He handed the phone back. "Maybe? Things were fine, and then they weren't. I can't for the life of me think about what I did or said or didn't…"

Dan nodded. "Don't look to me for advice. I'm still trying to figure this shit out."

Married for forty years, Dan and Angie Jimmy had three children. They weren't a model couple, but Cal was pretty sure neither would have it any other way. His mom said they'd never downsize because she didn't want to be too close to her husband. For his part, his dad said he hoped his wife would never retire.

"Did the girl make you go to the shindig last night? It's not your usual thing."

"Her name is Delia, and I volunteered. She's the one I hired to clean out Jimmy's Joint."

"And she hired Sid?"

Cal waggled his hand back and forth. "She created a place

for Sid to carve, and he helps her out some. He'd probably do it for free."

Dan snorted. "Wouldn't blame him. Still, Sid hasn't worked for a long time. Idle hands are not good."

"Yep. Speaking of idle, what did you want me to help you with today?" He made the trek home at least once a month at the behest of his mother.

"That damn tree needs to be braced."

Cal knew exactly what he was talking about. His parents moved into their house the day they got married. Together they had planted a Japanese maple. Its spreading boughs overtook the backyard, and the heavier ones needed support. His mother loved that tree and fussed at her husband to keep it healthy and strong. "When do you want to do it?"

"In a bit. The house will be swarming with kids. This will be the last bit of quiet I get today." He grabbed another doughnut and dunked it in his coffee.

*S*itting at the table in his parents' kitchen, Cal relaxed amid the chaos. Lisa and Laura, his two sisters, had just dropped off their kids and were headed to the grocery store. Their husbands, both commercial fishermen, were away, and the women were taking advantage of their mother's offer to look after the kids for a few hours before supper.

Angie Jimmy balanced a baby on her hip and swayed back and forth. She grabbed a chubby hand before it could snag her glasses. "Delia Duncan, huh?"

"What about her?" Cal's mother had the ability to reduce him to a twelve-year-old boy in minutes. This was why he didn't come home more often. He felt his father's smirk and decided to get it over with. "I was doing her a favor. She needed a plus-one for last night, and it gave me a chance to see how Sid's carvings did."

"The woman may turn out to be an axe murderer, but if she's got Sid headed in the right direction, I'll nominate her for sainthood." There were nods around the table at Angie's comment. Sobriety was a struggle for Sid and so many others.

"Is he coming over?" Dan asked.

"Yep." Angie passed their youngest grandchild to her husband. There were four so far, and they couldn't be happier. "Violet is bringing him for supper. I said you'd drive him back to the city." Cal nodded, understanding the pointed look she sent his way. Violet Fraser, Sid's mom, fought her own demons, and the relationship between mother and son could be difficult.

Three little girls ran screaming past them, and Dan stood, expertly shifting the little boy from one arm to another. "Right, I'll take them out back to the trampoline." He opened the kitchen door, called for the girls, and the stampede headed outside, leaving Cal and his mother in relative peace.

Angie caught him up on her work at the insurance office, sprinkling in updates on family members, which brought the conversation back to Sid. He had his own room at ODAAT and was reliably showing up at Jimmy's Joint, where he'd sit and carve. Customers in the shop stopped to watch and sometimes asked questions. At first, his answers were mono-syllabic, but as he gained confidence, he was coming out of his shell and was more talkative.

"What's he going to do when the store closes?"

Cal reached for another potato to peel. "Ivan Thompson is talking about opening up a space at ODAAT where Sid and others can have space to create their artwork."

"Is there a place to sell it?"

"I don't know. I think Delia is helping with that."

His mother flicked a glance at him, then back at the vegetables she was chopping. "That Ivan is something. A lot of energy and enthusiasm."

"Yeah. How long is his contract with the tribe?" Cal wanted him to head back up to Vancouver. Delia had been talking to him a lot last night. Maybe that was the reason she'd been distant at the end of the evening.

"Another six months or so. He's facilitating construction of the rehab center up near Snoqualmie, trying to get four tribes to work together, but it's not easy. Too many egos. Too many men." Angie winked. She was a natural-born leader and over the years held positions on the PTSA, tribal council, and community groups. Through her work as an insurance agent, her network was large, and she made a point of learning what was going on around her.

Cal snorted. She wasn't wrong. Like communities everywhere, drugs and alcohol had ravaged the reservations for decades. None were immune. It made sense for the tribes to band together, and it had taken forever to decide the location. As much as he didn't want him around Delia, Cal appreciated the work Ivan was doing to unite the tribes.

To keep his mind off Delia, he helped his mother with tasks around the house that she and his father didn't have the bandwidth for—updating their phones and computers, changing passwords. His parents were fairly savvy and not helpless. At times, Cal thought they asked for help simply as an excuse to check up on him. His sisters arrived, grilled him about Delia, then went into the backyard to rescue their father from the kids. Calm descended for a few minutes, then Hurricane Violet blew in.

Violet was seven years younger than Angie, the baby of the family. A pretty child, she'd grown into a beautiful woman. At least on the outside. Vain, self-centered, grasping, and lazy, she wanted the finer things in life but didn't intend to work for them. She was in the process of divorcing husband number three, who'd had the nerve to insist she get a job to pay for the shit she wanted—his words. For better or worse, Sid was her only child. Pregnancy and parenting were not things she enjoyed, so she had her tubes tied at a young age. In Cal's parents' opinion, it was the smartest thing she ever did. She may not have been the main reason Sid struggled with alcohol, but she was a contributing factor.

She strutted into the kitchen, dressed like a woman twenty years younger, trying to look an additional ten years younger. Behind her back, Lisa and Laura rolled their eyes. At one point, Violet had worked at the insurance agency as a receptionist. She couldn't be bothered to get her license but wanted to be paid the same amount as Lisa and Laura, the other agents. Cal wasn't sure if his mother had fired Violet. He just knew she left the agency abruptly.

Angie pressed her lips together at her sister's appearance but didn't say a word. Violet flirted with Dan and flipped her long hair back over her shoulders before sitting at the table and demanding something to drink.

Lisa filled a plastic tumbler with water from the tap and plunked it down in front of her aunt.

Violet glared. "No wine?"

Dan drank his tea and leveled his own glare at his sister-in-law. "No." There hadn't been alcohol in the Jimmy house in years. Angie and Dan weren't teetotalers but figured Sid didn't need the temptation.

"Where's Sid?" Angie asked.

Violet waved a dismissive hand, her beringed fingers tipped with long blood-red nails. "He'll be here in a minute. I told him to find out when he's going to get paid for the chess set. It sold for a pretty penny last night, and he should get a hefty cut."

Cal exchanged looks with his parents and sisters. They looked as confused as he felt. "Aunt Vi, did Sid sell a chess set last night?"

"The one at that event. You were there, you should know." She looked at him like he was a moron.

"That was a charity event. Sid donated the chess set. He's not going to get paid for it."

Violet gaped at him, then screeched. "What? Why the hell isn't he getting paid for it? Who's trying to screw him over? The goddamn whites are at it again. Going after—"

"Enough." Angie's voice was low and hard. "It was a fundraiser for ODAAT. Sid generously donated that chess set, and the money it brought in will help others in the program. No one is screwing anyone over."

That wasn't what Violet wanted to hear. "He should have been paid. He put a lot of work into that set." She swung around to look at Cal. "There's more at Jimmy's Joint, right?"

"Yeah."

"Well, put them aside. I'll be in tomorrow to pick them up."

"What for?" Dan rarely got involved with his sister-in-law but was protective of Sid.

Violet jutted out her chin. "I'm going to represent him. Galleries will be lining up for his stuff, and I'm going to find the best deals."

The bottom fell out of Cal's gut, and again he exchanged looks with his parents. "No disrespect, Aunt Vi, but do you know anything about being an artist's agent?"

"I've been working in the gift shop at the Hibulb Center. I know what sells." Sid appeared in the kitchen doorway, and Violet beamed at him. "My son is going to be famous!"

They crawled along I-5 with the Sunday night traffic. In the dull red reflection of taillights, Sid did not look good. He hadn't looked good all day. He spoke when spoken to, was polite to Dan and Angie, but every time his mother opened her mouth, Sid cringed. What should have been a celebration for Sid turned into the Violet show. Cal had intended to grill him on the screwed-up idea of Aunt Vi being Sid's agent on the drive, but seeing his cousin shifting restlessly in his seat changed his mind. "Do you, umm, need a meeting?"

Sid glanced his way, then back out window. "There's one every hour at ODAAT. I might sit in."

Normally, silence worked well for Cal. He was content to let his thoughts wander, was happy to listen to others talk, but didn't feel the need to do so himself. Tonight was not one of those nights. "How do you feel about pirates?"

"What?"

"A book idea I'm mulling over."

"Is Stacy Wrigglebottom starting a new series?" A spark of interest came through in Sid's voice. When he'd discovered Cal wrote for the famous author, Sid had been beside himself, wanting the inside scoop on upcoming books, suggesting plot lines and character pairings.

"Possibly," Cal lied. Stacy, the real Stacy, wouldn't deviate from the tried and true. "I'm going to pitch it to her, but I'm not sure where to set the story."

For the next hour, they discussed pirates. Using Cal's phone because Sid's was very basic, Sid brought up articles on French pirates, Cornish pirates, the difference between privateers and pirates, and how many female pirates made history. When Cal pulled to the curb outside ODAAT, Sid was in a much better space. He'd spoken animatedly and instructed Cal to purchase an eye patch to experience what wearing one would be like. Cal agreed but drew the line at a parrot.

Through the front window of ODAAT, Cal saw men meandering into the lobby. "Did a meeting just end?"

Sid nodded. "Some of them will go back into the next meeting."

"Have you ever done that?"

"Oh yeah."

"And tonight?" Having never felt the claw of addiction, there was only so much Cal could understand.

Sid shot him a wry smile. "I think one will be good enough." He opened the car's door. "I'll be in tomorrow. Thanks for the ride and…everything."

"Do you want your mom to be your agent?" Cal hoped he wasn't making a mistake by bringing it up.

Sid groaned. "God, no. She'll screw things up in some way."

"Do you want me to run interference?" He had a feeling Aunt Vi's presence in Sid's life would mess with his sobriety.

"You shouldn't have to do this for me. I should be able to take care of—"

Leaning across the console, Cal gripped Sid's arm. "Hey. One day at a time. One thing at a time. You've got the potential for something good here. And I hate to say it, but your mom is not interested in what's best for you. If you need me to play the heavy, I'll do it."

Sid looked down, blinking rapidly. "I'd appreciate it. You've done so much for me."

"Yeah, well, I'm keeping a tally. When you're rich and famous, I'll present you with the bill."

"I look forward to it." Sid huffed out a laugh and climbed out of the Jeep.

Cal watched his cousin walk into the center, wondering what to do about Aunt Vi.

$\mathcal{A}$ stack of books sat on the coffee table next to an empty coffee mug. Delia glanced down at the book in her lap, then up to the windows in her living room. The sun was shining, sparkling off the waters of the Sound. A large container ship made slow progress northward. Beyond it, the green trees of Vashon Island could be seen. For the first time in her life, Delia wondered about the original people who'd lived there, who'd lived close to the water in the summer, then retreated inland to longhouses in the winter. Longhouses that whites destroyed, believing that communal living was not conducive to productivity.

From what she'd read, she'd gathered that her ancestors had not personally relocated the Duwamish peoples, but they were sure happy to buy their land, clear the forests, and pollute the waters. They were most definitely complicit. Everything Naomi Sanchez had said was true. Through no fault of their own, the Duwamish had been forcibly moved from the thousands and thousands of acres they'd occupied around Lake Washington and the Seattle waterfront. They did not have a reservation of their own. No reservations were allowed close to what would be Seattle. Fast forward

170 years, and they now had three-fourths of an acre along the Duwamish River on a major arterial and were not recognized by the federal government.

Guilt settled heavily on Delia's shoulders. The Duncan family fortune was indeed founded on the misfortune of Cal's ancestors. She had no idea if Cal knew that but suspected he must. As much time as they'd spent together, they hadn't gone deep into their families and upbringing. For her part, Delia didn't bring it up, fearing he'd disparage her for being wealthy. Why she'd never asked him about his family was beyond her. She knew he was Indigenous, and that was about it. And yes, she'd made suppositions about Cal based on Sid being an addict living on the streets.

She looked at her watch. It was almost noon. Normally, she'd be at Jimmy's Joint by now. She was disappointed that Cal hadn't texted, wondering where she was, though because she set her own hours, and with the ODAAT event, she'd spent a lot of time away from the bookstore, and there was no reason for him to be expecting her at a certain time. The idea of hiding out in her apartment for the day, wallowing in shame, was appealing. There were orders for Delia's Closet to fill and emails to answer, things she could do from home, so it wasn't quite hiding out…

The phone's ringing dragged her out of her thoughts. "Hello?"

"Hey, it's Connie. I've got a delivery to bring up for you."

"Oh. If you don't mind, just leave it at your desk. I'll be by later to pick it up."

"Hang on."

There were muffled voices in the background, then Connie was back on the line.

"Yeah, that's not going to work. It's coming up to you. Bye."

Baffled, Delia stared at the phone. What was that? She shrugged and heaved herself off the couch. Maybe Connie wanted to get away from the desk for a minute and was looking for an excuse.

A few minutes later, the knock came, and Delia went to the door. She opened it to face a huge bouquet of sunflowers and daisies.

"What?"

The flowers were placed in her arms by a smiling Kevin.

Tommy said, "I didn't bother with a vase because I know you have masses of them."

The two men kissed her on the cheek and pushed past her into the apartment.

"Why am I receiving flowers? Not that I mind." Putting the bouquet on the counter, she went in search of a vase.

"For being awesome. For doing a great job on Saturday night. For forcing us to speak to each other." Kevin spoke over his shoulder as he went to stand in front of the windows.

"And to find out how your night with Cal went." Tommy leaned against the counter and waggled his eyebrows.

Delia ignored him. "You're dating? Excellent."

Tommy made a noncommittal noise that sounded oddly like a purr and smiled. "Let's not get ahead of ourselves."

Kevin joined them, nudging Tommy's shoulder. "We're exploring the idea."

"While exploring each other?" Delia said with a sly smile.

They grinned at each other, and Delia couldn't be happier for them.

"You know I'm always happy to talk about myself, but spill. How did it go with tall, dark, and handsome?" Tommy asked.

"Don't forget hot," Kevin added.

Delia concentrated on putting each stem into the vase. She tried for nonchalant. "Umm, good."

"Just good?" Kevin frowned.

"What'd you do?" Tommy propped his elbows on the

counter and rested his chin on one fist. "Spill. We're not going anywhere until we find out what happened. I honestly thought I'd be seeing pictures all over Insta with you and Cal."

Delia sighed and mirrored his pose. She had no idea where to start and whether she wanted to talk about it. Thankfully there was another knock on the door. "Hang on."

She'd barely opened the door when Connie blew past her. "Did I miss anything? I've got fifteen minutes, so speak quickly."

"Make yourself at home," Delia said as she trailed behind Connie.

"Happy to." Connie went into the kitchen and set about making tea. That done, she turned to speak to the men. "What did she say?"

"Not a damn thing," Kevin said. "You arrived just in time."

"What is this? An intervention?"

Tommy flapped a hand. "Don't be dramatic. Just tell us why you didn't spend yesterday in bed with Cal and why you're holed up in your apartment today."

About to protest, Delia eyed the three stern expressions in front of her and capitulated. "Fine. The evening started off well—"

Connie interjected, "You looked awesome."

"Did you see Cal? What that man does to a suit..." Tommy fanned himself.

"Ignore them," Kevin said. "Go ahead."

Delia tried to organize her thoughts, figuring out exactly what to share. Definitely not the kiss. It was too sweet and full of promise to sully its memory by dissecting it with friends. "It was a really good night. My parents liked Cal. He seemed to like them. Everything was great between the two of us, and Cal agreed to take me home. I stopped at the restroom and..." She looked at the expectant faces and finished in a rush. "My lawyer came into the bathroom, three sheets to the wind, and proceeded to tell me that my family had made their fortune on the backs of Cal's family, and the only reason they donated to ODAAT was out of guilt."

Her friends exchanged glances and turned back to her. "And then what?" Connie asked.

Delia shrugged. "I met Cal at the elevator, and he drove me home. That's it."

"That's it? You didn't drag him up here and make the beast with two backs?"

Delia rolled her eyes at Tommy. "Naomi Sanchez kind of put a damper on the evening. The worst part is, she's right."

Kevin, who'd worked for Duncan Properties up until a short time ago, tilted his head toward the couch. "Hence the books?"

"Hence the books." Delia nodded. "Cal said Naomi worked for the tribe and was a pit bull when it came to Indigenous rights, so I figured I'd do some research. Everything she said was true. My ancestors didn't physically force the Duwamish off their land, but they didn't do a thing to help them out."

None of her friends were derisive or dismissive, but neither did they envelop her in hugs and claim she'd been wronged. Two gay men and two persons of color, Tommy, Kevin, and Connie had faced outright discrimination and vitriol more than once, something Delia hadn't.

"You need to apologize to Cal." Kevin got up and went to pour the tea.

"For what Gweneth Duncan did?" Delia accepted her cup and wrapped her hands around its warmth.

"No. For not telling him what happened. Not trusting him." Kevin placed a mug in front of Tommy and leaned forward to kiss him. "You can't do much about your great-great-great-whatever, but you can tell Cal why you ditched him."

"I disagree," Connie said.

"What? You don't think she needs to apologize to Cal?" Tommy gaped at her.

Connie shook her head. "Not that. She definitely needs to do that. I think she can do something about Gweneth Duncan."

"How? It's not like the Duncan family will agree to give back the land they bought," Kevin challenged her. "I've seen those family board meetings. No offense, Delia, some of your relatives are useless money-grabbers."

"None taken," she murmured. She'd been to precisely one quarterly board meeting. The one when she'd received her trust fund. After that, she voted by email, going along with whatever her father told her to do. Something else to add to her list of personal failings.

"True, but she can do something useful with her skills and her money." Connie looked at her watch and frowned. "I need to get going. But Delia, I mean it. There are things you can do to make reparations. When you're ready, I'm happy to talk further about it." She came around the island to put her mug in the sink and wrapped an arm around Delia's shoulders before heading to the door.

After Connie left, Tommy took the vase of flowers and placed it on the dining room table. "She's right," he said. "You can't change history, but there are things you can do to improve the lot of the Duwamish and other tribes here in Washington State."

"What do you mean? Write them a check?" That seemed doable but way too easy.

"That's a start. I suggest you continue to do your research and find out what they need. Not what you *think* they need. Then talk to your family."

Kevin snorted and held a hand up when Tommy glared at him. "Babe, I agree with you. But the Duncan family…" He shook his head as if they were a lost cause.

Delia smiled for the first time that day. "You two can stay here and argue, but I need to get going. I have to talk to Cal."

❅

Shortly after noon, Delia arrived. For the first time in what felt like forever, Cal exhaled. His shoulders relaxed, and he struggled with whether or not to stay in place or wrap her in a hug. In the end, he stood and walked around the counter, coming to a stop a few feet away. She clutched a stack of books to her chest and looked up at him with a tentative smile.

"Hey." He held out his hands. "Can I take those for you?"

She glanced at the books as if she'd forgotten she was holding them. "Oh. Sure."

He took the paperbacks and deposited them on the counter. "I wasn't sure you were going to come in."

"I wasn't sure, either."

Something was off, and Cal figured he had two options: ask her straight out or pretend nothing happened and let Delia tell him when she was ready. Normally, Cal was inclined to let people figure things out in their own time, but not having slept two nights in a row and watching Delia walk around on eggshells was annoying the hell out of him. "Do you want to tell me what happened?"

His hand shot up when Delia shook her head. "Don't. Between the time I kissed you, and then meeting me at the elevator, something happened. If you changed your mind, and you don't want this"—he motioned a hand between the two of them—"I'm okay with it. Well, not exactly, but I won't push. We'll work together, but I won't pressure you into going any further. Just…tell me now." He shoved his hands in his pockets and rocked back on his heels.

Delia gusted out a sigh and brushed past him to drop her tote on a stool at the counter. He turned to watch her. She removed her coat and shook back her hair, releasing that hint of lavender that haunted him. She tapped the stack of books. "This is what's bothering me."

Cal glanced at the titles. *Chief Seattle and the Town that Took His Name, Reclaiming the Reservation, The River that Made Seattle, Dismembered.* Cal was familiar with some of the books, as the authors had accessed the databases at the UW library for parts of their research. "You're gonna have to give me more."

Delia crossed her arms and faced him squarely. "I've lived in Seattle my entire life, and I knew nothing about this."

"You didn't know that Seattle was named after Chief Seattle and the Duwamish were the original people here?"

"I knew *that*. I didn't know about them being forced out and sent to reservations. I didn't know about the destruction of their homes or that they weren't allowed to live in Seattle." She looked angry and embarrassed.

"History has always been written by the victors. The white settlers weren't about to make themselves look bad. That's why there were all the damn treaties."

"That weren't upheld. That the tribal leaders signed without understanding what they meant." Delia pointed a rigid finger at the books. "It was your ancestors who got screwed over."

"I know that." When the first treaties were signed, the Aboriginal leaders barely understood what they were doing, unable to read, write, or even speak English. Literacy and education were powerful, which was why his grandparents and parents stressed the necessity of school.

"And my ancestors"—Delia tapped herself on the chest—"my *family* profited from that. My venerated great-great-great-grandmother made her fortune buying land that was taken away from your ancestors. Did you know that?"

Cal scrubbed a hand across his face and stepped closer. "Yes. It wasn't hard to figure out."

"You researched me?" Now she looked accusatory.

"No. The development of Seattle is intertwined with the Duncan family. It didn't take much to put it all together."

She slumped down onto a stool. "I didn't put it together. I never bothered to learn about it."

Part of Cal wanted to hug her, tell her it happened a long time ago and she was at no fault. The other part, the part that knew tribal recognition was an ongoing battle, that rebuilding a culture was hard, that being considered less than for being Indigenous, wanted her to feel the guilt— the cost of understanding her privilege. "So what are you going to do about it?"

She didn't look surprised or affronted by the question. "I'm not sure. I do know I want to learn more, though."

"What got you interested in this?"

"I had a conversation with Naomi Sanchez the other night."

"Ah." He was beginning to put together what happened. "Did this happen before you met me at the escalator?"

She scrunched up her nose. "In the bathroom. She was…"

"Plastered and belligerent?"

"Yes! She was exactly what you said she was—a pit bull." She sighed. "It was rather uncomfortable, but I'm glad she told me."

Again, Cal didn't try to make her feel better. It was frustrating how many people lived their lives in a place without bothering to learn its history and about the first peoples who'd occupied it. He wasn't going to harangue her or climb up on a soapbox. If she wanted to go deeper, though, he was happy to help.

"So you didn't withdraw because of the kiss?" Despite being a writer, he had no clue how to ask the question without sounding like a teenager.

Delia's eyes widened, and she closed the space between them. "God, no. It was…"

Wrapping his arms around her, he smiled, pleased that she was speechless. "I was worried my technique was off, because I haven't done that in a while."

"Your technique is just fine." Her lips curled into a saucy smile. "Maybe a bit rusty, though. Perhaps I can help you practice."

Warmth suffused Cal as he murmured against her lips, "I'd like that."

*A*s much as she wanted to stay in Cal's arms and spend the day kissing him, there was work to be done. She waved at the front window. "What did you do to the chess sets? You can't possibly have sold them all?"

Cal grimaced and strode over to the window display. "Long story. For now, how fast can you change this display?"

"Half an hour or so. Why?" She moved to his side and started dismantling the vignette, knowing Cal wouldn't ask her to do so without a good reason. "Take that chair over to the carving station, then bring me the stack of books on the floor by the self-help section."

They worked quickly and efficiently, Cal accepting instruction without question. It helped that Delia had planned out different window displays knowing she would need to change them frequently. When the last book was in place, three pyramids of differing heights occupied the space, each topped with a book by a popular self-help guru. They headed outside to admire their work from the sidewalk. Cal looked at his watch. "Twenty-three minutes. That's impressive."

Delia grinned, pleased with both the outcome and the warmth emanating from the man beside her. He held the door open for her, placing his hand on her lower back as she passed him to enter the store. He was a writer of romantic fiction, and she knew that *he* knew exactly what that claiming gesture meant.

"Ordinarily, I wouldn't do this," Cal said as he reached to retrieve his wallet from his back pocket. "But would you go and pick up some lunch for us? I'm starved, and I can't leave the store right now."

"Okay." Delia accepted his card. "This has something to do with the chess sets, right?"

"Yeah. Sid's mom, my Aunt Violet, has appointed herself as his agent. She intends to take the chess sets and sell them for him."

"You don't sound happy about that."

"I'm not. Aunt Vi is self-serving and hasn't paid attention to Sid for years. And she's not a particularly nice person. So it's best you aren't by yourself when she comes by today."

"She can't be that bad."

Cal shook his head and opened the door for her. "Trust me."

Delia giggled as she went past him to pick up their lunch.

She returned to the shop to find a beautiful woman haranguing Cal. He stood silent, arms crossed, apparently letting her words wash over him. Sid was off to the side, shoulders hunched, looking embarrassed. At Delia's entrance, he bobbed his head in greeting. The woman whipped around, her long dark hair swirling like a cape before settling around her shoulders. It looked practiced, and Delia wondered if her own hair was long enough to pull off the maneuver. Above the woman, Cal caught Delia's eye and mouthed the words, *Aunt Vi.*

Lengthening her stride, Delia deposited the bag of food on the counter before approaching the woman. "Hello," she said, smiling wide and holding out a hand. "You must be Sid's mother. So good to meet you. Your son is extremely talented. I've been fielding calls from galleries, museums, and schools since yesterday. He can pick and choose where he goes from here." Still holding Violet by the hand, Delia led her over to sit at the counter. "Cal said you will be representing Sid. That's good. He needs a skilled agent. What have you got planned?"

Mouth hanging open, Violet stared at Delia.

Delia flicked a hand and stood. "Where are my manners? Would you prefer tea or coffee, and how do you like it? Cal can bring it for us, so let's go over to my office." She rolled her eyes. "It's not *really* an office. I took over this corner while working on the event and Jimmy's Joint."

Taking Violet's hand again, she steered her toward the back corner and kept up the chatter while she sat down and pulled out her planner. She leafed through pages until she found a bulleted list, hoping Violet wouldn't notice that it was her To Be Read list rather than a list of contacts for Sid. Cal had unearthed a tray and brought over the teapot, an assortment of mugs, milk, and sugar. Behind him, Sid carried a plate of the sandwiches Delia bought. Either Sid or Cal had cut them up, and while the presentation wouldn't impress Carol Lee Duncan, the men had done their best. As if rehearsed, they then stood behind Delia, and all three waited for Violet to speak. Her expression gave new meaning to the term "deer in the headlights."

Delia doctored her tea and sat back in her chair. "What were you thinking of first? Publicity for Sid or a private show? Perhaps a showcase of his work at the Hibulb Cultural Center with a class on carving?" Behind her, Sid let out a quiet groan. She'd have to apologize to him later. There was no way in the world she would subject him to that much attention so soon.

Violet shifted in her seat, then glared at Cal, as if suspecting he'd thrown her under the bus. "The cultural center. The gift shop, maybe?" She phrased the sentence like a question.

"Okay." Delia sipped her tea and nodded encouragingly.

"Excellent. Have you got a photographer lined up? In my experience, it's best to have one chess set on display and use images of the others. The photographer can zoom in on the details of the smaller pieces as well. I have some images of the sets. Do you want to choose which one now, or shall I email them to you? When you have the posters made for the exhibit, please send some my way. I would love to display some here and at ODAAT."

Violet shoved her chair back and stood. "I'll, um, get in contact with you. I need to check into some things first."

"Excellent," Delia said, smiling brightly, and stood as well. "Do you have a card? Here's one of mine." She blessed the day Carol Lee had insisted she have business cards printed. Pulling one out of a pocket of her planner, she held it out. Violet muttered something under her breath and turned to sail out of the store.

Delia slumped back in her chair and exhaled loudly.

"Wow," Cal said in a reverent tone. "That was freaking awesome. I've never seen Aunt Vi speechless before."

Delia twisted around to look up at Sid. "I kinda made things up. I did get some emails about you yesterday but haven't responded. You okay?"

Sid ran a hand across his sweaty brow, then settled into the vacated chair. "I've never thought about seeing my stuff in a gallery or teaching a class. Would people really want that?"

"Yeah." Cal pulled up another chair beside Delia's and faced his cousin. "If that's something you want to do, it could certainly happen. You have the skill. It's a matter of how committed you are to the business part. Showing up on time, following through on a job, taking care of the bills, speaking with people."

"That's the part where I screwed up." Both men turned to look at her. "My parents bankrolled a couple of businesses for me. I'd be really excited about an idea and the energy of the start-up, but the day-to-day work of running a business" —she waved a hand at the bookshelves surrounding them— "overwhelmed me and bored me at the same time. People were depending on me, and I let them down." She'd never spoken aloud about it. Her parents had quietly cleaned up her messes, everyone pretending that nothing had ever happened. "So if you want to make a living out of your art, make it your day job, be prepared for the scutwork."

Under the table, Cal took her hand and squeezed it gently before letting go. "She's right. I could have done so much more with Jimmy's Joint, but it was a helluva lot easier to let the dust gather while I sat and wrote."

"The nice thing is, you don't need to make this decision right away. I can employ you here at the shop until the building comes down."

Sid shot his cousin a grateful look. "Thanks, man. I know the training wheels have to come off some time. Right now, though…" He shook his head.

"Are you hanging out here today?" Cal asked.

Sid nodded at Cal. "Yeah. I have an idea I want to work on. Do you need me for something?"

Cal shook his head, then looked at Delia. She shrugged. "Not really. You two did a great job on your to-do list, so I'm doing catch-up on paperwork."

"'Kay. I'll think about what I want to do." Sid leaned forward and snatched up a sandwich. "Right after I eat."

CHAPTER 19

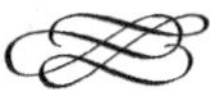

The phone went to voicemail before she could answer it. Her mother. Delia sighed, actually impressed she hadn't heard from Carol Lee earlier in the day. Hungry, she decided to eat and talk at the same time, knowing she would be doing more listening than speaking. She warmed up the soup she'd made the day before and settled at the counter. "Hey, Mom."

"Hello, sweetheart, how was your day? I've been hearing from people all day long about how great the auction was on Saturday night and how the displays were what drove up the bidding. So again, good job. You'll be happy to know I did not volunteer you for anything, although I certainly could if you gave me the say so."

Delia opened her mouth to say something, but her mother kept on talking, so she continued to eat.

"And Calvin Jimmy! What a handsome man. I saw the photos of you two. Is there something you'd like to tell me? Perhaps you'd like to bring him to dinner."

Delia choked on her soup.

"Are you all right, dear?"

Clearing her throat, Delia said, "I'm fine. Something went down the wrong way."

"You talk to him, and we'll sync our calendars with yours." Clearly done with that line of conversation, Carol Lee went on to the next topic. "The dedication for the Gweneth Duncan building. The date has been set for the ceremony. I'll handle invitations and catering. Hopefully, Grand Gestures can accommodate us. I'll contact Kevin and Jane today." There was silence for a moment.

Delia smiled. Her mother was tickled pink to be associated with the top event planning firm in Seattle and bragged to her friends that even she didn't have any pull with the owners, the firm was so busy.

"Your responsibility will be creating the PowerPoint presentation. Or do you think it should be a video with a narrator?"

"Do you have a preference, Mom?" Other than noting the date on her calendar, Delia had given little thought to the dedication.

"I'll leave that up to you, dear. Perhaps video. Maybe use one of those drone things for an aerial of the Seattle waterfront and zoom in on the building."

Delia pulled her planner toward her to write that down. "Good idea. Where is the building again?"

Her mother rattled off the address, and Delia wrote it down. It tickled something in the back of her mind in the process. "Hang on for a second, Mom." She retrieved her laptop and, opening up a browser, typed in the address. Switching to Google Earth, she zoomed in and found the building in its final phase of construction, adjacent to and towering over the Duwamish Longhouse and Cultural Center. Her hands went clammy. Could her family be more oblivious? "Why was that location chosen?"

"I'm a little fuzzy on my history, but I believe that was the site of the first Duncan sawmill. That land has belonged to the family forever. You'll have to confirm that. The archives are next to the conference room in the DP building. You'll find the details there. Your dad or Chuck can give you access."

She tried to wrap her head around what she'd just learned. Delia had to get off the phone. Over her mother's protests, she made an excuse and hung up. She stared at the image on her screen. The Duwamish Longhouse was situated on three-quarters of an acre. They'd spent years fundraising in order to purchase the property—from *her* family. Once again, her family had taken advantage of Indigenous people without a care.

The Gweneth Duncan building was close to completion. There wasn't much Delia could do about that. She could assuage her guilt by writing a check, however not in any amount that could come near the reparations owed to the Duwamish people. Delia closed her laptop, put it away, and then wandered restlessly about her apartment, wondering what, if anything, could be done.

Cal had flown to New York for his annual meeting with Stacy Wrigglebottom. Normally, he would have closed down Jimmy's Joint while he was gone, but Delia and Sid had talked him into leaving it open, assuring him they wouldn't run amok or set fire to the place. Sid quietly worked on his carving, and they took turns dealing with customers.

After spending the afternoon with Sid at the bookstore, Delia met Connie at a quiet bar equidistant from their two homes. They'd taken care of the work Connie had done for Delia's Closet and were now enjoying a glass of wine. Needing input from an objective third party, Delia told her about her day, needing to think out loud.

"The idea of opening another office building with fanfare on land they all but stole from their neighbors doesn't sit well with me."

Connie winced. "Stole is a bit heavy-handed, don't you think?"

Delia rolled her eyes. "Gweneth Duncan paid for the land well after the Duwamish were relocated. So, no, she didn't steal it. It's just…That property is worth a massive amount of money, and the original occupants, who didn't want to leave in the first place, can barely fund their cultural center."

"I get that you feel guilty, but what do you want to do with that guilt?"

"I don't know." Maybe talking to Connie wasn't such a great idea. "Making a video that sings the praises of a woman who profited from people who were taken advantage of feels wrong."

"I get it." Connie rose from the table and said, "I'll get the next round."

Delia watched her friend move toward the bar. She had no idea what she could do about the situation and hadn't a clue where to start. She was one person without influence against a history of sweeping distasteful subjects under the rug.

Placing the drinks on the table, Connie sat back down and crossed her arms. "If you and Cal weren't seeing each other"—she held up a hand to prevent Delia from protesting —"would you care so much?"

Delia frowned. She wanted to state vehemently that she wanted to see an injustice righted, yet she knew her discomfort was tied into Cal's heritage. He, himself, was doing well, but there was no denying that wasn't the case of other Indigenous people living in and around Seattle. "Probably not."

"What's happening with ODAAT? Did they hire you for another event?"

"No." She was surprised at the change in subject but happy to talk about something else. "I'm connecting them with gallery owners and museums looking for Indigenous art. ODAAT has some rooms that were originally event spaces that are currently underutilized. They can be repurposed to be classrooms and workspaces for the men in the program. There are some who are craftsmen and artists, and if they can work in a supportive environment, they can be successful in their sobriety and support themselves."

"How are you doing this?" Connie appeared to be doodling on an open page of her planner. Hers was more of a wire-bound notebook with a calendar on the left side and lined pages on the right. She didn't geek out over planners the way Delia did, but she was organized in her note-taking.

"I asked questions. Sid and his friends—I told you about the guys who come to the bookstore to carve with him—were talking about ODAAT and wishing they didn't have to lug their stuff around but could do their work there. I contacted Ivan about what they said, and he's taking care of it. After the fundraiser, there's no shortage of money. Now it's all about using it wisely. And updating the facility for workspaces is perfect. If the men have a place to work, and the galleries and museums can provide places to showcase their work, everyone is happy." Delia shrugged. It really had been a no-brainer on her part.

Connie leveled a gaze at her. "So ask the Duwamish what *they* need."

The next morning, Delia texted Sid to let him know she'd be late and drove over to West Seattle. She parked across the street from the Gweneth Duncan building and got out of her car. Traffic sped by her as she stood on the sidewalk, staring at the new building. Construction workers wandered in and out of the five-story structure, which dwarfed the Duwamish Longhouse beside it and made it look shabby. The archives of Duncan Properties provided documents detailing the purchases of property, records of construction, and what was done with the timber cleared from the land. Nowhere was it mentioned what had happened to the original inhabitants of the purchased land.

"Are you looking for some place?" A young woman with a pierced lip peered at her from beneath a big umbrella. She held a travel mug and a tote bag featuring an Indigenous image.

Delia smiled and shook her head. "I'm fine. Do you work there?" She nodded toward the longhouse.

"Yeah. I'm the volunteer coordinator. You're not looking to volunteer, are you?" A hopeful smile lit the woman's face. She looked to be younger than Connie, with bright blue eyes, fair freckled skin, and dark curly hair.

"I hadn't really thought about it," Delia said, tilting her own umbrella back to release a cascade of raindrops.

The younger woman narrowed her eyes and pursed her lips, giving Delia a calculating look. "Would you be interested in a private guided tour and hearing about volunteer opportunities?"

"Umm…" The woman looked harmless enough. "Sure."

"Excellent. Come with me." She snagged Delia's arm and hustled her across the street when a break appeared in the traffic. They went through the parking lot and around the building to the main entry. The woman fished through her bag and pulled out a set of keys with a triumphant grin. "You don't have to commit to anything, but I've been working on my spiel, and it would be great practice for me to deliver it to you."

"Okay." Delia collapsed her umbrella and followed the woman into the building, wondering what she'd gotten herself into. The last time she'd been there, a presentation on salmon recovery was finishing up, and the small lobby/gift shop/museum area was filled with people. Now, it was quiet and dim and looked slightly shabby.

The woman dumped her gear on the admission counter and flicked on light switches. She tsked. "Dammit, the cleaning crew didn't empty the recycling and wastebaskets again." She was speaking as if to herself. "Add that to the to-do list as well." She pushed a stray curl off her forehead and beamed at Delia. "Welcome to the Duwamish Cultural Center. I'm Ginny Clemons. Come this way and make yourself comfortable." She led the way past displays of Indigenous artifacts to a large multipurpose room, where she took a spot at the end of the room and spoke about the history of the longhouse, its purpose in the community, and opportunities for volunteers. "So what do you think?"

Delia nodded enthusiastically. "You did great. Maybe slow it down a bit. I noticed a lot of the volunteer work involves shifting things back and forth and moving furniture around. If you're targeting seniors, they may not be able to do that, so gear your appeal to the abilities of the volunteer pool. High school kids needing community service are great for physical labor, while seniors would be better for the gift shop and admissions desk."

Ginny whipped out her phone and entered the feedback with deft thumbs. "Thanks, that's very useful. So do you want to volunteer?" She shot a coy look Delia's way.

"Now? No. In the future, possibly. Is there a place on the website for volunteers?"

"No, but that's an excellent idea." Once again, her thumbs flew over the keyboard.

Feeling pleased with herself for being helpful, Delia asked, "Why do you need to shift things around so much? Is space at a premium?"

Ginny rolled her eyes. "This is pretty much the only room we can utilize. Chairs get rearranged, tables get set up and taken down and put into storage containers, then hauled out. On the upside, it's a great cardio workout."

"Can you enlarge the building, maybe add on to it?"

"I wish." Ginny's curls bounced when she shook her head. "We don't have the money to expand or the land to build on."

Delia knew this already but pretended ignorance. "How big is the tribe's land?"

"We're not even federally recognized. Don't let me get started on that, though. What you see"—Ginny extended her arms—"is it. Three-quarters of an acre."

"You said we. Are you Duwamish?"

Ginny held up a hand, her thumb and forefinger slightly apart. "A small amount. My great-grandmother was half. My great-great-grandfather was white. He worked at one of the sawmills around here. My family is a real polyglot. Makes for an interesting genealogy chart." She moved closer to take a chair next to Delia. "If you don't mind me asking, what were you doing out there? West Marginal Way is not the best place for walking."

"I was looking at the new construction next door. Any idea what it's going to be?" Truthfully, Delia didn't know what she'd been doing there.

"Not quite sure. I doubt it's residential. It would be nice if it was something that would attract visitors our way. It's probably office space of some description."

Delia cocked her head. "Could you rent space there to hold classes and stuff? The location is perfect for you."

"I wish. But again"—she rubbed her fingers together—"you need money for that, and we don't have it. And I seriously doubt the property owners will let us use it for free."

Feeling a bit awkward, Delia murmured something in commiseration and then changed the subject. "Maybe a fundraiser?"

Ginny rose and huffed out a laugh. She walked toward the lobby, Delia following behind. "We have a full-time staff of three people here. I was hired to do volunteer coordinating, but I also work the front desk, schedule events, handle the website and social media, and, more often than not, am the custodian. I have a laundry list of improvements I'd like to make, but no bandwidth to put on a fundraiser." She picked up her mug and drank deeply, then shot Delia a tired grin. "Sorry. I didn't mean to dump on you. It's awfully hard to make an impact when you're spinning in circles."

"If you had the money, what would you do with it?"

"I'd start with hiring a full-time custodian."

Delia pushed her hands together, then pulled them apart. "Go bigger."

Propping her elbows on the counter, Ginny clasped her hands together and leaned on them. "I'd start a class on building canoes the old way. Then we'd go up the canal in the canoes and learn about the ecosystem and how to restore it. I'd record the histories of all the tribal elders I can find so their stories don't get lost. I'd commission teachers to put together an Indigenous History unit to be taught in schools and pay for field trips so kids could know what it was like to live on the shore and in longhouses—which I would have built." She winked at Delia and continued, "I would unite the tribes to work together to combat mental illness, depression, and addiction. I would…" She sighed and looked at Delia.

"Change the world?"

"Yeah." Ginny straightened and swiped at her nose with her shirtsleeve. "If wishes were horses, beggars would ride."

Delia resisted the urge to wrap the girl in a hug. She was so young. Delia couldn't remember ever having the passion or energy for something other than herself. She plucked up a brochure from the front desk and held it up. "I don't know about all those things you talked about, but I will get back to you about volunteering. I promise. You did a great job on your spiel, and if I think of anything to add to it, I'll reach out. It was nice meeting you, and I wish you success."

Ginny lifted her chin in acknowledgment and held the door for Delia to exit.

The rain had stopped, and Delia stood on the edge of the sidewalk, waiting for a break in the traffic. Over one shoulder, she could see the longhouse struggling to represent the

Duwamish people in a place where no one cared. Over the other shoulder was the new construction representing... more money for her family. She darted across the street when there was an opening and turned back to look at the two structures again. An idea prickled the back of her mind, and she moved toward her car with a lighter step.

"Hi, Dad."

Chuck Sr. looked up from his desk and greeted his daughter with a smile. "Hi, honey. What are you doing here?"

Delia waved behind her. "Looking up some stuff for the video Mom wants me to put together."

Leaning back in his chair, Chuck Sr. motioned for her to enter his office. "Right. How's that going? You finding everything you need?"

Delia settled into a chair across the desk from him. "Yes, thank you. The records are in good order, and there are some great photographs."

"Choose photos that flatter your Aunt May. Otherwise, you'll never hear the end of it," he said with a wink.

"Got it." Delia smiled. "So, Dad, has Duncan Properties ever given up a piece of land?"

"We don't do it a lot, but we sell property now and then."

She shook her head. "That's not what I meant. It's more like, has DP ever donated a property to a nonprofit?"

"Do you mean ODAAT? They occupy the building for free, and we're good landlords. The place is in good shape, and if work needs to be done, we take care of it quickly. If they owned the building, the upkeep would take away from their ability to provide services."

"But if they owned the property, they could sell it and build a bigger facility somewhere else."

"True." Her father gestured toward the window. "But why

would we do that? Land is finite, and the Duncan family has owned that property for more than a century. It's not in our best interest to give it up."

Delia nodded in understanding and rose from her chair. "Thanks, Dad." She left his office and headed toward the elevator, mulling over all that she'd learned that day.

CHAPTER 20

Cal accepted the cup of coffee from the flight attendant with a smile and settled back into his seat. Stacy Wrigglebottom had paid for him to fly first class, and he appreciated it. On the red eye from New York to Seattle, the seat next to him was empty, an added bonus. Stretching out his long legs, he pulled his notebook out of his backpack to review the hastily scribbled notes he'd made for his pitch.

Usually on these annual trips, he would meet up with Stacy at a writers' conference, where she would schmooze with industry professionals, talk with aspiring writers, and sign books for readers. She and Cal would hash out the story arcs for future books as well. Cal had no complaints about the contract he had for ghostwriting her books, but he was getting restless and bored with Regency novels. It was a combination of Delia's comment about pirates and finding the chess pieces carved to represent Coast Salish images that had fired his imagination. With Stacy's blessing, he'd arranged a meeting with her editor and presented his pitch for a series of books. They would follow a young girl who is separated from her family during a raid and takes shelter in a cave with a hermit. The girl would grow up to become a pirate, traveling the coast of Washington and British Columbia and raiding villages with a crew of animals.

The editor was cautiously receptive and asked for a query letter, the first three chapters, and a full synopsis. Cal agreed to deliver them in two weeks' time, even though he had nothing in writing yet. This would be his first solo project under his own name. He was both ecstatic and scared spitless at the same time. He would deliver. There would be no dukes, no ball gowns, no castles, or carriages. He couldn't wait to get started.

Thanks to Delia, Jimmy's Joint no longer felt like an anchor weighing him down. The inventory of books, the leftover crap from when it was a diner, and his family's castoffs were slowly going away. Thinking about her made him smile. They hadn't said it aloud, but they were moving slowly toward a relationship. He wanted more than stolen kisses, and at his age, he wanted the whole package. He and Delia together. Cal resolved to take her on a real date. No networking, no maintaining polite distances. He wanted to know about childhood pets, favorite vacations, first crushes.

He'd seen her confidence grow with each of her successes. She didn't speak about her trust fund, but Cal knew that retaining it was important to her, if for no other reason than a point of pride. He liked the woman she had become because of the threat of loss. Her original purpose in working for him may have been to keep her trust fund, but it had evolved. Delia genuinely seemed to like working at Jimmy's Joint. She seemed to like helping others in ways they didn't even know they needed help, like Sid and helping ODAAT set up space for people with addictions to work with their hands. Finding a way to help themselves was good for both the individual and the community, regardless of background. With Sid settled and Jimmy's Joint closed down, where would *he* go? Delia's apartment flashed into his mind, but he shook his head. Maybe. But not yet.

Once home, he grabbed a few hours of sleep, then walked with eager steps to Jimmy's Joint in the rain. He didn't mind. The cool, fresh air helped clear his head after the long flight. He shook off the raindrops before entering the store and removing his coat.

The place was empty, but he could hear voices. Using the mirrors, he spotted Delia at her table, talking to a dark-haired woman. She looked up, and their eyes connected through the mirror, and Delia's beautiful face became *more* beautiful as she smiled at him. She held up a finger, and he nodded once, then moved quietly to hang up his jacket on a hook at the back of the store and drop his backpack near his usual stool at the counter. While Delia continued her conversation, he looked around the store. He'd been gone four days, but the time and distance had given him fresh eyes.

The window display was the same three pyramids of books, but the books on the top had changed. Only because he was so familiar with the place was it obvious that the shelves were barer. A couple months ago, books were crammed together and the shelves were packed. Now, most of the shelves were no more than half full, and empty spaces were used to display books on easels. Delia had continued to arrange by category, but also by color. The shop looked artful and aesthetically pleasing. For a store going out of business, it looked inviting and not at all forlorn.

Closing it down would be closing a chapter of Cal's life. A dark chapter where he had remained in stasis, held in place, and going through the motions of life without really living, yet it had served its purpose. He had a place to earn a living while reconnecting with his writing, and Sid found his way back to life through Jimmy's Joint. A laugh brought Cal out of his thoughts. Delia had been responsible for both. Before her, Jimmy's Joint was an albatross, a weight around his neck. The store had served its purpose, and now it was time to move on. And he was going to do so with her.

"Thank you for coming here. I really appreciate it. And I'm glad Jane recommended you."

Cal moved toward Delia's voice. She and the woman, who was taller than Delia, with short no-nonsense hair, and wearing a no-nonsense dark pant suit, were standing next to the table that functioned as Delia's desk. The woman was packing up a briefcase and turned at the sound of Cal's steps, giving him a perfunctory smile.

"Calvin Jimmy." Delia performed the introductions. "This is Marti Castillo, my accountant. Calvin is my, umm, client."

He bit back a smile and held out his hand. "Pleased to meet you."

"And you as well." Marti shook his hand, then stood back and looked at him appraisingly. "Ms. Duncan will be needing a 1099 form from you. I'm assuming you'll have it ready in a timely fashion?"

Delia caught Cal's eye over Marti's shoulder and mouthed a silent apology.

"Yes, ma'am. I will indeed," he said.

"Right then." She fished a business card out of a pocket and gave it to Delia. "If you have any questions, give me a call."

Delia nodded, studying the card. "I thought you were with Snyder, Otterholt & Hill. Do you have your own office now?"

Marti's cheeks reddened, and she looked down before speaking. "I took a leave of absence when my father was in an accident, and then I made it permanent."

"Oh. How is your father now?"

"He died."

Delia stepped closer to Marti, her expressive face full of sympathy. "I'm so sorry for your loss."

"Thank you." Marti cleared her throat. "It's been almost a year and…umm, my mom is getting stronger, and I'm back at work so…yeah. But working for myself, which is interesting because I've always worked with a firm." She stopped as if realizing she was rambling. Then she picked up her briefcase and raincoat and turned toward the door. "I'll find my way out. Delia, nice to meet you. You, too, Mr. Jimmy." With a quick nod, she was gone.

"Your accountant, huh?" Cal leaned against a bookshelf, hands shoved into his pockets. Delia shuffled papers on her desk, looking embarrassed.

"Yeah. I want to make sure I do things right, and Jane speaks highly of her, and I'm not great with—"

Cal stepped forward and placed a finger against her lips. She turned wide eyes up to him. "Successful businesspeople hire professionals. That's what makes them successful." He pulled his finger back, wanting to replace it with his lips, but didn't. Instead, he moved his hand down to her shoulder and gave it a gentle squeeze.

"Right," she said, turning her gaze back down to the papers but looking pleased. "How was New York? I'm surprised you're here. You must be exhausted."

He shrugged. "I'm good. I wanted to see you."

Again, she looked pleased, and he moved closer, taking her into a loose embrace. "I missed you," he said. "The time away made me realize how much I like being with you. If you aren't busy, I want to take you out tonight. Somewhere quiet, just the two of us. No talk about Jimmy's Joint. No networking for you. Just us."

He felt her knees go weak, and he tightened his hold. Her hands came up to rest on his chest, and she tilted her head back to meet his gaze, her eyes warm. "I'd like that, too. Are you sure you won't be too tired?"

"That's why God invented coffee. I'll be fine."

Her phone pinged with an incoming text, and Delia patted Cal's chest and pulled away. "You may have time to stand around making big eyes at me, but *I* have a business to run and work to do." She waved him off. "Go mutter at your computer, and you can tell me how much you missed me later on."

"I don't mutter at my computer."

Delia gave him a look and settled into her chair.

"Fine," he said. "I get the message." He kissed her on the nose and sauntered off to the counter to get to work.

That evening, at a table in the corner of a busy restaurant, Cal shared his plans for the new books. Chin propped on her fist, Delia leaned forward, listening attentively.

"Does this mean you'll stop writing for Stacy Wrigglebottom?"

"Eventually. Stacy wants to retire. She's got a bunch of grandchildren to spoil and a husband who wants to start traveling."

"She knows that you pitched to her editor?"

"Oh yeah. I wouldn't have done it without running it past her. One, because she's my friend as much as she is my boss. Two, because she has a lot of influence, and I'd be shooting myself in the foot if I went behind her back." Cal sipped his water and sat back in his chair. "So that's my big news. What have you been up to while I was gone?"

Delia shifted in her chair, a slight frown creasing her forehead. "I started working on the video presentation for DP."

Cal nodded. She hadn't gone into great detail about it, but he knew it was a dedication for a building being named after Delia's business-savvy ancestor, commemorating 150 years that Duncan Properties had been in business. "Is it not going well?"

Before she could answer, someone called her name. They both turned to see a man striding toward them, looking harried and relieved at the same time. Cal looked at Delia's welcoming smile and stood to greet the tall, good-looking man.

"Hi," he said, his gaze bouncing between Cal and Delia.

"Liam, it's nice to see you." She looked up at Cal. "Calvin Jimmy, this is Liam Cross. He works at Duncan Properties and is good friends with my brother."

The men shook hands and exchanged greetings.

Liam stood back and pushed a hand through his hair. "This is incredibly awkward, and I understand if you say no, but there was a mix-up with our reservation and they don't have a table for me, and Jane just finished an event and will be here momentarily. Is it possible for us to join you?"

Cal blinked in surprise, then looked at Delia. He'd planned on having a quiet dinner with her, then seeing where the night would take them. His place, her place—as long as they were together and *alone*. She looked at him in silent inquiry, and he shrugged. Groaning inwardly, he gave her a slight smile.

She turned her smile on Liam and gestured at the table. "Sure. We haven't ordered yet. Go ahead and tell the hostess you two are joining us."

"Thank you," Liam said on a sigh. "I will owe you big time."

No shit, Cal thought, settling back into his seat. He looked at Liam's retreating back and said, "It sounds like he's afraid of Jane."

Delia giggled. "Jane Beckett is a badass, and Liam is happily twisted around her little finger. There isn't much he wouldn't do for her."

The waiter chose that moment to add the extra place settings, and Cal studied Delia in silence. She sighed, sending him on alert. Was Liam Cross a former boyfriend? Maybe an unrequited love? They hadn't dug deep into each other's dating history, and Cal wasn't quite ready to meet someone from her past. As was his habit, he brought up what was on his mind. The waiter left and Cal leaned forward.

"Did you and Liam ever date?"

Delia rolled her eyes. "No. He's best friends with Chuck,

and I *did* used to have a crush on him when I was fifteen. Over the years, I may have flirted with him, because, you know, he is good-looking." Then she looked Cal straight in the eye. "But he has nothing on you, and you have nothing to worry about."

"Good to know," Cal murmured. Perhaps the night wasn't totally lost.

Liam returned, his hand placed on the lower back of an athletic-looking brunette who said something to Liam that made him blush. While Liam wore a tailored suit and tie, albeit undone, the brunette, who must have been Jane, wore gray slacks, an emerald green button-down shirt with a logo on the upper chest, and flat shoes. When she spotted Delia, she hurried toward the table with her arms outstretched.

"Ohmygod, you're a lifesaver." She collapsed into her chair and grabbed Delia's hand. "You have no idea how good this feels."

Delia held up her glass of wine. "It looks like you could use some of this."

"Yes!" Jane sipped the wine with a dramatic moan, causing Delia to grin and Liam to shake his head.

Liam pushed in Jane's chair, then rounded Delia's chair, before settling into his own seat. He leaned toward Cal and spoke in a low voice. "Seriously, man. I'm in your debt. It was an event from hell, and the only thing preventing Jane from throttling the client was the vision of the chef's special here at the end of the night."

Cal relaxed a bit, seeing the women's animated conversation. "I'll keep you in mind if I need help."

"Did Marti get in touch with you?" Jane asked Delia.

"Yes. Thank you. When did accountants start making house calls? She came by the bookstore today."

Jane grimaced. "She's building up her own practice after taking personal time, so I think she's bending over backward for new clients."

Delia sobered. "She mentioned her dad's passing. That would be hard to move on from."

Beside Cal, Liam shifted in his seat, and the women turned sympathetic faces toward him but didn't say anything. Cal thought about his own father and the void his death would leave in his life. "I'm sorry for your loss," he said.

"Thank you." Liam lowered his head, then looked around the table with a slight smile. "It's been a while, and it helps that I have good memories of him."

Jane took his hand and kissed his knuckles, while Delia blinked back tears. Cal reached over and rubbed her shoulder, and she turned a watery smile his way. Cal raised his glass and looked around the table. "To good memories."

The others did the same and the moment passed.

Jane and Liam knew what they wanted to eat, so when the server returned with their drink order, all four made their dinner requests.

"The event didn't go well?" Delia asked.

Jane flapped a hand. "It was fine. The organizer for the nonprofit was a nightmare."

Cal watched as she and Delia talked about event planning in general and the evening's function in particular, noting Delia's interest. It was more than casual, and he filed that thought away to bring it up again on the way home. It wasn't what he'd planned, but he enjoyed the evening, nonetheless. Despite his appearance, Liam Cross was not a stiff suit, and it was hard not to smile at the obvious affection between him and Jane. Cal learned a little bit more about the dynamic between the Beckett sisters and Duncan Properties, and Delia's role in exposing the predatory practices of a big-box church. The night ended with hugs between the women and handshakes between the men.

Worried that Cal would be too tired from his trip, Delia had picked him up in her car. Now, on their way home, he asked his question. "Is event planning something you want to do?" To his way of thinking, she could do just about anything.

Focused on driving, Delia bobbed her head side to side. "Yes and no. Before I started working for you, I asked Kevin if Grand Gestures would hire me. He said no."

"I'm glad he did."

Delia grinned. "I am, too. I like the energy of event planning and bringing attention and funding to nonprofits."

"I'm sensing a but in there."

"I think I want to do more. I like the work I've done with ODAAT. I like being able to help Sid and other craftsmen find workspace and venues for their art. I guess I like the variety, and I think event planning would become one party after another."

Cal turned her words over as he studied her profile in the lights from the car's dashboard. "It sounds like you want to go a bit deeper, maybe work only for one nonprofit."

She nodded slowly.

They were at her building, and instead of pulling up to the entry, she drove to the entrance to the underground garage. "I forgot to ask. Are you, um, did you want me to take you home?"

Seeing her white-knuckled grip on the steering wheel, Cal reached out to shift a skein of hair off her shoulder. "No. I haven't spent enough time with you tonight."

Her hands relaxed, and she drove up to the keypad to enter the code, through the raised gate, and into a parking spot. Cal climbed out and waited for her by the trunk. When she reached him, he took her hand, and they walked toward the elevator together. Inside, she pressed a button, then stared at it while he watched her. When the doors opened at her floor, he put his hand out to prevent them from closing. "I can leave now and take a cab home if you're uncomfortable. Is that what you want?"

She shook her head, wide eyes focused on his.

"If I come in, I'm not gonna want to leave until morning. Are you good with that?" If she wasn't interested in his company, with or without sex, he wanted to know now.

She leaned up to touch her lips to his. "I want you to stay. Stay with me." Then she guided him out of the elevator and to her door.

CHAPTER 21

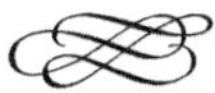

*D*elia thanked the stars she was a tidy soul. Entering the apartment, cool night air from a cracked window greeted them, and the soft glow of a table lamp by the sofa drew them down the short hall from the door. Delia entered the living room and stood to the side as Cal moved past her. The one and only time he'd been there was when he'd carried her drunken ass home. What had he thought then, and what did he think now?

He stood at the window. "Your view beats the hell out of my view."

"It helps when your family owns the building."

He twisted to look her way. "Do they live here as well?"

"No." She dropped her purse on the glass top of the table and draped her wrap over a chair, then joined him. "They have a house in Magnolia and one in Maui. Your parents?"

"They have a house in Tulalip. They used to have a time-share, but Dad talked Mom out of it and bought a boat."

"Sailboat?" Delia's parents had worked at the Ballard marina when they first met in college and owned a sailboat.

Cal smiled down at her. "No. Dad's a retired commercial

fisherman. He bought a boat he can take fishing but is comfortable enough that Mom will go with him."

"Does she fish as well?"

"Not so much. Dad catches and cleans the fish. Mom cooks them. She reads while he fishes. Sometimes she reads aloud to him."

Delia looked up at him with a sly smile. "Are they Stacy Wrigglebottom fans?"

"They've never mentioned it. And don't bring it up when you meet them." He scowled at her, but there was no heat in the words or the look.

He wanted her to meet his parents. Delia schooled her expression to not show her excitement. "What other things am I not allowed to mention?"

"Well…" He stepped closer and slid the hair off her shoulder, his thumb tracing her collarbone. "I wouldn't tell them that it's hard for me to keep my hands off you. That I spend my days following you around the store."

"No, you don't. You're always sitting in front of your computer." It was hard for her to concentrate when he was so close.

"I follow you with my eyes. I can see more of you from my spot behind the counter."

"Do you…" Delia cleared her throat. Her flirting game had disappeared, and she floundered with her thoughts and words. "Do you like what you see?"

His thumb moved up her throat and traced the curve of her jaw. He stopped with his hand cupping the back of her neck. "Very much. I like what I see when I look at you, and I like what I see when you're working with Sid. I like what I see when you're excited by an idea and when you're happy with what you've done. I especially like looking up and seeing you working away at your desk. I used to think I needed to be alone to write, but now that I've had you close by, I don't think I can go back to that. I think when I close down the shop, I'm going to need a place where you and I can work together. Where I can see you every day."

His words were a statement, but there was a question in his eyes. Biting her lip, she gave the slightest nod, maintaining eye contact the whole time.

He continued, his voice getting lower, "Perhaps we could extend your contract? Add another task to your to-do list?"

"You want me to find an office we can share? I thought you were going to work out of your apartment."

Taking her hand, they moved over to the couch. He sat her down and took a seat on the coffee table in front of her, then removed her shoes and pulled both her feet into his lap, cradling her feet in the palms of his warm hands. She groaned as his thumbs pressed into the balls of her feet. "My apartment is too quiet, and I've decided that a writer working in a coffee shop is a cliché. Besides, you need me."

"I do?"

"You need someone to organize. You need someone to rescue you from clients who've overstayed their welcome. You need someone to bounce ideas off of and talk things over when something's bothering you. I want to be that person." His thumbs stopped moving, but he still held her feet like they were precious. "Will you let me be your person? Share an office with me?"

She was agreeing to more than working beside him in the same space. He wanted to be part of her life. "Yes." She held out her hand, unsure what to do next.

He dropped her feet and accepted her hand, using it to draw her close. Their lips met, and he slanted his mouth over hers. She opened, accepting him in, welcoming the promise of his kisses, the tease of his nipping teeth, the playful lapping of his tongue. He pulled back and pressed his forehead against hers.

"I have energy for one of two things tonight. You can tell

me what's been on your mind, or you can lead me to your bed and have your way with me."

Delia giggled. "Have my way with you? No one says that anymore."

He shrugged. "Romance writers do."

Her fingers drifted through his hair, and she tugged at an errant curl. "I think I want to have my way with you. We can talk in the morning."

Rising from the couch, Cal scooped her into his arms. "Good answer."

A small smile curving her lips, Delia stood in the kitchen, watching coffee drip into her mug. Her bare feet curled against the cold of the tile floor. She'd forgotten her slippers but didn't want to risk waking him. Flat on his back, one well-muscled arm curled up and under his pillow, the copper of his skin contrasting beautifully with the white sheets. She'd imprinted the scene in her memory right next to the memory of making love with him.

In the quiet of the morning, she processed their conversation. Being with him every day. Looking up from her desk to see him muttering and pounding away at his keyboard. A quiet man, Cal was not a quiet typer. She wondered how many keyboards had been sacrificed during his writing career. She liked the idea of bouncing ideas off him. Is that what she'd been looking for? Someone to share her thoughts with? Someone who cared enough to want to know her thoughts? Yeah, she liked that a lot.

"Is one of those for me?"

Delia turned her head to smile at Cal, then whipped completely around, mouth hanging open.

Grinning, he stepped back from the counter, holding out his arms and twirling around. "What do you think? Is it me?" He was wearing a short black-and-white tiger-striped robe in satin that strained across his shoulders and barely covered his butt.

Crossing her arms, Delia said, "Turn around." He did her bidding, and she focused on his long legs. "Oh yeah. It works for you. I bought the wrong size and was too lazy to return it. No one else has ever worn it. I thought…" Her words drifted away as Cal rounded the counter and headed toward her.

"Thanks for putting it out for me." He kissed her on the nose, then reached for a coffee mug. "But I may put on my pants. I don't want you distracted by the view." He grinned.

Apparently, sex made him cocky in the morning. She giggled at the double entendre but didn't share when he looked at her quizzically. Instead, she asked, "Are you hungry? Would you like an omelet?"

"Not yet." He tagged her coffee mug as well as his own and led the way to the couch, Delia following behind.

He gave up on trying to cover his crotch with the robe and snagged an afghan to drape over his lap. "Hot coffee and bare testicles are not a good way to start the day."

Delia buried her grin in her own mug, and they both stared out at the view. Clouds chased across the sky in the early morning, and the water was choppy. No ships or boats of any size had ventured out yet.

Cal nudged her shoulder. "You have my complete attention."

Delia smiled and nodded, choosing her words. "Lumber mills," she said.

"What about them?"

"That's how the original Duncans made a living. They had a small mill over near the Duwamish Canal. They bought the land, displacing the original people, the Duwamish. Some stayed in West Seattle and worked at the sawmills or fished, but others moved away to reservations at Port Madison, Tulalip, and Muckleshoot." She held up a hand. "I know this isn't new information to you. I think some of your ancestors were affected."

Calvin said, "My great-great-grandmother and her sister were sent up to Tulalip. After their parents died of smallpox."

"Right," Delia murmured. Having no immunity, many native peoples fell victim to the diseases accompanying western expansion. "Did any of your family members go through the boarding schools?" From 1819 to 1969, four hundred Indian boarding schools operated in the US, fifteen in Washington State. Native Americans were required to attend until the 1920s. "I've read about the unmarked graves they've found at former residential schools in Canada. And…well…"

Cal nodded. "My great-grandfather went to the one near Chilliwack in BC. My understanding is he never talked about it." He looked grim.

Delia's gut twisted. No one in her family experienced having their child taken away from them and sent off to live miles away, sometimes in another city. Children were stripped of their language, stripped of their culture, mistreated, and often died far away from home. Many people wanted to sweep the stories under the rug and ignore the impact, but the intergenerational trauma was real and wouldn't disappear anytime soon.

"Do you think that's why Sid turned to alcohol?"

"For Sid? I doubt it. But the lingering effects from the boarding schools—more than one hundred years of being abused and told you're not worthy, then passing that down to your kids—impacts a lot of Indigenous people around here. People on the reservations, some who attend ODAAT, and others you see down at the waterfront. Is it any wonder we don't trust the education system? On either side of the border?"

His questions were rhetorical and despite wanting to, there wasn't much she could add.

"The building that commemorates the work of Gweneth Duncan is right next to the Duwamish Longhouse and Cultural Center. It's not ostentatious. But there's a grand opening ceremony, and I'm supposed to make a video about the foresight and determination of Gweneth to buy up land and develop it, while in the shadow of this building is the only land that the Duwamish have left. Less than an acre. Because people like my great-great-great-grandmother wanted it. Yes, I know it was legal at the time, but it wasn't…" Delia waved a hand in frustration. "It wasn't ethical, or humane, or—right."

Cal rose and, taking Delia's mug with him, refilled their coffees. In the too-small robe, he should have looked ridiculous, but he didn't. Appearance didn't bother him at all.

"Does your family understand the significance of the juxtaposition?" he asked, before sitting back down.

"I don't know. I think most of them are like me, happy to take their monthly check regardless of where it came from."

"This video could be a powerful tool. You said you have to show it to the board for their approval prior to the ceremony?" At Delia's nod, he continued, "What if you educated them on what that land used to be and used to mean? Any chance they would deed some of the land back? Other companies have done so."

He was referring to the resource company that had deeded back an ancient cemetery—land that was used as a lumber mill that had ceased to operate in the 1990s—to the S'Klallam tribe, the original inhabitants of the Port Gamble area.

"I'm not sure I can convince them to give the land back, but there is a precedent for giving a building."

Cal raised his mug. "There you go."

Delia raised her own. Shoulders relaxing, she stared out at the day, thinking about the project ahead of her.

al got dressed, and they drove together to the bookstore. Delia parked in the alley and unlocked the door to the back room. Without the memorabilia and collected junk, their footsteps echoed as they walked through the empty room and into the bookstore itself. The nook that had held the washer and dryer was now empty. The appliances went to a shelter for queer youth as well as the supplies that Cal had kept on hand for Sid to use. Delia had arranged for many of the books to be sold but not picked up until the day before closing. Thus, the store did not feel desolate. Sadly, neither the Museum of History and Industry nor the Hibulb Cultural Center were interested in the diner counter and stools. But a restaurant supply store agreed to pick them up, sell them, then donate whatever they could get for the items to another nonprofit. Methodically, Delia had arranged for and overseen the removal of everything inside Jimmy's Joint, something Cal had been unable to do. Others might call it nostalgia, but truthfully, it had been inertia. Cal had used Sid as an excuse to hide out in Jimmy's Joint and write for others. He didn't know where he was going to do it, and he didn't know if it would get picked up by a publishing house, but he would be writing his own stories, under his own name.

"Will Sid be in today?" he asked before dumping his backpack on the counter and pulling out his laptop.

"Should be. The space at ODAAT won't be ready for them for another week. Sid and his fellow artisans will continue to work here until we close up shop. I don't want this place to be a hollow shell. Oh, and they're taking the side tables and chairs with them."

Cal tipped his chin in acknowledgment. The artisans might be working in a new space, but at least they'd have familiar objects with them. He pointed at the industrial coffee maker. It was functional but outdated. "What about that?"

Delia patted him on the shoulder as she moved past him to switch the power on the old machine. "Don't worry. I found it a good home. Sid's gonna take it with him, as well as the teapot and mugs. Except for yours. I will treat it like the important artifact it is and take it to my place."

That warmed his heart, his beat-up coffee mug in Delia's kitchen. Months ago, when she'd stalked into the bookshop, he couldn't wait to get rid of her. Now, he couldn't fathom not seeing her on a daily basis. Waking up alone in her bed this morning had stopped his heart momentarily as he wondered if she was full of morning-after regrets. Then he'd found the robe, if that skimpy piece of fabric could be called a robe, and he stopped worrying. Starting the day with coffee Delia made for him, then sitting beside her on the couch was perfect, and he looked forward to many more days like it. Definitely at her place, though. His apartment was functional but had no ambiance or the silky soft sheets she must have spent a lot of money on. He thought about making it permanent, her wearing his ring, then his mind skittered away from the image. They had time. Right now, he had a new book to outline, and Delia had a presentation to prepare.

CHAPTER 22

The week passed with the two of them working on their own projects, Delia at her table, Cal at the counter. Items were picked up, while Sid and the other artisans—they weren't all woodcarvers—worked away with quiet conversations. On Friday, Cal looked up from his computer to see Delia standing by the front door, holding one of her many planners, eyes scanning the shop. "Do I want to know what you're thinking?"

She walked toward him with determined steps and sank down on the stool opposite his. "Would it be weird to have some kind of ceremony to say goodbye to Jimmy's Joint?"

He narrowed his eyes and spoke slowly. "No...What do you have in mind?"

She twirled on the stool, gesturing broadly. "Nothing big. I've heard you and Sid talk about your grandparents and hanging out here when you were kids. I bet your other cousins and relatives have similar memories and might like to get together to share them. Maybe invite some of the shopkeepers who've been here for a long time and knew your grandparents as well." When he remained silent, she turned back to face him and studied his expression. "It's just a thought. We don't have to do anything."

Standing, he leaned across the counter and plucked her off her stool. "Hey!" He ignored her protest, lifting her clear over the counter and settling her in his arms. Her eyes were big, and his heart was full. This thoughtful woman fixed things he didn't even know were broken. He pressed his forehead against hers. "Thank you."

"Does that mean yes?"

Cal huffed out a laugh and pulled back to look at her. "Yes."

Grinning, she squeezed him and then moved to stand beside him, looking out at the mostly vacant shop. "Will your parents come?"

"I think so. When do you want to do it?" His mother had a busy schedule but would want to be present.

She grabbed her planner and flipped to a calendar page. Using different colored inks, she'd written in notes on most of the dates. She pointed at the second to last day of the month. "The day before you turn over the keys. That's two weeks away. Late afternoon, early evening. Maybe an open house where people can pop by and—"

"Can you make it a fixed start and end time? I don't think I can be polite and social for an extended period of time." He wasn't kidding. He much preferred to be in in the background. With the exception of Delia, he did not draw energy from being among people.

She squeezed his arm. "Of course." She found a fresh page in her planner and started jotting notes. "I thought I'd invite my parents." Leaning over the counter, her hair hung down, hiding her face.

Cal understood what she was saying. "Sounds good," he said.

She stood to face him, a small line forming between her

eyebrows. "Mom's been asking about you since the dinner. So them being here and your parents being here…She's going to put two and two together and draw your mother aside and…"

"And what? I don't see the problem. I've met your parents, and I like them. They're good people. Dad will find a corner, drink coffee, and make pithy comments. My sisters will tell embarrassing stories about me, and my mom and your mom will get along like a house on fire."

Delia blanched. "I'll be meeting your sisters?"

"Yeah. With or without their husbands and probably with small children in tow." Now she was chewing on her lip, not looking nearly as enthusiastic. "Is that a problem?"

"Do you know if they're on Instagram? Follow much social media?"

He snorted. "Yeah. Laura wanted to know where you got that dress the night of the party. She asked me if I'd seen your closet." At Delia's somber face, the penny dropped. It had been a while since he looked, but prior to Delia working, she'd spent a lot of time posting selfies at parties and events, and then there was the video of him carrying her out of the bar. He moved closer, forcing her to look up at him. "They've seen it all. Lisa said that if things didn't work out with you, she would use the video on a dating profile for me. She thinks I might land someone if I promote my ability to carry women around." She dropped her head and banged it softly against his chest. "Is there anything else in your closet besides the world's most orga-nized collection of socks? Something I don't know about? 'Cause if there isn't, don't worry about meeting my family. They have lots of skeletons and lots of embarrassing stories." She lifted her head and met his gaze, looking a little more settled. Like every other family in the world, Cal's had its share of nutbars. Anyone who believed normal existed was fooling themselves. "You still want to do this? Not just this party, but me and you? I have a big family, and they come with me. Loud dinners, noisy kids, and nosy sisters."

"If I share you with my family, they're going to like you better than me." Delia's lips turned up in a teasing smile, and she turned back to her planner, adding another note.

Cal's shoulders relaxed. "I *am* pretty awesome." Looking at the list she was working on, he said, "Will a party interfere with your board meeting?"

She waved away the question. "Nope. That's the following week. I have it covered."

"'Kay." He kissed her on the temple and went back to work.

❄

"It's brilliant. But those board members are going to lose their minds." Connie lounged back in her chair, hands laced together over her stomach. Today was her last day on the job as a concierge, and Delia had made her a celebratory dinner. She'd finished the MBA program, but instead of seeking a job in the business world, she was working part-time for two nonprofits and dog-walking and pet-sitting, many of those gigs in Delia's building. Connie had approached the head concierge with the idea, and he'd all but hugged her. None of the concierges liked walking dogs and picking up poop, so to contract it out made them very happy. Many of the jobs required overnight stays. So while Connie wouldn't be moving out of her childhood bedroom any time soon, she wasn't spending nearly as many nights there.

Now she sat at Delia's dining room table in spruce green yoga pants and a hoodie, looking more relaxed than Delia had ever seen her. She picked up her tea and cradled the mug in her hands. "What are you offering?"

"What do you mean?"

"You've put together facts and figures and images that will make them feel about this high." Connie held her thumb and forefinger a millimeter apart. "Rich people hate to feel responsible and guilty. And after this, their guilt level will be through the roof."

"Good. That's what I want." She'd spent the last twenty-four hours crafting the presentation. All she needed to do was layer her voice over it. That way, she wouldn't have to speak in front of the board. It would be smooth and professional. Now, she scowled at Connie, feeling like an obtuse child.

"Babe, when you went to the longhouse, what was your first reaction?"

"I wanted to make a donation."

"Why didn't you do that?"

Delia flapped an impatient hand. "Because it's a Band-Aid solution. Doesn't do anything in the long term."

Connie pointed at the laptop's screen where an image of the DP logo was superimposed over the Seattle skyline. "That's exactly what the board members are going to do. Whip out their checkbooks, assuage their guilt, and go back to cashing their dividend checks."

"We don't get dividends."

"You know what I mean." Connie drank her tea while Delia stewed. She thought she'd done a great job. "What's the ask?"

"I don't know what you mean. I've detailed how Duncan Properties has thrived while the presence of the Duwamish has diminished and how the building that they'd fundraised for forever is in the shadow of Gweneth Duncan's building. The juxtaposition is so obvious, they can see the problem."

"True."

"Well then, what have I done wrong?" She pushed her chair back and stomped around the table, picking up the dirty dishes. Connie was supposed to be her friend, give her advice, not make her feel inadequate. Make her feel like she'd done a half-assed job. She'd worked hard on this, and she thought it showed. She dropped the cutlery in the sink with a clatter and yanked open the dishwasher.

"You haven't done anything wrong. It's simply not finished."

Delia harrumphed.

"You've found out what the Duwamish need. What's standing in the way of their success. Now you need to communicate that to DP in a way that's going to make them want to fulfill that need. They want to feel good, not guilty." She came around the counter to give Delia a swift hug. "I have to take off. I have a sleepover with a schnauzer."

Delia dried her hands and walked Connie to the door.

When Delia turned from the door, she noticed plastic from a dry-cleaning bag was sticking out of the closet door. She opened the door to retrieve the item and take it to its proper home—her closet. It was the dress she'd worn to the ODAAT dinner. She removed the plastic film and hung the dress up, thinking about the night. Being in Cal's car. Tommy and Kevin getting together. The triumph of the fundraiser. She gasped. Dropping the plastic to the floor, she raced back to the dining room table and sat in front of her laptop, knowing what was missing.

CHAPTER 23

Standing on the stepladder to hang the backdrop for the video station, Delia ignored the ding of incoming texts. Fastening the fabric to the wall required both hands. Whoever it was would have to wait. She climbed down and stepped back, eyeing her work critically. Not bad. In the corner where the carvers normally worked, she'd arranged a chair, a video camera, and a ring light. Anyone who wanted to share a memory of Jimmy's Joint could make a video recording. Delia would do the editing in the future and send it out to whoever was interested. Memories needed to be preserved, and this old place held a lot of them.

Picking up her planner, she placed a tick behind "Video Corner" and mentally patted herself on the back. The party was coming together nicely. She had six hours before it began, and all her ducks were in a row. There was time to go home for a shower and maybe a nap. She glanced over to where Cal was packing away his laptop. Perhaps she could convince him to join her. The ring tone of her phone alerted her to an incoming call from her brother Chuck. Hopefully, he wasn't backing out of coming to the party. She was looking forward to introducing him to Cal and was hoping they'd hit it off.

"Hey, what's—"

"Where are you?" Chuck asked in a panicked whisper.

"Uh, Jimmy's Joint, prepping for the party. Why?"

"You're late," he hissed. "The board meeting started ten minutes ago. You're on the agenda in twenty minutes."

"No. No, no, no." Delia found the page in her planner. "The meeting is scheduled for next Friday. I wrote it down."

"Well, you wrote it down wrong. It's happening now."

The bottom fell out of Delia's stomach. She must have made a noise, because Cal looked up, eyebrows raised in silent inquiry.

"I'll stall them as long as I can, but get here as soon as possible." Chuck hung up, and Delia stared at the phone in horror.

"What is it?" Cal was at her side, wrapping an arm around her shaking shoulders.

"I'm supposed to be at Duncan Properties. The board meeting is today, not next week." Unable to think, unable to move, Delia stared blankly at Cal. What the hell was she going to do? The slide presentation was complete, and she'd interspersed aerial footage of the Seattle waterfront as well as old photographs, but she hadn't recorded the voice over. She hadn't completed the script.

Holding her by the shoulders, Cal bent down. "Look at me. Hey. It's fine."

"No! It's not fine." She shook him off and backed away. "It's not finished! The handouts are still at the printers, and the voice over isn't done. They'd be staring at a silent screen, wondering what the hell they're looking at. Oh God!" Once again, she hadn't followed through on a promise. Pacing the floor, Delia visualized the disappointed and embarrassed expressions of her father and brother as they sat at the conference table with the other board members. She had no excuse, just plain stupidity. Wallowing in her pity party, she'd tuned out Cal's movements until he thrust her bag and sweater into her hands. "Hey!"

He picked up his laptop and strode over to the front door to lock it. "Give me your keys. I'm driving." He propelled her through the back room and out the door to the alley.

Delia gaped at him. "I'm not… We can't…"

"Give me the damn keys. I know you've got your talking points in your planner, and you sent me a copy of the video. You've got everything you need."

Delia pulled her keys out of her purse and handed them to him. He beeped the car open and pushed her into the passenger seat, then leaned over to buckle her seat belt. "You've got this. I know it's not the way you wanted to present it, but you're going to do a great job." She nodded dumbly as he closed the car door and walked around to the driver's side and climbed in. "Right. Where are we going?"

*H*e was surprised to discover that he'd walked past the Duncan Properties building many times without knowing what it was. He'd even bought coffee from the coffee shop on the bottom floor. Standing in front of the bank of elevators, he glanced over at Delia. White-knuckled, she gripped the handle of her bag and stared up at the numbers above the elevator. The doors opened, and they entered. "What floor?" At her answer, he pushed the button for sixteen, then tipped her face up to meet his gaze. "Breathe. You'll be fine."

She nodded, chewing her lip. Then her face fell in dismay. "What?"

She gestured at the mirrored wall behind him. "I look like crap. No one will take me seriously."

He thought she looked sensational. In slim-fitting jeans

tucked into tan, suede boots that looked like hipster hiking boots, she wore a faded Nirvana T-shirt she'd stolen from his drawers. It was too big for her, so she'd cuffed the sleeves and tied a knot in the waist, which she'd tucked into the back of her jeans. Over that, she'd thrown a long, soft green cardigan.

"Show me your teeth," he said.

She frowned.

"I'm serious. Smile and show me your teeth."

She rolled her eyes but complied, flashing him more of a sneer than a smile.

"Great. You've got nothing stuck in your teeth. You'll be fine."

Once again, she rolled her eyes, but her shoulders relaxed, and she'd lost the deer in the headlights look.

The elevator dinged, and the doors opened. Delia didn't move. With a gentle hand, Cal guided her out of the elevator and into a plush carpeted hallway. "Which way do we go?" She nodded to the left, and they walked toward two closed dark wooden doors. He turned her to face him. "Got your planner?"

She dug it out of her bag and held it up like a shield.

"I'll set up the laptop for you."

She blew out a breath. "Thanks."

"It's not going to happen, but if you get nervous, focus on me. I'm the only one you need to look at. 'Kay?"

"You're going to stay?" Her eyes held equal amounts of surprise and hope.

"Any reason why I shouldn't?"

"None at all." For the first time since answering her phone, Delia smiled fully. She straightened her shoulders, then grabbed the doorknob.

"Thank you for your patience."

Eight people seated around the large conference table made from reclaimed lumber murmured greetings as Delia strode to the front of the room. She patted the arm of a man who looked so much like her, it had to be her brother Chuck. She waved at Liam, then kissed her father on the cheek. Cal didn't recognize the others, two late middle-aged white men, one Asian man also of late middle age, and two white women who looked to be in their late forties. He positioned his laptop close to where Delia stood, then, with Liam's assistance, hooked it up to the large presentation monitor on the wall. When he took a chair off to the side and close to the doors instead of exiting, more than one eyebrow was raised in curiosity, but nobody spoke. Delia's father glanced between Cal and Delia, then lifted his chin and smiled. "Good to see you, Cal."

"You as well, Chuck." Cal settled into the chair, aware that more than one pair of eyes had noticed the mismatched laces on his battered hiking boots and his faded flannel shirt.

Delia cleared her throat. "Again, thank you for your patience. The finished video will have a voice over and can be used in subsequent presentations. For today's purpose, I'll be reading from the script." The first slide came up on the screen. "I'd like to acknowledge that we are meeting on Indigenous land, the traditional territory of Coast Salish peoples." Eyebrows were raised, and bodies shifted. Delia ignored them. She recounted the early history of the Duncan family, how they started off with a small sawmill, and the death of Gweneth's husband, and her selling the sawmill and buying a mercantile near the Seattle waterfront. Delia incor-porated familiar photographs of old Seattle, and she spoke of growth and prosperity. "Combining images from this presentation with others from our archives and displaying them in the lobby of the new building will be a way to show the interconnection of Duncan Properties and the growth of Seattle." The board members relaxed and nodded along.

Then an image came up of an Indigenous family, surrounded by belongings, standing in front of the remains of a longhouse. Delia spoke about the deliberate burning of longhouses, the dissolution of communities, and the push to move natives away from Seattle. The next slide showed a map of Elliott Bay, Lake Union, and Lake Washington. Highlighted were the original home sites of the Duwamish and their traditional fishing grounds. As whites moved in and built businesses and homes, the Duwamish were forced out and relocated. The next map showed the current location of the Duwamish. Then a photograph of the Duwamish Longhouse and Cultural Center, with the new Duncan building rising next door to it. The height of the new building, and the angle of the sun, meant the Duncan building literally overshadowed the longhouse. Delia finished by saying, "One hundred and fifty years later, Duncan Properties owns six hundred acres of land in and around Seattle and is opening their newest building on the original site of the first sawmill."

Cal watched the board members exchange wide-eyed glances before looking at Delia's father for guidance. "That's not exactly what I was expecting," he said.

Delia put her notes down on the table and clasped her hands. "My purview was to show the alignment of the city's growth with Duncan Properties' growth. And I did that."

"That"—Chuck Sr. waved at the screen—"makes it look like we're responsible for driving out the native population. We never took property from the Duwamish. Your great-great-great-grandmother bought those properties legally."

Delia bobbed her head side to side. "True. The first peoples here—the Duwamish, Suquamish, Lummi, Skagit, Snohomish, Snoqualmie, and Swinomish—did not understand what they were doing when they signed the Treaty of Point Elliot in 1855. They had no idea that they weren't sharing the land with the whites but, rather, being evicted."

"That was long before Duncans came to Seattle," one of the women said.

"You're right, Alice. Our great-great-great-grandparents

didn't get here until years later. But they knew who originally occupied those lands and that they were never compensated for them. The original inhabitants were forcibly moved out. There are so few of the Duwamish left, they aren't even recognized by the federal government."

Alice looked like she wanted to say more, then turned to look at Cal, and then back at Chuck Sr. "Why is he here?" She then addressed Cal directly, "What do you want from us?"

"I'm tech support."

Lip curled, she waved her hand up and down. "But you're…"

Cal stretched his legs out in front of him and crossed his arms, aware that the light reflected off his silver bracelet against his copper skin. "Yes?"

Alice persisted, "Board meetings are closed to outsiders."

"Duwamish means people of the inside, so I guess that's not a problem," Cal said.

Chuck Sr. raised a placating hand. "This is an informal informational meeting. Cal is with Delia, so it's not a problem."

Cal wanted to stick his tongue out at the glowering woman, but he settled for a smirk.

"Delia, I'm sure everything you've said is based on fact. Those facts don't paint a good picture of Duncan Properties. What's your reasoning behind this?" Her father looked perplexed.

This was the part Cal was unfamiliar with. He had a vague idea what Delia was leading up to, but still. Like the others, he leaned forward in his seat.

Delia stood tall. "Like the other family members, I've benefited from the shrewd business practices of Gweneth Duncan and those who followed her. Land is a limited commodity, and we have profited from that. DP is on track to have its best year ever. Our wallets are getting fatter."

"So make a donation if that makes you feel better," Alice

shot back. "DP has a philanthropic arm. We make generous donations all the time."

"I'm aware of that." Delia raised a hand and ticked off the many nonprofits Duncan Properties had supported over the years. "My point is, we can do more. Chuck, what's going into the newest building?"

"Right now, we have tentative agreements with an insurance agent and a telemarketing firm." Chuck looked over at Liam, who nodded in affirmation.

"Really? I thought we had more for it?" Chuck Sr. asked.

Chuck shrugged and answered his father, "Demand for commercial office space is down with so many people working from home."

"So Gweneth Duncan's commemoration will be an empty building. Is that correct?" Delia pushed.

"Yeah, for now," Chuck said.

"Get to your point, Delia." Alice spoke through tight lips.

Delia stepped back and pointed at the slide on the screen. "Right next door to this empty building is the Duwamish Cultural Center. It's bursting at the seams. They have one big room for making presentations and holding workshops. They're a nonprofit with great programs and no place to facilitate them. They need space, and we have it."

Alice shrugged. "They can rent from us. What's the big deal?"

"The optics." Chuck Sr. looked up at his daughter. "Am I right?"

"Yeah. The Duwamish are struggling to be a presence on their ancestral land that they had to buy back. If we charge them rent to use the new building, DP epitomizes all the ways Indigenous people have been taken advantage of and used."

The room erupted in a buzz of conversation. Cal raised a surreptitious thumbs-up to Delia, who acknowledged it with the slightest of nods. She raised her voice. "The thing is, DP has set a precedent for lending their properties to nonprofits." She clicked the slideshow to bring up an image of the ODAAT building. "You can do the same thing again."

Chuck Sr. made a noise that sounded like a chuckle mixed with a covering cough. He waved for Delia to continue, looking like he was biting back a smile.

"Few people know that DP owns the ODAAT property and doesn't charge them rent. You can do the exact same thing, or you can make a big deal about partnering with the Duwamish and providing a site for the services and programs they provide to the community. I don't know the exact details, but I'm pretty sure DP would get considerable tax benefits. Liam?"

The CFO nodded.

The last slide came up, featuring an artist's rendering of the lobby of the Gweneth Duncan building, with Pacific Northwest artwork and a land acknowledgment lettered on one wall.

"Duncan Properties can't restore the land that was lost by the Duwamish, but they can help them rebuild their culture by providing a space to grow." Delia clicked off the slideshow and shut down the laptop, while the board members sat, looking thoughtful.

Her father rose and gave her a one-armed hug around the shoulders. "Thank you, Delia. You've given us lots to think about."

She smiled and nodded and made her way to the door. Cal rose and held it open for her, closing it behind them. They made it a few yards down the hallway before she collapsed against the wall and gusted out a sigh.

"Thank God, that's over."

Cal wrapped her in an embrace. "You rocked it. Well done." He stood back and relieved her of the computer and planner that had been trapped between them.

She pushed a hand through her hair and grinned. "I never want to do that again."

"You looked like a pro."

"I think I hit all the points I wanted to make. I wish I'd been able to have the handouts. They looked really good." She took hold of Cal's wrist to look at the time. "No time for a nap, but we can stop by my place so I can shower and change for this evening."

They started for the elevator when a voice called from behind. Turning, they waited for Chuck Sr. to catch up with them. He gave Delia a full hug and kissed her on the forehead before stepping back.

"Good job, sweetheart. The board is buzzing. That wasn't what they were expecting."

Delia scrunched up her nose. "Sorry, Daddy. I just—"

"Don't apologize. You brought to the forefront something we should have been doing long ago: acknowledging the original peoples and making amends for the disruption to their lives." His gaze encompassed both Delia and Cal. "I need to get back in there, but I'll see you tonight. Cal, I'm looking forward to meeting your parents." He retraced his steps, then stopped and said, "Your cousin Alice asked if you'd edit the video so we don't look…"

"Yes, Daddy. I'll make DP look good."

CHAPTER 24

The video corner was a success, to the point that a time limit had to be set as some people had many stories about Jimmy's Joint they wanted memorialized, including her parents. Apparently, they had waited out a rainstorm, sitting at the counter and having, in the words of Carol Lee, "the most amazing cinnamon rolls."

Cal's sisters, Laura and Lisa, came without their husbands or children. They were warm and effusive, giving their brother crap at the same time being openly affectionate toward him. His mother, Angie, watched over her kids with an indulgent smile and greeted Delia with a warm smile, big hug, and complimentary words. It was Cal's dad, Dan who stole Delia's heart. Not tall or imposing, he made no effort to draw attention to himself. He had a ready smile, a quiet voice, and listened more than he spoke. He seemed to like being in the background and was obviously proud of his family, enjoying their company.

Delia shifted from one foot to the other. Putting on heels was a mistake, but the way Cal had looked at her when she'd first walked out of her closet made it worthwhile. She looked over to where he and Sid stood talking. He'd swapped out his flannel shirt and ragged jeans for a white button-down shirt and newer jeans and looked yummy. His mom had given him grief about needing a haircut, though. Delia didn't agree. Running her fingers through his hair was one of her favorite things, but she kept that thought to herself. She buried her nose in her wineglass to hide her smile.

"You must be exhausted, speaking to the board this morning and then this shindig."

Delia looked up at her dad and decided to confess. "I'm glad it went well, because I screwed up the dates. I thought it was next week and wasn't as prepared as I wanted to be."

"Ah. That explains the Nirvana T-shirt." Chuck Sr. chuckled. "We had quite the discussion after you left."

"And?"

"The board voted unanimously to offer the Gweneth Duncan building to the Duwamish rent-free."

Delia gaped. "The *whole* building?"

Her dad smiled. "Yep. The whole damn building. Your brother will approach the Duwamish leadership next week with the offer. You were right. We've set the precedent with ODAAT, and that partnership has turned out well. We can work together to accommodate their needs, provided they don't want a helipad on the roof of the building."

She bumped his shoulder. "Yeah, I can see where that might be a bit much."

"Your mother and I were talking about it, and we're very proud of you. Duncan Properties doesn't do enough for the community. I'm going to approach the board about hiring you to do community outreach. Finding organizations we can partner with and support, without a lot of fanfare for the company. No hoopla."

Delia was shaking her head before he even finished. "Thank you, but no."

"Honey, you've proven you're good at this. And your trust fund date is coming up, so you need—"

She put a hand on his arm. "Dad. I'm going to be fine."

"Are you sure? You've got the documentation the lawyer wants? I can go over it and—"

"Dad! Seriously, I'll be fine." If she didn't love him so much, she'd be annoyed. His fallback was to reach for his wallet, and she'd never batted an eye before but simply held out her hand. Now, she was holding her head high. Did she have everything nailed down? No. Was she scared poopless? Yes. Would she do this? Damn skippy.

"So you've got a lot of clients lined up? Friends of your mother or places like this?" He gestured to the cleared-out bookstore.

Delia bobbed her head back and forth, not quite ready to tell her dad the whole story. The door opened, saving her from further explanation.

Tommy, Kevin, and Connie arrived and came toward her for hugs. Chuck Sr. knew both the men, and Delia introduced him to Connie.

Shaking her hand, he cocked his head. "I'm sure we've met."

Wearing a pink wrap dress with nude pumps, understated makeup, and large hoop earrings, Connie looked nothing like her former self. She laughed. "I worked as a concierge in Delia's building."

"Ahh, yes. You're not there anymore?"

Wrapping an arm around Connie's shoulders, Tommy spoke up, "This girl recently finished her MBA while working full-time and is now done with that horrid uniform."

Connie gasped. "It wasn't that bad."

Tommy clutched his pearls. "Are you kidding me? It did nothing for you, and don't get me started on the horrors of polyester."

Kevin groaned and took Tommy by the hand. "Let's find you a drink and leave these nice people alone."

"You do look great," Delia said to Connie.

"Thanks, because this dress is wasted on my clients."

"Who are you working for?" Chuck Sr. asked.

"I'm doing consulting work with a couple of nonprofits. My goal is to help small businesses owned by people of color navigate red tape and bureaucracy and improve their business practices."

"That's impressive," he said.

"Thank you. Right now, it's part-time with very little money, so I'm dog-walking and pet-sitting. Thus, no need for heels and dresses."

"She also helped me iron out billing and inventory. Between help from Connie and Marti my accountant, Delia's Closet and my contract work are both running well." Delia was thankful for the women who counseled and supported her.

Her father pulled out his wallet and handed a business card to Connie. "If you decide to shift gears, give me a call. Meanwhile, if you have questions about commercial realty, you're welcome to call as well."

Connie accepted his card and, in turn, handed Chuck Sr. one of her own. "I'll keep that in mind. Thank you."

Cal joined them at that moment, Sid at his side, sending shy, admiring looks Connie's way.

"Hi, Connie," Cal said. "Well done on finishing school." He then drew Sid forward and introduced him to both Chuck Sr. and Connie. "Sid is the artist who carved the chess pieces for the ODAAT fundraiser."

"Your work was exceptional. It was the only item I was interested in but was outbid on it," Chuck Sr. said with a one-sided smile.

"Kevin showed me a picture. It really is awesome," Connie added.

Sid ducked his head and said thank you. Delia wasn't sure if he was uncomfortable with the praise, the attention, or being close to Connie. She suspected the latter. Her dad wandered off to get something to eat, and the circle closed in.

"I'm bummed I didn't get down here more often. I love used bookstores," Connie said, looking around at the room then back at Cal.

"What do you like to read?" he asked.

"Romantic suspense, some thrillers. No horror, though. It keeps me up at night." She gave an exaggerated shiver.

"Do you ever read historical romance?" Delia ignored the nudge Cal gave her and winked at Sid. He grinned.

"Some. That's what my mom reads. She really likes Stacy Wrigglebottom, but I could never get into her. Dukes and damsels in distress traipsing around England are not my thing."

"Her writing has actually improved over the past few years. The female main characters have a lot more agency."

Connie looked at Sid with interest. "Sounds like you're a fan."

"I'm kind of close to the author." He grinned.

Delia snorted.

Cal sighed and crossed his arms over his chest.

Connie gestured between the three of them. "I'm missing something. What is it?"

Delia clutched her hands in supplication and gave Cal big eyes. "Please…"

"Fine," he said, then grinned when Delia bounced on her toes.

She wrapped a hand around his bicep and waved the other in front of him like a game show host. "Allow me to introduce Stacy Wrigglebottom."

"What?" Connie gaped.

"Cal's been writing under her name for a few years now. And Sid's right. The story lines and writing have definitely improved, although it bums me out that nobody swoons anymore."

Cal accepted the compliments and ribbing with good grace, then shoved his hands into his pockets and rocked back on his feet. "There are two more books to come, and Stacy Wrigglebottom will be announcing her retirement."

"Does that mean…"

Cal's lips twitched. "It does."

Delia jumped into his arms with a squeal, drawing the attention of everyone in the room.

"It's fine," Cal said. "She's overreacting a bit."

Carol Lee and Angie approached them with anticipation in their eyes.

Stepping back, Delia spotted them. She turned apologetic eyes on Cal. "Sorry about that."

He rubbed her shoulders. "Now's as good a time as any to tell them."

Angie made a rolling gesture with her hands. "Tell us what?"

"A major publishing house has offered me a contract to write a five-book series under my own name."

Angie gasped. "Oh, sweetheart. That's awesome." She turned to Carol Lee, who wore a look of polite confusion. "My son is an amazing author. He's been ghostwriting for years, and now it's his turn."

"That is fantastic news! "Congratulations, Cal," Carol Lee said. She turned to Angie while gesturing between Cal and Delia. "I'd been kind of hoping…"

Angie winked. "Me too."

Their mothers were not being subtle. Delia and Cal exchanged glances. It would happen, but they weren't in a hurry.

While Carol Lee and Cal became engrossed in a conversation about thrillers versus suspense novels, Delia did a circuit, checking on the buffet table and picking up empty dishes. Rounding a corner, she bumped into Angie. Delia winced. "I'm so sorry. I wasn't watching where I was going."

"No problem. My glass was empty." Angie gestured at the full tray of dishes. "Can I help you with that?"

"Sure, follow me."

The two women went into the back room, where empty boxes from the caterer were stored on a folding table. Delia put down the tray and pointed with her chin. "We can put all the dishes in there. The caterers will pick everything up tomorrow morning, and they said not to worry about separating the clean and the dirty."

"What about food scraps?"

"They've provided a compost bucket for that."

"Wow," Angie said. "They thought of everything."

This was the first time Delia had been alone with Cal's mother, and she tried not to let her nervousness show. They worked well together with few words and were finished quickly.

From a pocket, Angie pulled out a small packet of wet wipes and held it out.

"Thank you," Delia said. "Great idea."

Angie smiled. "I have four grandchildren. I should buy stock in the company." She dropped the used wipe into a wastebasket next to the compost bucket. "I overheard you speaking to your father about donating the newest DP building to the Duwamish. That's a very generous move."

Delia watched the other woman. She was looking everywhere but back at her. "Thank you. Am I sensing a 'but' there?"

Angie rolled her eyes and smiled at her. "My husband says I should never play poker."

"I don't know about that. I do know that Cal believes in being direct, and I think he gets that from you." She gestured to two large coolers against the wall. "Do you mind if we sit? My feet are killing me."

Angie nodded. She sat, and Delia pulled the other cooler around to sit across from her, sighing.

"When I was in high school, I worked as a hostess at a restaurant in the casino." Angie pointed at Delia's shoes. "I wore a pair of heels like those, only higher, my first night. Then I switched to flats. I only wear heels now when I won't be standing very long." She leaned back against the wall. "I heard your father say that your brother will approach the Duwamish leadership next week about the new building?"

"Yes." Delia's pressed her clenched hands between her knees, feeling more nervous than she had making the presentation to the board.

"Giving the Duwamish a larger space for cultural programs is not going to turn back the clock two hundred years. The Treaty of Point Elliot caused irreparable damage to the first peoples and the way they lived, but also *where* they lived as well. Forests wiped out, rivers dammed up and dried up and paved over—" Angie stopped herself, her words echoing in the largely empty room. "I get a little passionate about this."

Delia bobbed her head and cleared her throat. "Do you have a suggestion? A different use for the building?"

"When Naomi confronted you"—Angie held up a hand at Delia's startled expression—"Cal told me about it only after I pushed. He'd come to see us the day after the ODAAT fundraiser, and I knew things hadn't ended well. I was concerned that he'd done something to put you off."

"No. Naomi took me by surprise and was…"

"She's very good at her work but has no diplomatic skills."

"I think she had a thing for Cal. Do you know if they ever dated?"

Angie tilted her head and stared off to the side. "Not that I know of. Other than Julie, I never met any of his girlfriends and never their parents." Eyebrows raised, she smiled at Delia, who blushed.

"Getting back to the topic," Angie continued. "After your confrontation with Naomi, what did you do?"

"I felt like an idiot. I didn't want to believe her. I figured I needed to learn more, so I did some research."

"You educated yourself."

Delia shrugged. "I guess you could put it that way."

Angie leaned back against the wall and stretched out her legs. "You learned about the first peoples and the treaty and its impact on the Duwamish."

"Yes."

"I have Duwamish blood. My great-grandmother was sent to Tulalip after her parents died from smallpox, and she married a Snohomish man. On most of the reservations around here, Muckleshoot, Puyallup, you'll find people with Duwamish roots. People whose ancestors were part of the diaspora. So devoting a building specifically to one group— and I am not going to get into federal tribal recognition— negates the impact of contact on other Coast Salish people."

Delia turned over Angie's words in her mind, then spoke her thoughts aloud. "Are you suggesting opening the building to all the tribes, perhaps those who were signers on the Point Elliot treaty, and giving them each a space for their own use?"

"You can certainly invite them." Angie sighed. "You may be surprised to know that the tribes don't always get along. Even when we're working toward a common goal, it can get tricky."

The door opened and Cal entered, closely followed by his father. "Hey," he said, looking between the two women. "Everything okay? Do I want to know what you're talking about?"

Angie smiled, raising a hand toward her husband, who took it and pulled her to her feet.

"Did you solve all the world's problems?" Dan asked, keeping hold of her hand.

"Almost." She stretched out her other hand toward Delia.

Delia rose, accepted Angie's hand, and impulsively hugged her. "Thanks. Can I call you in a day or so? I might have some ideas to run past you."

"Absolutely." Angie leaned up and kissed Cal's cheek before leading Dan back to the bookstore.

"Everything okay?"

Delia reached up to smooth the furrow between his brows and smiled. "Yes. I'll tell you about it when we get home."

At noon the next day, Cal did a final sweep of the store, his steps sounding loud in the empty space that looked so much bigger than it did when packed with books and the old lunch counter. Even though the building was slated to be demolished in the next few days, the store was spotless. He went to investigate a shadow in the display space of the front window. A chess piece. The pawn, a field mouse, looked tiny in the palm of his hand. He tucked it in the pocket of his jeans, then let himself out the front door, locking it for the last time.

CHAPTER 26

Using her phone as a mirror, Delia reapplied her lip gloss and fluffed her hair. When going through her wardrobe, trying to decide what to keep and what to toss, she'd hesitated over the dress. It invoked memories, both good and bad. She wasn't wearing the boots she'd worn the last time, but the dress and the bag were the same. She shook out her hands and straightened her shoulders before exiting the elevator and walking down the hall. She knocked on the open door and waited to be invited to enter.

And waited.

Naomi Sanchez banged away at her keyboard, eyes focused on the screen.

Giving her the benefit of the doubt, Delia knocked again.

Naomi flicked a glance at her, then went back to the screen, the pace and sound of her typing increasing. Like with Cal, Delia wondered how often the lawyer went through keyboards and if frequent replacement was part of her employee benefits.

Delia leaned against the door and waited.

Naomi stopped typing. "Right, you're here."

"I am." Delia strutted over to a chair, seating herself

gracefully and crossing one leg over the other. Her face a polite mask, she waited.

"Daddy's not here with you?"

Delia knew that Naomi knew because Delia had been cc'd on the email from her father. Naomi wouldn't be acting like a class-A bitch if she'd been expecting Chuck Sr. "No."

While Naomi busied herself with finding a file folder and tapping a chewed-up pencil against the desk, Delia studied her. Work Naomi was no-nonsense in her appearance. No makeup, no jewelry, hair pulled back in a tight bun, nails short and unpolished. Her light gray suit and matching high-necked blouse were of good quality, no doubt chosen to convey a serious attitude without drawing any attention. If Delia hadn't seen her at the ODAAT event, she wouldn't believe that Naomi cared about appearances at all. There was a slight sneer on her face as her gaze traveled over Delia, taking in the artfully tousled hair, figure hugging dress, and nude heels with the distinctive red soles. Delia kept her face blank.

"You've been busy," Naomi said. "I've corroborated your income statements with your bank statements, and you've done quite well with your business."

Was she imagining an emphasis on the word business? Delia let it go. "Thank you," she said.

"I've seen your credit card statements up until last month's." Naomi looked pointedly at Delia's shoes. "And your expenses are down as well."

The shoes were two years old. Delia said nothing. Her shoe closet, which originally held over one hundred pairs, now contained fifteen. She no longer needed the clothing racks in her dressing room and had recently sold off the custom-made shelves for her sweaters and jeans. All of her wardrobe, including shoes, now fit into one closet. She and Cal were arguing over who would be using the now-empty room for their office. In truth, Delia wanted to reconfigure her home office to accommodate both of them. Looking up to see him muttering at his laptop was one of the best parts of her day. She was pretty sure she could convince him that the extra bedroom would make a great library or, maybe, in the future, a nursery. None of this she told to Naomi.

Naomi nodded toward the computer screen. "Jimmy's Joint is now closed. Delia's Closet is likewise, and I don't see how you will be able to maintain the inflow of money to support your lifestyle." She seemed incredibly happy by this.

"You mustn't have received the documents about my LLC." Delia reached into her bag and drew out a candy-apple red folder with hearts all over it. Naomi studied it like it might bite her.

"No, I didn't," she clipped out.

Opening the folder, Delia laid a page on the desk and angled it so both she and Naomi could see it. "3D Systems brings order into people's lives. Declutter, Downsize, and Distribute are principles that can be applied to storefronts needing to relocate or close down, handling estates, or persons choosing simpler lifestyles. Objectivity is often needed to determine the necessity of keeping one item over another and how and where to deal with the overflow. Streamlining a space relieves stress and can increase productivity." Delia resolutely kept her eyes on Naomi, not letting them stray to the untidy stack of folders littering the credenza behind her. She took out another paper. "We start with a phone or video conversation to discuss needs and timeline. Then a site visit to the current space and, if needed, the future space. We use the same tools we employed with Jimmy's Joint, finding buyers for collectibles, online auction sites, and businesses that upcycle. We minimize the amount that goes to landfill as much as possible. We organize and set up the new space if asked." Flipping to another page, she went on, "Our first job will be moving an eighty-five-year-old woman from a three thousand square foot home filled with sixty years of memories into a four hundred square foot apartment in an assisted living facility. When that's completed, I have clients booked for the rest of the year. Depending on the scope of the job, I anticipate being able to handle three clients per month."

Delia handed this paper over to Naomi. It detailed the name of the client and the particular task they wanted to hire her for. From her raised eyebrows, it was obvious Naomi recognized some of the names.

"You keep saying we. Do you have employees? Is Calvin Jimmy schlepping boxes for you?"

She refused to be anything but professional and chose to ignore Naomi's snide question. "I have contracts with a handyperson, a moving company, and a virtual assistant. So yes, I say 'we.'"

Naomi lined up the documents Delia had given her and, using them as reference, typed some entries into her laptop. She pushed them back across the desk when she was finished. Through compressed lips, she announced, "You've satisfied the parameters of the clause, and your trust will continue."

"May I have that in writing?"

Naomi glared.

Delia waited.

Naomi banged away at her laptop, and the printer behind her came to life. She slapped the resulting paper on her desk. "Here's a hard copy, and I've emailed my findings to the board of Duncan Properties."

Delia nodded and stood to gather her belongings while Naomi ignored her.

Turning back at the open door, she said, "Thank you for opening my eyes." Then she headed down the hallway to the elevator.

In the lobby of the building, Cal sprawled on a couch, his backpack and a tote bag beside him while he scowled at his laptop. He looked up at Delia's approach. At her broad smile, he rose and wrapped her in a hug.

"Good job. Did you tell her what you plan to do with the trust?"

"Nope. She doesn't need to know." She picked up the tote bag. "I'll go change in the restroom, and we can get going."

"Take your time." Cal settled back down.

Ten minutes later, she was back, now wearing a white T-shirt and emerald green knit blazer over dark wash jeans, tucked into the boots Cal referred to as urban hikers.

"Let me finish this paragraph, and I'll be right with you," he said.

"No rush." Delia sat and watched him shut down his laptop and stow his things away in the battered backpack. He was wearing the same shirt and jeans he'd been wearing the first time they'd met. Was it deliberate or just the fact he had a small wardrobe? The hiking boots were the same as well, but with new shoelaces. Delia had bought them.

"Let's go." He slung his backpack over his shoulder and picked up her tote bag. When she stood, he took her hand and led her to the elevator and down to the parking garage.

Cal drove while Delia pulled out her planner, pleased to check "Meet with the witch" off her to-do list.

"We're picking up Sid. Are we picking up Connie as well?"

"No," Delia said. "Connie will meet us there, which is a bummer because those two in the backseat tripping over their tongues is too cute for words."

"Leave them alone. If something happens, it will happen."

"I know." Delia shifted to look at Cal. "Maybe we'll have to go somewhere afterward and Sid will need a ride home."

He darted a narrow-eyed look at her before returning his attention to traffic. After picking up Sid from ODAAT, they made their way to West Seattle. The lot under the Gweneth Duncan building and behind the Duwamish Cultural Center were full of vehicles for the construction workers and employees, so Cal parked a few blocks down. They stood across the street, and while waiting for a break in traffic, Delia was pleased to see the progress and changes. A gravel path lined with native plants now linked the two buildings. The planting of young trees, shrubs, and grasses were the same around both buildings, and the storage containers behind the longhouse were gone. Similar understated lighting was used on both buildings, and the signage was the same.

Today, she and a team would be designating which offices in the GD building would be used for what. The DP board unanimously agreed to naming the new building The Coast Salish Educational Center. The lobby would be lined with historical images (including one of Gweneth Duncan and the original sawmill that had been on the site) as well as Indigenous artwork that was available for sale.

Entering the building, Sid startled beside her, and Delia looked to see what caught his attention. A glass-topped plinth displayed one of his grandfather's chess sets. A small card next to it gave details of its provenance, as well as a photograph of a very young Sid carving next to their grandfather. Delia watched Sid studying the image. "In the art room, there will be an enlarged image of that photo. Would you like a copy for yourself?"

Sid nodded. Five artists had been engaged to teach weekly classes in a shared space. Next to the classroom would be a drop-in workshop, where students and artists alike could work on their projects. They were following the design in place at ODAAT, tweaking it to allow for children rather than all adults. Sid peeled off to inspect the workshop's progress and provide input on purchasing tools and supplies.

Taking Delia's hand, Cal brushed his lips across her

knuckles. He nodded toward Sid's retreating back. "He walks with purpose now. Thank you."

She returned the kiss. "Thank you and your slovenly ways. If Jimmy's Joint had been up to par, none of this"—she indicated the building and the two of them—"would have happened."

Cal's lips twitched. "Yeah? I guess I was waiting for you to boss me around."

"Indeed." She tugged on his hand. "Let's go check out your space."

He and three others would be part of the storytelling program, a combination of visual arts and the written word. Next to a classroom, a soundproof room was set up to make audio and video recordings of elders telling the stories of their ancestors, many of which had never been written down. Some of these stories would be transformed into graphic novels, and others would be turned into animated films.

At one end of the classroom was a podium with a projection screen behind it. The podium was built to accommodate a laptop and the necessary wiring. Rows of tables and upholstered chairs filled the space. It was both inviting and accommodating. Cal looked impressed. "How is all of this being funded?"

Since their conversation at the party, Delia and Angie had spent countless hours emailing, Zooming, and talking on the phone. Delia convinced her father and brother to hold off on contacting the Duwamish until she had a fully formed plan. With Angie's help, she'd reached out to the tribal organizations around the Puget Sound, inviting them to use the new building for meeting and educational purposes. It wasn't easy to convince them that Duncan Properties did not have an agenda beyond giving back. By retaining ownership of the building, DP was responsible for upkeep and taxes, and the tribes were on an equal footing as joint tenants. Delia tried to convince Angie to serve as executive director, but Angie demurred. She had no desire to relocate to the city and was making noises about retiring. At Angie's suggestion, a search firm had been engaged to find an executive director for the center. While that was going on, Ivan Thompson—much to Cal's chagrin—had been engaged to serve as interim executive director. His first move had been to hire the volunteer coordinator from the longhouse, Ginny Clemons, as well as Connie.

"That's where Connie comes in. CSEC has hired her to do grant writing, as well as sorting out the website and scheduling events and classes. She has a long list of foundations she's reaching out to for funding. She's also approaching the tribes and nonprofits about partnering on programs that are beneficial to them both."

"I thought she wanted to work with small businesses?"

Delia leaned against the podium and gestured at the chairs. "She will be. CSEC will be offering classes and services that benefit the whole community. Connie will be working one-on-one with people needing assistance with their small businesses, connecting them with the right agencies, finding interpreters, and a bunch of other things that I can't remember right now. She, Ginny, and Ivan have so many ideas, it's exhausting and exhilarating at the same time."

Cal opened the door, and Delia followed him out into the hallway. "And she's earning a wage that allows her to give up pet-sitting?"

"Yep. Tommy and I are taking her shopping for a professional wardrobe next week." It had to be on a budget because Connie was making plans to move into her own place for the first time. Delia was up to the challenge.

As if conjured by the conversation, Connie came around the corner, carrying a clipboard and walking like a woman on a mission. "Hey," she said. "How did it go today? Did you slay the dragon?"

Delia tossed her hair over her shoulder. "I did indeed."

"Yay!"

Delia's parents had asked a few questions, made a few suggestions, then wrapped her in a hug when they heard her plans for her monthly income from her trust fund. A quarter would go to a local nonprofit, and another quarter would be set aside for long-term care and health insurance. The other half would be used to pay back her parents for the apartment and car. For the first time, Delia was truly self-supporting.

The official opening of CSEC would be in three weeks, and her job of coordinating the furnishing, equipping workshops, and installing electronics would be done. The new project would be a challenge, and she was thrilled with the variety of work coming her way. Discussing ideas with Cal when he was done writing was the best part of the day.

Cal spent more nights than not at her place and wouldn't be renewing his lease. They'd talked about subletting the apartment to Sid, but he wasn't quite ready to leave the safety of ODAAT. Delia made a mental note to mention the apartment to Connie.

"Is there going to be a party?"

Delia narrowed her eyes at Connie. "Why?" Throwing a party because she hadn't lost her trust fund did not seem like a good idea.

"Ah…your birthday?"

"Oh!" Delia shook her head and looked up at Cal. They didn't want to add another event to their calendar. "We're headed up to the peninsula for an overnight hiking trip."

"Oookay." Connie was very much a city girl and looked dubious.

Cal nudged Delia's shoulder. "She needs to get those boots muddy."

"He's promised me a spa day when we get back, so I can

live with a camping trip." She'd pretty much follow him anywhere by now.

Connie laughed. "Well, watch out for bears. I'll see you when you get back." She turned and walked off.

"Hey," Delia called. "Any chance you can give Sid a ride back into the city? Then we can start our trip a little earlier."

"Shouldn't be a problem."

Looking like the cat with a canary, Delia turned to see Cal scowling at her. "She's just giving him a ride home."

"Um-hmm."

"I thought you'd like to get an earlier start on our trip."

"I do." He took her in his arms and touched her lips with his own. "You sure a camping trip is what you want for a birthday present? It's not too late to change your mind."

That was true. However, the car was packed with their gear, and she knew what this meant to Cal. "I'm sure."

He kissed her again. "Happy birthday, Delia."

She stepped closer into his embrace. "Happy birthday to me."

ABOUT THE AUTHOR

Lynne Hancock Pearson writes stories of people finding their way, even if it takes a while to get there. She lives near Seattle with two finicky felines and one long-suffering husband. She is a left-handed middle child who grew up in the Great White North and is a proud member of the Métis Nation of Canada.

To get more of *Fraudulent Trust,* learn about Connie and Sid's upcoming story, and about Lynne, go to www.lynnehancockpearson.com and join her newsletter. You can unsubscribe at any time.

You can also follow her here:

facebook.com/lynne.hancockpearson
instagram.com/lynnehancockpearson